Reunion

Ken Lizzi

Twilight Times Books
Kingsport Tennessee

Reunion

Paladin Timeless Books, an imprint of
Twilight Times Books
P O Box 3340
Kingsport, TN 37664
www.twilighttimesbooks.com/

First Edition: June 2014

Library of Congress Control Number: 2014933958

ISBN: 978-1-60619-295-5

Cover art by Brad Fraunfelter

Printed in the United States of America

To Isa.

Te amo, Gatita

Chapter 1

THE EARTH SHOOK. AS A SEISMIC EVENT IT WAS NOT INTENSE IN EITHER motion or duration, just a momentary jostling. Truth is, I barely noticed.

I looked up from my coffee and the crossword puzzle in my lap, both illuminated by the penlight in my mouth. Through the windshield of my squad car I saw a brief shiver run down the brick wall of a four-story building. The ground floor was occupied by a convenience store. Through its large picture window I could see my partner stocking up on beef jerky. The window quivered but held as the ripple of motion reached the lower floors.

The lights in the store flickered, then winked out. So did the rest of the lights in the building, and the street lights standing sentinel along the sidewalk.

I unclenched my jaw to let the penlight drop, grabbed the heavy flashlight from the seat beside me, and exited the cruiser. I turned up my radio as I left to keep abreast of the expected chatter. Something was happening and I didn't like it. The hairs at the back of my neck were standing to attention. I could do with a few words of reassurance from the squawk box.

It was quiet. The radio, I mean. But the city around me was also still. And it was dark. This was an infrequently trafficked street, so no car headlights aided the bright cone of my flashlight. I ran the light across the store window. My partner, radio to his lips, averted his gaze as the beam rolled over him, and tossed a half wave in my direction. I pivoted slowly about heel and toe, scanning the building. I continued on to the next building along the street, and then across to the other side.

A row of genteel Victorian houses appeared to have birthed a—what? A pyramid? Not precisely, not the Egyptian variety; it was more the South American type. A—what would my buddy Gordon, who insisted on wasting his life as a college professor call it? A ziggurat? A ziggurat, if that was the word, that out-massed the building at my back. I could see coils and wisps of steam or smoke rising from the crushed remains of the houses.

Crushed? No, the bizarre edifice before me hadn't fallen on them. I certainly hadn't heard it, and the quick tremor I'd felt hadn't seemed sufficiently vigorous for such an aerial advent. And I certainly would have heard it. Looking closer, the gingerbread-work and trellis-bedecked Victorians seemed to meld into the cyclopean pastel-hued stones of the lower tiers of the ziggurat. The higher reaches of the step-pyramid receded upwards and backwards beyond the limits of my flashlight beam.

The silence ended about that time, or I just then noticed the resumption of noise. It consisted primarily of screaming. I backed towards the convenience store, feeling behind me for the door. The curls of smoke rising from the wreckage were multiplying, and I began to smell gas.

"...the hell?" I muttered. No, I wasn't seeing this. I wasn't hearing this. I wasn't smelling this.

Overwork. Too many night shifts. The tremor had just tweaked my senses for a moment. Temporarily. Just have a quick chat with my partner, get my head straight. When I looked outside again everything would be back in its proper place.

The expected electronic chirp failed to greet me as I pushed my way into to the mini-market, the equipment at the rear of my Sam Browne digging into my back and hips.

"Odd night, Sean," I said, trying to keep my voice steady. I gave the store a quick sweep of the torch. Sean was the only customer. The clerk was blinking at the light, punching repeatedly and futilely at the buttons of the cash register.

"Subtle shit don't escape you, does it Nick?" Sean answered. "I can't get nothing from dispatch."

"Try Downtown," I said, then, "Interesting evening, Ngyuen," addressing the clerk, a casual acquaintance of several years.

He focused on my voice, something familiar to latch on to. "Going to play hell with the receipts tonight," he said. "What do you think happened?"

"I dunno," I said. "Earthquake, maybe. Mount Hood finally blew its stack. Any insights, Sean?"

Sean paused his fruitless attempt at radio contact. We'd shared the squad car for years and had seen our fair share of the bizarre. Sean was senior to me by a half-dozen years and so had observed that much more. But this was a new one even to him. "Earthquake sounds good. But it beats me, college boy." College boy? Still, after all these years. "You're the one oughta have insights."

Maybe. But I was fresh out of insights. Too little data to base any sort of hypothesis on. A little tremor. Power kaput. Some serious, instant, neighborhood renovation. I had no clue.

Well then. Time to face it. Was I out of my gourd or would Sean see it too? I took a deep breath. Exhaled. "What do you make of that?" I said, and pointed my beam out the window...at the mysterious ziggurat. Damn.

Sean had his head down, twiddling with the frequency knob of his radio. "One damn thing at a time, Nick." Then, as his head came up, "What the fuck?"

What the fuck, indeed. I could understand him employing the baffled, querulous profanity from what I'd already seen. And he'd seen it too. So, confirmed. But now, as if that weren't enough, marching in lockstep toward us came a troupe of renaissance fair players, or a troop of costumed combatants from some live-action role playing game.

The flashlight revealed them in clear detail: a half-dozen figures decked out in high gloss lacquered armor, the chest covered in small, orange and black checkered squares–ceramic perhaps. The extremities were protected by interlocking pieces of a brassy hue, maybe actual brass, or highly polished wood, or shaped ceramics or goddamned plastic for all I could tell. Their faces were concealed by full helmets, elaborate, arching beehive affairs, like rounded ziggurats.

What concerned me more than the constituent components of their outfits were the spears they toted. Each five-foot shaft was topped with a blade nearly as wide as it was long, and slightly curved, the inner, concave edge sprouting hooked spikes or barbs.

"What the hell have we got here?" asked Sean. "Chinese army reenactment society?"

He pushed open the door and strode out to keep the peace. I followed, keeping my light trained on the advancing group.

Sean held out his left hand, palm up, keeping his right on the butt of his service Glock.

"Hold it right there gentlemen," he said, continuing to close the distance. "Go on back to your homes. I know you want to help out with–whatever this is. But leave it to the professionals. Go on home."

I held my ground, giving him room, and edging to one side to keep my line of fire clear. I popped the restraining strap on my Glock. There was too much craziness going on at one time. I needed to focus on my job, let my training and experience guide me, and forget about what exactly the hell was happening.

An orange light blazed up away to my left, eastward, toward the Willamette, like a great ball of flame. A moment later a rolling rumble hit my ears, the sound of something massive hitting the ground in steady sequence, the tolling death knells of a tall building.

My light wavered briefly. The disturbance must have distracted Sean too, for when I brought the beam back on line I saw his broad profile, the white of one eye bright and wide. I also saw the platoon of make-believe soldiers–if that is what they were–breaking into a trot, then a charge. Their armor chimed a glassy tinkle. Sean pulled his piece free and took a two-handed grip, dipping to a slightly bent-kneed stance.

"Far enough," he said, then began to fire as it was immediately obvious they had no intention of complying.

He dropped two of them before he was lifted up off the ground. Six inches of bloody metal protruded from his spine.

My pistol was in my hands and I was firing. If I have implied I was acting without volition, that is very nearly the case. I cannot recall any deliberative process. One moment my Glock 21 was holstered, the next my right hand was pointed down range with a fist full of pebbled grip, my left hand crossed beneath illuminating the targets, and I was squeezing off double-taps.

The last of them fell at my feet, the chinstrap of his helm snapping as his head hit the road surface. I felt an absurd sense of relief that the face revealed was human. He could have been anyone, at least anyone with a taste for blue tattooing in abstract patterns. And, this being Portland...

I scrambled to Sean's aid. But it was too late. It had been too late the moment the blade tore through his ribcage.

"Officer down," I radioed.

Only static answered.

ꕥ

I've since felt bad that I left Sean's body there, but really, what was the point?

ꕥ

The mini-market clerk didn't answer my hail, nor did he appear in the sweeping beam of my flashlight.

I climbed into the squad car and tried the radio there. Still nothing from Central. I switched frequencies. The radio relayed panic, confused pleas, shouts, screaming, crackling that could be distant gunfire or flames, or static. I did not try to send. What could I contribute? And I was beginning to feel that I was lingering too long in the vicinity of the ziggurat and the dead soldiers.

I turned the key and to my relief the cruiser churned to immediate, vigorous life. I suppose some part of my mind feared that whatever had killed the power had also affected the engine's electronics. That was ridiculous, of course. My flashlight worked. The radios worked. Why wouldn't the spark plugs?

Then again, what was rational about any of this?

I pulled a u-turn, slowly, as I had only headlights to illuminate the road. The turn would take me past the bodies and the strange building, but that was the quickest route to downtown and Central Precinct.

I realized I'd just made a decision without any conscious debate: to check in with headquarters before checking in on my wife. Well, I'd make it brief.

The twin beams of my headlights picked up another squad–no, a whole damn company–of the armored spearmen double timing it down the street. They filled the street and sidewalks, the outer files up on the lawns carried orange torches that burned clean, with nary a flicker. They trotted straight toward me.

Well, let's see what they make of a ton of fuel-sucking, Detroit steel... I never finished the absurd rodomontade. The gas leaking from the twisted ruins of the row of once charming houses ignited in a window-shaking *whoomp* that left only charred human wreckage. I drove through and over it like meat speed bumps.

The burning houses augmented my headlights, displaying a chilling landscape. More burning buildings added to the hellish illumination as I picked my way eastward through what was no longer recognizable as Portland. Some buildings remained whole and familiar. Others were unfamiliar. The new structures of blocky, heavy geometry, uniformly of stone construction, but of varying architectural styles. Some of them squatted in what had once been the middle of the street.

They all looked alien to me.

The streets themselves were no longer trustworthy. Or even there. A wide flagstone plaza spread out in the middle of Eighteenth Street. Half a church aligned along one edge of the plaza was revealed in cutaway view by a tree burning nearby. I'd eaten lunch beneath that vast, shady oak many times when on day shift.

Sometimes I found myself driving over cobblestones, surprisingly smooth as though age worn. A creek crossed the road at a bias. I forded it gingerly, not daring to exit the perceived safety of the squad car.

The front tires dipped, descending to the center of the hubcaps. I held my breath. I felt the car level off, and I hit the accelerator, punching it up the far side. I couldn't see beyond the far bank, but it was worth the risk of striking an unseen obstruction on the far side to avoid getting stuck in the stream.

The cruiser bounced safely back onto asphalt and I puffed out the breath I'd almost forgotten I'd been holding.

I crossed over I-405 beneath the menace of another of those ziggurats. A scattering of arrows rattled off of the roof and hood, flushing a burst of profanity from my fear-clenched jaw. Much of the immediate neighborhood was completely unrecognizable. All of the familiar old buildings–offices, hotels, restaurants–had been replaced or somehow transformed. Bits of architectural features I recollected poked out from the sides of alien constructs. After a few blocks of this chaos I drove through the Portland I knew for a few streets running, the roads and buildings unscathed. I saw no fires here, but no electric lights either, and drove by headlights alone.

The beams caught brief snapshots of battling figures. More a massacre than a battle. Unarmed Portlanders were being hacked and stabbed by armored soldiers who displayed no mercy.

Somebody ought to call a cop, I thought, and knew I was bordering on hysteria. I pounded on the steering wheel. I had to get a grip.

I did not stop to help. I can explain that rationally: I did not know the tactical situation. I was heavily outnumbered. It was dark. I could just have easily shot a civilian as one of the invaders. It was my duty to get back to headquarters.

The rationalizations just kept coming. Maybe they were all true. Maybe I was scared and only interested in saving my own skin. Take your pick, it makes no difference to those butchered citizens. The entire journey had felt dreamlike, none of it seemed quite real, not even the people dying outside the illusory safety of my squad car.

I rolled up at long last to Central Precinct headquarters. It wasn't there. Well, part of it still was–a corner of the structure rose up out of the beams of the cruiser's headlights, a corner protruding like the prow of an immense ship from the side of an even vaster construction. It was as if the two had collided at high speeds. I turned on the spotlight, and swiveled it up and around, taking in the hulking mass that stretched along several blocks of what had once been Second and Third Avenues. I could make out lights twinkling from windows along the stone wall, too reddish and flickering to be electric, the sentry lights of some colossal fortification.

What was my duty now? The answer came immediately and without reservation: home and Trina. Assuming I still had a house and a wife.

Was she safe? Was our house now a component in some alien amalgam?

I got moving again, edging around the edifice that currently blocked my route to the river. I thought briefly of working my way south toward the campus, making a quick check on Gordon, but dismissed the notion. Trina was unquestionably priority one, and I doubted any such thing as a quick check-in was still possible.

I hoped I would find a bridge still standing. But after all, Portland is Bridge Town. The Steel Bridge, at least, remained in place, though it now abutted the thick piers and wide arches of a stone bridge that would have made the ancient Romans sit up and take notice.

It was hard to be certain in the dark, but it looked to me as if the river was rising. I risked exiting the cruiser again, pulling up next to an abandoned Prius. I leaned over the rail and shone my light down.

Yes, the river was rising. Two sailboats were held fast by the current against the side of the bridge by the tips of their masts, both vessels threatening to capsize. That, however, is all they had in common. I was familiar with the gleaming fiberglass crafts always visible in the marina. The other was a wooden affair, elegantly curved fore and aft, with a single broad sail, and what looked to me like a bank of oars. Each boat appeared uncrewed.

A shout from the nearby stone bridge reminded me not to linger. I didn't understand the words, but I wasn't going to wait around to learn the language. A line of torches promised another company of soldiers, and I didn't want to risk more arrows.

ꝏ

The east side of town proved as fucked-up as the west. It was a slow, frustrating drive to my hillside neighborhood in Northeast Portland. I tried to put together some coherent plans while I drove, but I could not. The uncertain roads and frequent detours required my full attention. And whenever an open, familiar stretch of street allowed, questions–unanswered and seemingly unanswerable–toppled my constructed thoughts as rapidly as I assembled them. So I surrendered to useless anxiety over Trina.

That worry increased as I began ascending the rising grade near home. The houses and well-manicured lawns and topiary were now hopelessly merged with low, flat-roofed structures. My headlights allowed glimpses of unadorned pillars, narrow windows, and trapezoidal doorways melded into brick walls, picture widows, and gables. Had the same happened to my house? And what had happened to the inhabitants when it–whatever 'it' was–occurred? Had it happened to Trina?

I'd lost my partner. Was I to lose my wife as well? Was I being selfish? From the available evidence, anyone still living in the neighborhood–hell in the whole city, in the whole damned world–had lost someone.

Where did that come from? What kind of thinking had I picked up, feeling guilty about my own grief? So what if I was being selfish? What else could I be and still be human?

I reached the crest of the hill and turned into my driveway. My driveway was still there. That gave me hope. The headlights swept up the incline, then leveled to reveal my split-level ranch. Intact. Unmerged. Whole.

I parked, unlocked the shotgun, and climbed out of the cruiser, careful to close the door quietly behind me. It occurred to me that undamaged houses might soon become objects of interest. So why accelerate the process by loudly announcing my presence? Of course, force of habit would have been just as compelling a reason. I liked to let Trina sleep, and I prided myself on being able to ease into bed without rousing her.

I let myself in, removed my shoes, and tiptoed to the bedroom. I edged the door open, stepped in, and let my eyes adjust as far as possible. I could hear her before I could see her, the sweet susurration of her breathing assuring me that she was alive. I unclenched a previously unnoticed fist that had been squeezing my adrenal gland. I let myself relax–just a touch, mind–for the first time since the weirdness had commenced.

I now faced a new, lesser, dilemma. Did I wake her right away? Did I shake her awake and pour out the story of a twisted cityscape and untold deaths? Would it help? Did every moment count? Was there some unknown deadline to flee? Or would waking her only serve to ruin what might be the last decent night's sleep of her life?

I thought about it for a moment, standing there in the blackness of our bedroom and listening to Trina sleep. I fought every instinct that years of police training had instilled, the protective, proactive urges of the public guard dog to sniff and bark. The immediate neighborhood had struck me as relatively quiet. I'd seen no fires, no bodies. Perhaps the merger of the houses and strange buildings had done for all my neighbors as well as the...the occupants of those alien-looking buildings–death and entombment in one efficient package. If any were left alive then, maybe, like Trina, they still slept. If so, perhaps we were safe for the moment. I could let her sleep, and, if I could manage, get a couple of hours myself. I could take stock in the morning, discuss the situation with Trina, and make plans in a less frantic state of mind.

I gave in to the temptation, unburdened myself of Sam Browne and uniform, and snaked into bed.

ᘓᘐ

Trina is a picker. She finds blemishes–bumps, tiny cysts, ingrown hairs, etc.–and she worries at them with her fingernails. By blemishes I mean specifically my blemishes, which for a basically clear-skinned man in his early thirties don't amount to much. Hers (if such a dainty, porcelain princess could be said to ever endure temporary, minor skin imperfections) she treats gently. Me she picks at. I've had one spot on my left shoulder that is now essentially permanent scar tissue from her ministrations.

Now, in the clear light of early morning that flooded in through the gap in the curtain, she was steadily drawing blood. I doubt she was even remotely aware of it. She lay next to me in the bed, absorbing my story, and looking out the window at the Millers' back deck. The deck now terminated in a single story ocher and yellow structure, windowless on this side. The peak of the Millers' colonial emerged from the roof, the top half of the circular rear window tantalizing with the mystery of what lay within.

And all the while her fingernails worked at a purple pinhead of skin on my arm, currently oozing a dribble of blood.

"So Sean is dead?" she asked after long, silent reflection. "And...and the Millers? And Tom and Kathy? And...oh my God!"

The tears bubbled up then, and I held her, watching the light creep along the wall. I tried to imagine what terrors she was experiencing, what losses she was assuming.

Counting the dead.

Was she thinking of her co-workers at the restaurant? The people she would never help plan menus with again, never shop for at the local farmers' market. Was she missing her maiden aunt in St. Johns? Was she mourning our friends, especially Tom and Kathy? That seemed likely; we'd been close throughout the duration of our relationship, both dating and marriage.

Or did she spare a thought for my old college buddy Gordon, the terminal student, academic, and third wheel? Did she piece together a series of snapshots of my night of horror from the narrative I'd given? I liked to think so, that she was thinking of the living, especially of me.

Finally she lifted her head, looked at me with eyes puffy but dry, and asked, "What do we do?"

There was my Trina, a few layers of sentimentality, irrationality, and spontaneity wrapped around a solid core of practicality.

"Good question," I said. "First, we don't panic. We think this through. We're still alive, so there's no reason to suppose that plenty of other people aren't as well. Second, we secure the house. Camouflage it somehow, I guess, make it look abandoned. We don't want a visit from...from whoever these people are. Third, I see if I still have a job."

"What? Nick, look outside. There's no more Portland. If there's no more Portland, there's no Portland Police Force. Nick! Nick, listen to me. You are no longer employed. Your job now is to serve and protect *us*."

"Integrity. Compassion. Accountability. Respect. Excellence. Service," I recited. "Protect and Serve is LAPD, not Portland PD."

"Goddammit, Nick! You said we need to think this thing through. You're the one not thinking. You're not a cop anymore. I'm not a chef anymore."

"I hear you Trina," I said, though it was exactly what I didn't want to hear. The foundation of my world was disintegrating beneath me. Dismissal of my core identity wasn't a subject I wanted raised. "Let's take care of points one and two, and worry about point three later."

I recognized the exasperated flare of her nostrils as she recognized my evasion. It meant she'd let it go for now, but the matter wasn't forgotten. Well, good. It wasn't forgotten for me either. After receiving my Criminology diploma from PSU I'd spent all my working years on the force. How could I just wake up one morning and walk away?

Walk away like I'd done last night, slinking away from my duty to the people I was supposed to serve.

ꕥ

We crawled out of bed and dressed. I took my time to carefully scan up and down the street. The desertion seemed complete, nothing moving except for birds going unconcernedly about their business. A pall of smoke from last night's fires thickened the air, carrying odors of destruction. But the occasional noise of mechanical nature promised that people were still alive: A car engine in the distance, a gunshot, and–inciting a momentary burst of hope–the far off rush of a jet.

When I was convinced we were unobserved Trina helped me push the car into the garage. I don't know if our new visitors had any concept of what a car in the driveway might mean, but I wasn't going to risk it. Then Trina began inventorying our food stocks and performing triage on the freezer and refrigerator. I went on a reconnaissance of our immediate neighborhood, riot gun under my arm.

Behind our house, on the other side of the fence, was the Millers' place. To the left of our house, as viewed from outside, was the Diaz ranch-style home, on the right the Martens' colonial. Across the street was the Clarks' craftsman bungalow, and to their right the sweeping brick pile of the Fultons' on the corner lot.

At least, that's how it used to be.

My house now rested within an open section of what appeared to be a rather dense housing complex. The blocky structures, mostly low to the ground, colorful, were now hopelessly intertwined with what had been the houses of Edgar Miller, Bernardo Diaz, John Marten, Adam Clark, and Mr. Fulton (I could never bring myself to call him Frank; he'd always exuded too much gray-haired dignity for first-name familiarity.) The structures brought to mind the Roman urban villas I'd read about in school, but with a colorful touch that reminded me of Mexico, or paintings of Babylon. I imagined that if I took the grand tour I'd find central courtyards in each of them.

I found a door, a thick wooden affair recessed about a foot into massive, salmon-pink stone walls. A section of wall and most of the upper floor of John Marten's place protruded through the door. His garage was now melded with what appeared to be a fountain, the base a series of gargoyle heads or some sort of abstract representation of humanoid beings that struck me as vaguely Mayan. The door I pushed open was to the right of the garage and situated where Karen Marten had tended her prized flower bed on either side of the Martens' front entry.

A maze of stone walls and drywall confronted me. I could edge my way here and there, though I suffered a faint twinge of claustrophobia. I found a few open spaces, emerging gratefully into about eight square yards of the Martens' living room. Later I stumbled into a more or less equally sized section of a sparsely furnished sleeping chamber, with a low bed frame stretching taut a closely woven leather mattress.

I doubted I would get very far, and it wasn't long before intersecting walls of the two merged buildings blocked my progress. But I didn't want to go any further anyway, because emerging from the side of a stone wall, fresco-ed with a geometric wave pattern, was the lower half of the Martens' bed—and the lower half of the Martens.

I leaned against the corner where two alien walls met and I retched.

As I let my arms take more of my weight I felt a section of the wall shift. Glad to take my mind off of the Martens' demise, I set down the shotgun and probed further, pushing at either side of a square block of stone. It seemed that it had loosened when the two houses interlocked. I found that I could work it free, scattering bits of mortar. The piece was pretty heavy, about forty pounds at a guess. Too heavy, at any rate, to manhandle back out of this maze. But if I could find similar weakened spots outside the buildings...

࿇

By early afternoon I'd convincingly disguised the front of our house. With blocks piled on blocks it now appeared that yet another of the strange houses was folded into ours. I boarded up the windows for good measure.

We ate a terrific lunch that Trina had assembled from the perishables. And then we went looting.

Chapter 2

I WANTED TO GO ALONE. I KNEW FIRSTHAND HOW DANGEROUS THESE NEW-comers were, not to mention the hazards of the altered roadways. But Trina persuasively argued that it would also be dangerous for her alone at home. Well, it wasn't persuasive; she almost certainly would be safer hunkered down and unnoticed. But I could see the panic growing in her eyes at the thought of being alone permanently. Widowed.

She wasn't going to leave my side until she'd adjusted to the new status quo. So I pretended to be convinced. Honestly it was a bit of a relief. It was absolutely selfish of me. She was my wife and her safety should be paramount, but I felt awkward without a partner watching my back. I was glad to have her along but felt guilty about it at the same time.

During the night the altered landscape had been terrifying, the unseen or hinted amplifying the strangeness that I could see. During the day the new world we lived in was horrifying–horrifying because in the stark light of the sun it was now so undeniably *real*.

We rolled down the hill quietly, the transmission in neutral. I could see Trina staring about her wide-eyed, taking in the new neighborhood that had supplanted her own overnight.

Turning right at the bottom of the hill I was forced to yank the wheel hard to avoid an unexpected obstacle: A towering pine had toppled, unable to bear the burden of abrupt merger with a statue, or idol, of Olympian proportion. Both lay sprawled now, fragments and splinters of wood and stone strewn across a broad plaza of closely spaced flagstones. Amidst the flagstones appeared the tops of fire hydrants, cable boxes, and mail boxes. The head of the statue had remained almost intact, rolling free of the wreckage. It was about the size of my patrol car, presenting a visage reminiscent of the faces decorating the base of the fountain outside the Martens' house.

The public square, or whatever it was, had cut through the foundations of the neighborhood houses like a scythe. The houses, deprived of support, had pancaked, roof sections splaying out from the collapsed ruins. I had seen pictures of earthquakes that had caused less devastation.

Trina clutched at my arm as we drove by the first body. The upper torso of a young woman emerged from beneath the remnants of a fallen deck. Had she been coming home late from a night out? I cut off that line of inquiry as we saw the next body. And the next. That kind of speculation was unproductive. They'd died. How wasn't immediately relevant.

I picked my way across the plaza, threading the cruiser through a maze of fallen houses, then taking another left, I picked up an untransformed street that descended through a burned over swath of land.

Not even the weird stone buildings whose advent had caused the conflagration had escaped unscathed. Their walls were scorched a uniform tarry hue and were misshapen from the heat. No one, newcomer or resident, could have escaped this firestorm alive.

God. How many thousands had died here? How many people had perished instantly, suddenly become a physical part of one of these strange buildings? Had the population of Portland been cut in half overnight? Or was the possibility of half remaining alive an optimistic assessment?

The torched zone terminated at a blackened wall of stone, probably twenty feet high. The street we were traversing passed under an archway in the wall, or at least one lane did, the other half of the road now one with the huge, shaped blocks that composed the wall.

The driver's side of a Kia Soul jutted out a couple of feet, the driver forever stuck within the curve of the archway, like an ornamental feature.

Beyond the wall appeared small, well tended gardens sprouting from manicured lawns, and squat stone houses melded into Colonial Revivals and Cotswold Cottages. And amidst this confusion lay strewn the remnants of a pitched battle, a chaotic scrum that had been fought in the darkness between the baffled survivors.

I could only imagine the terrible struggle that had ensued as bewildered combatants met by flashlight and torchlight, exchanging blows with baseball bats or axes. Here lay a man on his back, a pitchfork protruding upwards from his chest like a shrimp fork from an appetizer. He still clutched a shotgun in one hand. The five corpses sprawled about him, unclad save for blood soaked linen kilts, told a grim tale.

After a few seconds Trina looked down at her hands folded in her lap, and stared fixedly at them, saying nothing until I'd passed through the battlefield.

Just past the last of the bodies I glimpsed movement. An old woman in a shapeless white tunic was sitting on a triangular, three-legged stool, fanning herself with a wide-brimmed, shallow hat. The stool rested against the wall of one of the low, simple stone buildings that I was beginning to suspect meant "peasants live here."

In front of the house was a Prius. A shirtless man was gruesomely *in* the car, his head and shoulders emerging from the roof, his torso melded with the front seat. A cow was similarly fused, its head and front legs emerging from the hood and front bumper.

The old woman just sat there and fanned herself, as I imagine she'd done all morning since emerging from the front door and seeing her man's grotesque demise. She did not look up as we neared.

I pulled to a stop. "What are you doing?" asked Trina.

What was I doing? Responding to a situation, a citizen in distress? These people, whoever they were, were the enemy. And I was no longer, according to Trina, a cop. Still...

"She's an old lady," I said, "looks near catatonic. I don't think I'm in any danger. Maybe I can learn something."

I got out and approached her. She didn't notice until my shadow broke her concentration, or fixation. A sunburned, wrinkled face peered up at me from beneath the straw hat. It was a weather beaten face, but one that suggested it wasn't quite as old as I'd first guessed. This was a woman worn down by hard labor and neglect, not age.

"Your husband?" I asked, nodding my chin towards the macabre display.

Her shoulders pulled in slightly and her face shrank back a fraction beneath the shade of the hat. However, other than this expression of fear, I received no reaction. I hadn't expected her to understand, but–'know your enemy.' Anything I could glean might be useful.

I squatted on my haunches. "Is that your husband?" I pointed with my finger this time. Nothing. I pointed at myself. "I'm Nick. Nick. What is your name?"

This first contact shit sounded stupid to me, and I guess it did to her as well. She stood up without a word, turned her back, and walked back into her house.

"You were right, I was wrong, Trina," I said, climbing back into the cruiser. "It was a pointless exercise."

She rewarded me with a smile and a condescending pat on the knee.

We rolled on through Wonderland, passing out of the new belt of agricultural land and back into the disastrous melding of two alien urban environments. The frequency of corpses rendered them just another aspect of the scenery. The I-84 freeway made a gentle curve south here, just to our right. But now it appeared that the freeway was sharing space with a canal, the road surface submerged beneath thirty feet of sluggish brown water.

Trina and I got out of the cruiser and walked to the railing. Things–dead things–bobbed in the murky current, spinning in slow orbits about each other. They bumped gently, linking temporarily or drifting off on different tangents.

A barge, a heavy timbered affair with a single squat deck house at the stern, crept by low in the water. A single crewman stood on deck, looking up at me open mouthed, the long pole in his hand, temporarily forgotten, beginning to slip behind. He was shirtless, wearing only the peasant kilt, though I noticed this one was a pale green. I gave him a little wave as he floated by.

We drove on, hoping at least one of the freeway crossings remained intact. We entered a small pocket of normalcy, a half a block that appeared unaltered, though not untouched. A body lay splayed across the hood of a car, the back of his head stove in, the back of his Trailblazers jersey a stiffening mess of crimson.

A man emerged from the front door of a split-level ranch as we crept along the street. I recognized the expectant look of hope. He'd seen the patrol car. Someone to help him. Authority. Stability. I saw that look fade as he neared and took in the lack of uniforms.

I lowered the window. "Good afternoon, sir," I said.

"Are you a cop?" he asked with a last flicker of hope.

"No, he is not," said Trina, leaning across my lap.

"Are you OK? Did anyone else survive?" I asked.

He nodded. "My wife and daughters slept through the whole thing. I heard a commotion and got up to check." He pointed at the body. "I saw LeRon fighting with a bald-headed dude in a robe and two guys in skirts. One of the dudes in skirts busted LeRon's head with a hammer. I tried calling the cops, but you know." He gestured with both arms, taking in the totality of the new circumstances.

"Yeah, I know. Look, gather in what supplies you can, but keep a low profile. Watch out for these, whatever they are, especially any wearing armor and carrying spears or other weapons."

"Aliens, man. Fucking aliens."

"OK, watch out for the aliens. Do you know 62nd, 63rd Avenue, around Davis Street?"

He nodded.

"Well, it's pretty much burnt to the ground. Good lines of sight now, you can see anyone coming for a long way. If you can, go there tomorrow, about eight in the morning. Maybe we can find other survivors, start organizing."

"Yeah, OK. Thanks." He turned and shuffled back to his house, his shoulders stooped from disappointment.

ഇ൦

"They're not aliens, Nick," Trina said as we drove away.

"What?" I was lost in half-baked plans of armed resistance and building a new society, a jumbled mess of conflicting concepts and nonsense.

"I don't think we should call them aliens. I mean, they're obviously human, we both see that. That's not what I'm talking about. I think..." She stopped for a moment, allowing her thoughts to coalesce into words. "I think they belong here, or something like here, or some other here, just as much as we do."

I didn't precisely follow her, but I was getting used to a constant state of befuddlement and let it go.

"What do we call them, then?" And what did it matter anyway? Other than convenient nomenclature for our use, what was the point in assigning appropriate names? Was she worried about offending them? It seemed important to her, so I tried to mask any dismissiveness in my response. Keeping certain thoughts to myself, and not betraying them by pursed lips, raised brow, or other facial signs that women are so adept at reading, was a skill I'd long practiced. I won't go so far as 'mastered.'

"I don't know. But not aliens. It's like when I was in the dorm, I was assigned a roommate. Neither of us wanted the other to be there, we were just forced upon each other."

"I'm not calling them roommates," I said.

"I'm not suggesting that. I'm just trying to explain what I'm feeling about the situation. I mean, from our point of view they are interlopers. Maybe from their point of view, we are."

"It's a little early for me to begin feeling empathy," I said. I steered around the fire gutted remnants of a church and something that reminded me of a warehouse (though what the elongated, colorful stone edifice might have stored I couldn't guess.) One end of the 'warehouse' was thrust across the entire width of the street, forcing me to drive onto the sidewalk to bypass the obstacle.

"They probably don't want to be sharing Portland with us, but where can they go now? They're like refugees living in an abandoned building. Squatters."

"We called them 'adverse possessors' in crim," I said. "I never thought that was accurate. It was like the instructor was compensating for not making it through law school and kept trying to shoehorn inappropriate euphemisms onto half-remembered concepts." I eased the cruiser off of the sidewalk and back onto pavement that was now checker-boarded with broad paving stones. The alternating stone slabs of slate gray and dusty rose glittered with specks of quartz.

"Neither of those are quite right, anyway," Trina said. "We're like competing claimants for the same land."

"Well, those claimants are going to lose the competition,"

I don't think my words carried conviction. Fair enough. I was far from convinced myself. And I don't think it mattered at the time. I think we were both talking just to avoid thinking too closely about what we were viewing outside the car. The sight of bodies was becoming commonplace, but that didn't make it any more pleasant. Thinking about why or how all these people died only led to maddening whirls of speculation.

Better to just talk.

ഊഗ

We found the 39th Avenue (or Cesar E. Chavez Boulevard, as I was slowly accustoming myself to refer to it) freeway overpass still in one piece, apparently unaltered. We crossed, and turned westward again, driving down the remnants of Northeast Broadway, looking for likely shops to ransack while picking our way closer and closer to the shops at Lloyd Center.

Broadway proved at first as much of a hopeless amalgam as most of the rest of the city, the buildings no longer discrete, coherent units, the roadbed comprised of varying surfaces. After a few hundred yards I noticed a row of stone buildings flanking one side of a section of cobblestone street–the type of structures I was now beginning to think of as 'Claimant buildings.' These particular edifices stood two stories tall and were narrower than the peasant housing or the elaborate villas I'd mostly observed today.

A trio of men sat on a neatly fashioned stone bench. All three were kilted, but these weren't bare-chested. They wore short tunics, and one bore a leather apron over the top of that.

I kept my speed constant, cruising slowly by. Their heads turned as we rolled past, faintly lifted eyebrows suggesting a certain dulled curiosity, but nothing more.

A fourth man emerged from the door of one of the Claimant buildings. He was adorned in an embroidered, split-skirted robe of turquoise hued silk. A small, three-lobed hat–reminding me of a matador's headgear–perched on his head.

He displayed none of the others' dull curiosity; his response was unhesitating. He roared out something to the three spectators. They leapt to their feet with alacrity, demonstrating the sort of instantaneous, ingrained obedience I associated with recent boot camp graduates. They sprinted after the cruiser, workman's tools clutched in their fists: a heavy pair of shears, a hammer, and some implement I couldn't make out.

I gunned it and left them behind.

"Did you see that?" Trina asked.

I assumed it was a rhetorical question, but I answered anyway. "Yes. Those guys sure hopped to it. Whoever the Claimant in the hat was, he sure had some juice with the other three."

"I think he was a priest, a Claimant priest. When I see a robe and a hat, I think priest."

I could see by her grin that she was pleased I'd adopted her appellation for the newcomers.

"I am in awe of your analytical powers, professor," I said. "Robe and hat."

I pulled to a stop at what I can best describe as one-third of an auto-parts store. I'm not sure what the other two-thirds consisted of now. Maybe it was a bakery. The upper section was more rounded than I'd come to associate with Claimant buildings, and it appeared open at the top, like a chimney.

I managed to salvage a half-dozen car batteries. I figured a quiet power supply could be useful.

"Nick!" Trina called.

The urgency in her voice brought me sprinting. The last two batteries swung from my hands by their handles, threatening to dislocate both shoulders.

Incredibly, the three Claimants hadn't given up. Trina had spotted them jogging down the street. Had they just assumed we'd continue along the same road? Or had they carried on running because they'd had no orders to the contrary? "Go," they were told. And they went.

I didn't know and I didn't wait around to speculate. They didn't worry me; I could just shoot them if I had to. But I certainly wasn't going to let it come to that, especially with Trina along for the ride. So I cranked over the engine and pulled away from our frustrated pursuers.

ꙮ

Shopping for the apocalypse was not something I'd prepared for and the vast cattle pen now inhabiting the same space as the mall didn't make it any easier.

I found a place to park underground near one of the entrances to Sears. By that I mean I backed up to the door and opened the trunk.

Neither of us were prepared for the smell that assailed us when I pried open the locked doors. It was a musty, wet, earthy smell–the scent, we soon discovered, of feces and frightened cows. Some lowed and stalked in bewildered fashion past the Binyons, Hot Topic, and Banana Republic. Others floundered helplessly across the ice-skating rink.

There was something odd about the cattle, other than the setting that is. I'm no country boy, but I've seen cows, and these seemed bigger than the grazing dairy cows I'd glimpsed through car windows.

Still, we carried on looting as efficiently as we could manage.

I caught a glimpse of another group of 'shoppers' in Sears. I waved, but upon sighting me they scrammed through the nearest exit.

"What the hell?" I said.

"Think, Nick. Even out of uniform you still scream 'cop.'"

Smart woman, my wife. I guess the new paradigm hadn't sunk in. These folks–in the midst of a massive five-finger-discount junket–saw a police officer. I guess I shouldn't be surprised they didn't stop to think that law and order was on hiatus. They didn't stop to consider that I was doing the same thing they were.

I began to wish I'd boosted a pickup truck; the cruiser's cargo capacity was limited. I manhandled a small gasoline-powered generator into the trunk and added an assortment of tools.

Trina stockpiled blankets and warm clothing for the winter. We weren't going to have the luxury of relying on central heating. We ransacked the outdoor department. We picked our way through wandering cows, giving the massive bulls a respectful distance, trolling the shops for any oddment that struck us as useful. It was a spree, a downright guilt-free lark. I found myself grinning foolishly, tried to hide it, and then gave up when I caught the same gleeful expression on Trina's face.

After cramming the car full from floor mats to ceiling liner, we found we still had a bit of room on the front seat. And with the bungee cords I'd picked up, we could make even more space by strapping a few items to the roof. So we drove across the street to the grocery store, loading up on non-perishables and pharmaceuticals. Antibiotics and the like.

The shelves, I noted, were already conspicuously sparse. A positive sign I hoped.

"Don't forget condoms and birth-control pills," Trina said.

"Huh?" I replied. I'm not stupid, I don't believe, but at times I do open my mouth before taking time to ponder my words.

"I don't think I'm going to be able to receive a new birth-control injection anytime soon. I don't really think we want to bring a baby into this situation. Do you?"

"Oh, right. Condoms and the pill, check."

The sun was beginning its decent behind the West Hills when we commenced our drive home. I noticed evidence of looting at some of the other more-or-less intact storefronts that we passed. I was amused by the conflicted response the smashed plate-glass windows evoked in me. I was relieved by this additional sign of survivors, but the cop in me was irked at such lawless, uncivilized behavior. I mean, sure, people needed the supplies. But did they need to break the windows?

Is it possible to be both consistent and human?

Points of light glowed on Mt. Tabor, like candles on a giant birthday cake, growing brighter as dusk deepened and we wended eastward toward that ancient volcanic remnant. I wondered what had ignited these new fires.

Nearing home we stopped at an unscathed liquor store. By the orange light of the increasing conflagration we stuffed the remaining crannies of the cruiser's interior with looted booze. The end of the world was nothing to face sober.

Chapter 3

THE NEXT DAY I ENLISTED THE FIRST RECRUIT OF MY RAG-TAG, ROUGH-and-tumble resistance force.

Trina was opposed to the idea from the beginning.

The recruit wasn't LeRon's neighbor; he didn't show up at the rendezvous. I did show up, a little bleary eyed from a late night of unloading the car–a labor that demanded frequent liquid relief from a recently liberated bottle of top-shelf bourbon.

I hid the cruiser in a garage that now abutted what I took to be a grain silo–judging from all the grain inside–though it looked nothing like any silo I'd ever seen. Toting the riot gun, I moved from shelter to shelter until I reached a concealed observation point from which I could survey the rendezvous point and its environs.

Nothing moved. Nothing stirred the blackened ashes of this once vibrant stretch of Portland but the occasional gentle breeze. I sipped a bottle of water and pondered the demise of the world I knew.

Trina had been resistant to my traveling alone. But our excursion the day before had demonstrated that while it was by no means risk free, it wasn't suicidally perilous. Trina was used to my daily absence on patrol–a job that was never entirely free of danger–so solo excursions in this new world were really just a matter of degree. I hoped that she was at least resigned to the idea, even if she didn't entirely buy my argument. Given the recent upheaval I was going to be compelled to forage on my own if we were to survive. It was best that she accustom herself to the inevitable now.

Or so I consoled myself while waiting and nursing my morning-after flu.

ꕥ

I first caught sight of Jim Cantrell limping along the blackened remains of the street, supported by a baseball bat he was using as a cane and stirring up a dark gray trail of ash in his wake. The barrel of the deer rifle slung over his shoulder bobbed in rhythm with each halting step.

I observed his gradual progress for ten minutes, wary of I don't know what. Perhaps the Claimants were using him as a stalking horse to flush out other survivors. Maybe–hell, maybe anything. At this point paranoia struck me as a vital survival skill. So I let him hobble along unaided until I felt reasonably certain he was alone and not being pursued.

I figured he was likely to be a bit jumpy–I was–and I could see he was armed. So I kept to my concealment behind the bed of a gutted pickup when I hailed him.

"Sir, are you OK?"

The rifle was off his shoulder and traversing toward me in an instant, one-handed but relatively steady.

"Relax, I'm not one of them," I said. My voice was calm, but I wasn't about to move from cover.

The barrel wavered for a moment. Then he swung it back to a shoulder arms position. "Hell, you're speaking English. I guess you couldn't be one of those bastards. You startled me is all."

His words came in an easy going flow but were slurred a trifle by swollen lips. At this distance I could see he was mottled with contusions and webbed with abrasions. He'd either been in a car wreck or a fight.

I laid the shotgun across one corner of the bed of the truck in a gesture of peace before I hoisted the rest of me into sight. "Yeah, whatever language they speak, it isn't English," I said. "I'm Nick. Nick Gates"

"Jim Cantrell." He limped over, slipping the sling of his rifle back over his shoulder.

"You look like you took on the Winterhawks and lost," I said.

"I feel like it too." He eased his butt down on the bumper of the pickup and leaned back against the scorched tailgate.

"What happened? I mean to you, not this," I said, clarifying by an all encompassing gesture.

He laughed. "I know what you mean. I saw it happen, though, but I couldn't tell you what happened."

"You were awake? I was too, but I didn't actually *see* any changes."

"Yeah, I was, and I did." He paused, and I don't think the pain I saw cross his face was entirely from his injuries. After a moment he said, "'kay, here's the story from the top. Understand that times have been a little rough for me recently, and I'm not talking about this shit. Job, wife, house–gone. I'm not going to bore you with it, don't worry. A friend of mine let me stay at his house with him and his wife while I started putting my life back together. I was up late when it happened. Greg–my buddy–was up with me, not letting me brood and drink alone."

He stopped again, and I waited patiently. One of the things you learn as a cop is how to listen and, anyways, I could appreciate the picture he was sketching with only a few lines. I have–or had–only a few good friends, but I could imagine the best among them staying up late with me if my life had utterly collapsed, listening and keeping me from falling into solitary, alcoholic mopery.

"Greg was standing in the den, beneath the rack of the big six-pointer he'd bagged last season. Then the air sort of thickened, like it became water or something. It *rippled.* And then, where Greg was standing, there was a stone wall, painted a sort of salmon pink. The ends of antlers still poked out, and below them, the tip of Greg's nose and his shoes.

"One second he was alive, the next he was part of a wall. No time to scream, no time to think 'here it comes.' Just dead, like that." He snapped his fingers.

"So," he continued, "I discovered that Greg's house was now part of another building, all mashed together like. It was a temple, I think. And I wasn't alone in it. I worked my way through the mish-mash of walls, like a maze you know, and I ran into some skinny dink in a robe and a funny hat–what?"

"Nothing, just got something down my wind pipe. Go on."

"Anyways, he starts yelling some gibberish and two guys in armor, toting spears, come running. I'm in this big hallway lit up by torches, with these big gargoyle-looking idols throwing shadows. Spooky, you know. Anyways, I turned around and ran back the way I came. Greg's gun case was in the den. It hadn't been...absorbed. I grabbed the 30.06

and loaded it before the tin soldiers could catch me. They tried to stick me with their spears, so I shot them. I filled my pockets with cartridges and tried to get out.

"It... it wasn't easy. There were a lot of them." He didn't elaborate. He didn't need to. The marks on his body told the tale well enough.

"Do you have a place to stay, Jim?"

"You cruising, Nick? I know I'm pretty."

I laughed. I told him my story as we drove back to my house.

ꝏ

"Trina, this is Jim Cantrell. Jim, my wife Trina."

"Oh, God. Come in, sit down. I'm sorry, we have no ice. Let me get some disinfectant and bandages. We just looted a pharmacy, so we should be able to fix you up." Trina can ramble a bit when flustered, but simultaneously she's thinking rapidly, working through the problem. She disappeared into the bathroom to rummage through our now fully stocked medicine cabinet.

"I like her," said Jim as he eased his battered frame onto the couch with a grunt of pain.

ꝏ

I recruited my next two freedom fighters two days later while Trina was nursing Jim back to health. She declared that he needed a crutch in place of a baseball bat–a reasonable request.

I was glad of the excuse to get out of the house. I'm a restless sort, and I was reluctant to face having to bunker down, either in hiding or under siege (a question more of 'when' than 'if'.) I determined to take advantage of as much freedom to roam as possible.

I once again navigated through the weirdly altered thoroughfares of Portland, this time working my way south and a bit west. I stopped once to siphon gas from a parked Subaru Forester. The house behind, a rundown Craftsman Bungalow, was now merged with a shrine and public fountain. Frowning statues slightly in excess of life size stood guard over a bubbling font and square stone catch-basin. Each statue was posed with outstretched arms terminating in cupped palms. I was beginning to recognize specific facial types in the statuary.

There was an orderliness, a sameness, about the Claimants' architecture that was at odds with Portland's eclecticism. Soviet-era apartment blocks as designed by ancient Egyptians, looming idols standing in for the commies' colossal figures of heroic workers. What kind of people built like this?

The medical supply store I'd intended to plunder was now a burnt-out shell, as were its immediate environs. So I continued south, steering for a convalescent center, and hoping the Mt. Tabor fires hadn't engulfed the entire hill.

I was happy to discover that the conflagration had not been total. The convalescent center rose into view, seemingly unharmed, as were the buildings and trees nearby–unharmed, though not entirely unchanged. I was not happy to see the top tier of a ziggurat peeking above the pines farther south.

I was staring at the ziggurat as I crept nearer to my destination, so I almost didn't notice the young woman who leaped clear from her hiding place behind the decorative hedge framing a bus-stop shelter.

I hit the brakes before I hit her. Luckily, my recent habit was the slow crawl. The streets were too hazardous now to drive the posted speed.

Over a no-longer white, ribbed tank top she wore an oversized denim jacket with the sleeves rolled back. Her dark hair was pulled back in a pony tail. She was flagging me down with both arms, unnecessarily at this point.

I kept the engine running, but lowered the window. She came around the side.

"Thank God," she said, then, "Are you a cop?"

"Up 'til a couple days ago." I still kept the motor chugging and my eyes roving.

"Tonio, it's OK. Come on out," she called over her shoulder.

Another figure appeared from behind the topiary. He was dark complected, didn't stand much taller than she, and was dressed much the same. I noticed the leather sheath of a machete emerging from beneath the hem of his jacket. He kept his head on a nervous swivel. I didn't blame him a bit.

He came around to her side. My hand eased down to rest on the .45 at my hip.

"Luisa, I told you, anybody could be driving a cop car," he said.

"Yes, but not one of *them*," she answered.

I made my decision. "I'm going to pull into the lot. Let's talk out of the street. It's too exposed here."

They walked behind me as I maneuvered the cruiser to a spot in the parking lot between a panel van and a Mercedes SUV. I grabbed the riot gun and got out. "C'mon. Talk to me while I hunt for a crutch. And whatever else useful I can find in here."

They exchanged glances. "A crutch?" she said.

"Just as likely to find one of them," he said.

"Maybe so, but the wife said I need to bring home a crutch, so I'm going to bring home a crutch." Besides, it couldn't hurt to augment our pharmaceuticals. And now I had a couple of vigilant sorts watching my back. Probably.

We climbed the stairs to the old brick pile and entered the front doors. It smelled like death inside.

"I told you," said Tonio, though to the best of my recollection I don't believe he had. "They were here. They've been hunting us down, fucking hunter-killer patrols, man!"

I didn't betray any nervousness, I don't think, though I did bring the shotgun to a ready position. "Why don't you tell me your story? I don't think there's anyone here alive but us right now. You'd have noticed."

"I think he's right, Tonio. And anyway you've got, like, animal instincts; you always see them coming." Something in her tone suggested to me that her compliment was barbed.

We moved through cavernous, antiseptic corridors, walking over buffed white floors scuffed by the impact of some sort of hard soled shoes. We breathed the odor of dried blood and the early stages of decay, deliberately staying in the hallways and avoiding the rooms. Tonio and Luisa began relating their story of surviving the change.

"We were staying with Tonio's parents," Luisa said.

"They had an apartment on Stark, over that way," Tonio said, "with two bedrooms."

"We didn't see it happen, we were sleeping."

"We was tired, man. Luisa, she work two jobs, and I work overtime every day last week."

"But we woke up near dawn when the screaming got too loud."

"It was fucked up, man. Houses burning and shit. Buildings just different. You know."

"Tonio's mom and dad were sitting on the couch in front of the TV."

"It wasn't even on and they were just, like, staring at it."

"We sat with them until dawn. Then we went outside to take a look. All four of us."

"We saw that big pyramid, like they have in Mexico, you know?"

"And we saw lots of soldiers. Not regular soldiers–no guns, no camo uniforms."

"Big fucking spears, man. And they were killing everybody!"

"They were just marching down the street. And at every house four or five of them would break off from the group and knock down the front door."

"Every house that was still a house, and not one of those Fred Flinstone-looking places."

I didn't think his description of the Claimant's construction was very apt. The stone structures were elegant, in their way. They were regularly and exactly constructed, and elaborately decorated, not the crude huts of Bedrock. But I let it go.

"Tonio's folks went back into the apartment. We went with them to grab some stuff."

"They didn't want to leave, man. They was just hugging each other and crying. Luisa got some food in a grocery bag and I got my machete. Then we tried to drag my papa and my mother downstairs. He was hitting me and she was crying..."

"We had to let them go. Tonio did everything he could, but they weren't moving. It wasn't your fault, baby. The soldiers were almost there."

I found a likely looking room. Glass windows sandwiching a wire protective grid allowed a glimpse of stocked shelves. I went in, giving my two young companions a moment to compose themselves. I stuffed my pockets with small bottles, the labels of which I didn't bother reading.

I saw no crutches. But there was another door. I pulled that open. There I found a wheelchair, and, leaning in a corner several pairs of crutches. But I didn't notice those for a moment.

What captured my gaze was the old man sprawled on a bed, arms flung wide. A cloud of flies hovered over the corpse, centered above a gaping slash in his abdomen from which dangled a loop of intestine. A splatter of dried blood tracked along the floor leading to a door that would adjoin the main hallway.

I stood motionless for several minutes. I was piecing together moving images from Tonio and Luisa's story with what I'd imagined had occurred here in the convalescent center. The soldiers themselves I could picture easily; they were permanently engraved in my memory. I could see them trooping in lockstep down the center of the street, a column streaming from the front entrance of the ziggurat, gaping like the mouth of hell. Their wide-bladed pole arms glinting above them, like the flickering points of light across a river's ever shifting surface, and their armor rippling like the scaled fish darting below. The front of the column begins peeling off left and right, like the mouth of a delta, each separate strand flowing into a house. Blood then puddles from beneath the doors and out each window. I could see them filing into the convalescent center, tramping down the halls, smashing open doors and butchering helpless old men and women in their beds. It was all remarkably vivid, a lucid daydream.

"Hey, man, you OK...oh, shit!" Tonio said, from behind my shoulder.

I stepped to the corner and grabbed a pair of crutches. "Yeah, I'm OK. Let's get out of here. Luisa doesn't need to see this."

But I was too late. Her eyes grew wide, and then narrowed into slits of pure hate.

"Come on you two. Like you said there is a ziggurat nearby. In that case, we've been in one place too long." I placed one hand gently on her elbow and shifted her about. She didn't resist. Tonio was already moving.

"Do you have a place to stay?" I asked as we descended the front stairs.

"No," Luisa answered, "we've been on the move since...damn!"

I followed her glance and concurred with her epithet. We had been in one place too long. About two dozen Claimant soldiers marched toward us, still about two hundred yards away.

Tonio stepped in front of Luisa and dragged free his machete.

"The hell with that, Tonio," I said. "There are too many of them. Get in the car."

We hustled. Tonio crawled into the back seat and I tossed the crutches in with him. Luisa hopped in beside me and I left thick streaks of rubber to memorialize our visit.

Reaching ramming speed and tearing through the Claimants like bowling pins was tempting, but foolish. I'd seen what they could do with those spears of theirs, big ungainly things like something out of a badly dubbed martial-arts movie. It wouldn't take too much for one of them to take out a tire, or smash through a window to cleave open one of our heads. No, it was back home with two more foundlings. I wondered what Trina would say.

Despite my best intentions the little horror docudrama I'd just envisioned wouldn't stop running through the projector in my head. And I remembered the rage in Luisa's eyes. And I remembered Tonio's grief as he described leaving his parents to be slaughtered.

I pulled a u-turn, gunned the cruiser toward the marching soldiers, then with a practiced ease that would have made my police academy driving instructor proud I spun the wheel and slid to a stop perpendicular to the head of the column.

I lowered the window, leaned as much of my head and shoulders out as I could to ease the impending noise inside the car. Then I leveled the barrel of my shotgun at the front rank and hammered them with five rounds of buckshot, leaving four Claimants sprawled on the asphalt, bleeding out.

Then, listening to the cheers of Tonio and the delighted growls of Luisa I drove us home.

ꙮ

"Well," said Trina, "it will be nice to cook for several people again. I was beginning to miss it a little bit."

I hugged her close. "You are the best, baby," I whispered. "All these people–I'm just dropping them on you without warning."

She smiled a 'we'll talk about it later' smile and took Luisa under her wing like a sister.

We set up Tonio and Luisa downstairs. The front of our house presented only a single story facing the street. But a slight depression in the hillside opened like a bowl behind the house, dropping at a steep enough angle to allow us two stories at the rear of the house. Jim bunked in the spare bedroom (den, study, library, whatever the hell it was) upstairs. Sitting in the living room after a terrific supper–Trina worked wonders with canned food and rice–I could envision the house beginning to feel a might cramped soon.

We were plenty cozy in the living room. The couch and padded reclining chair required augmentation in the form of a couple of chairs from the dining room table. We sat grouped around the coffee table. I sat with Trina on the couch facing the fireplace with the antique Civil War saber hanging above the mantle. That was Trina's one concession on the living room furnishings. She felt that instead of it being unduly masculine it added an old fashioned character to the room, providing a hint of class from a bygone era that elevated the IKEA dominated decor a notch.

We'd avoided discussing the day's unpleasantness over dinner. Now Trina and Jim listened–Trina horrified but trying not to show it, Jim enraged and not bothering to hide it–as Luisa and Tonio recounted their story again, adding the new details from the convalescent center.

"What are we going to do about this, Nick?" Jim asked. "I mean about the Claimants? Do we just hunker down and wait for them to come kill us?"

Trina gripped my arm, hard. "What are we going to do about it?

Nothing. There is nothing we can do. This is too big a problem for five people to solve. We hide. We wait."

"Wait for what?" Jim asked again. "You heard Tonio and Luisa. Those Claimant soldiers aren't waiting."

"We wait for our own soldiers," said Trina. "We heard a fighter jet the other day. That has to be ours. The Claimants don't have that kind of technology."

"I don't know, Trina," I said as gently as I could, placing my free hand over her two white-knuckled hands. "Maybe if we were up in Seattle. Fort Lewis is right down the freeway from them. Assuming the whole base didn't get transformed into a lake or something there's probably enough left to start fighting back. But we don't have a big military presence nearby. There's the Air National Guard stationed at PDX—that's probably where the jet came from. And there are a few Guard and Reserve units scattered about, but they aren't active—they aren't staffed 'round the clock with armed men."

"So we wait for the troops from Fort Lewis," Trina said, but I could hear the doubt in her voice. She was a realist if you probed far enough beneath the surface.

"Waiting doesn't sit right with me," said Jim. Tonio nodded and Luisa growled.

"Baby, I don't know," I said to Trina. "If there were more of us, maybe we could bunker down, defend ourselves when they come. But there are just the five of us. We can't hold the house for long against a real assault. Five are too many to really hide for long, and too few for a big fight."

"Then what does that leave us?" asked Trina, still looking for a safe resolution.

"Hit-and-run," said Jim. "Guerrilla tactics."

I nodded. "Keep them off balance. Make them worry more about their security than hunting down survivors."

"Sweetheart, you were a cop, not a soldier," Trina said. "You weren't trained for this." She turned to face Jim. "You going to tell me you were a Green Beret, or a Seal, or some shit?"

"No ma'am. I served, but I'd never lie about a thing like that. I just fixed tanks. Didn't drive 'em, didn't fight 'em. Just fixed 'em. But I know one end of a rifle from the other. I shot Expert every time. And I imagine if we put our heads together we can figure out a way to do some damage and get away clean."

"What about you two?" Trina asked, turning on Tonio and Luisa. "Do you know anything about fighting?"

"I wasn't in no gang," said Tonio defensively, as if Trina had accused him of something. "I ain't never shot a gun. But I can learn."

"Good," put in Jim. "You won't have to unlearn anything. Gang-bangers can't shoot for shit."

Trina ignored him. "Come on, Luisa. You're not seriously thinking about this."

It was a fruitless search for an ally. Luisa locked eyes with Trina and to me her reply sounded earnest and unfeigned. "I'm dead serious. You didn't see what they did to that old man in the hospital. I'm sure you've seen enough of the bad stuff that happened. Maybe it wasn't on purpose. This whole thing could be some big accident. But what they–the Claimants–did after it all started...I just want to hurt them."

"Nick, it's not safe," Trina tried, a faltering, rear-guard gambit.

I lifted her hands off of my arm and held them both gently between my own. "Baby, you know I never wanted to change the world. I never worried about leaving the world a better place. I just wanted to make a good life for you and me, and maybe help a few people, get a few bad guys off the street. But now, if there is any hope left of making a good life for us, I need to try to change the world. Or at least a little part of it."

"What a load of horseshit, Nick," she said. "What movie did you steal that speech from?" That hurt and she saw it. So, being Trina, she added, "Still...maybe somewhere, buried under all the crap, you have a point."

"Not buried that deep, baby. You won't need hip waders. I'm preaching nothing but the truth. If we do nothing, eventually they are going to find us and kill us. If we take the fight to them maybe,

maybe, we can buy enough time for whatever is left of the armed forces to get its act together and save our asses."

She sighed and leaned her head on my shoulder.

"So," asked Jim, "how are we fixed for guns?"

Chapter 4

Guns didn't prove to be much of a problem. I had my service pistol and the shotgun, a Remington 870 Police Model. I also kept a little snub-nose .38 in a box in the closet, but I didn't count it among our assets–it wasn't much of a battlefield weapon. Even the .45 was too much of a close quarters tool for the safe distance, hit-and-run tactics I was envisioning.

Jim had his deer rifle, though we'd need to scrounge up a couple boxes of ammunition from a sporting goods store, if we could find one intact. A gun store would be even better, solving a host of problems in the armory department. But given the extent of the changes I wasn't going to hang our hopes on such a fragile hook.

As it happened, we sorted out our armaments deficiency in short order. In the morning we split up and explored the warped mazes that had once been my neighbors' houses. The altered architecture caused problems, of course. But we persevered. The Diaz house was frustrating–the bottom section of Bernardo's gun cabinet bellied out from a stone wall, and above it the merest skin of glaze from its glass front sheened over the dull ocher fresco that now encased his collection of rifles. I gritted my teeth, regretting the loss of the Winchester .270 and especially the Ruger Mini-14. I remembered Bernardo showing them off to me, his cop neighbor, with a mixture of pride and–not fear exactly, but that lightly buried concern I had long ago become accustomed to. It happened when conversations with civilians edged the slightest bit toward entirely innocent, (yet somehow fraught) territory: guns, fast cars, taxes, etc.

The search of the Clark's house was more fruitful. Disturbing, but fruitful. The bedchambers of Mr. and Mrs. Clark and Mr. and Mrs. Claimant had somehow existed in juxtaposed spatial coordinates or the same point in alternate universes, or something. I really had no idea. Whatever the reason, they now occupied the exact same spot. As did their beds. As did–more or less–they themselves. It wasn't pretty, so I won't dwell on it, or the smell. But Adam Clark's closet was untouched. Leaning in one corner of the closet, behind a couple of winter coats, was a pump-action Mossberg twelve-gauge.

We turned up a couple of 9-millimeter pistols in the course of ransacking the neighborhood, a Beretta and a Ruger. A couple of backup pieces couldn't hurt if things got too hot. But the real treasure was in Mr. Fulton's basement–once we got beyond a vast sunken wading pool, its tiled bottom a mosaic of the ubiquitous Claimant gods. Mr. Fulton had possessed a Korean War vintage M1, maintained in immaculate condition, rust free and still reflecting light from its last coat of oil. He may have owned other guns as well because we found a reloading press and sufficient variety of brass to keep all of our various calibers supplied with cartridges for anything short of a war. We were never able to locate the other weapons, but the day's haul was quite satisfactory.

"Hot damn," was Jim's verdict, and I concurred.

The search allowed me a closer inspection of Claimant habitations. Of course I could only observe odds and ends. The Claimant jigsaw pieces had been thoroughly jumbled up with ours in the world's puzzle box. Still, the remains of the Claimant estates contained more intriguing matter than the dull, utilitarian peasant dwellings I'd observed in passing. There should be quite a lot to glean.

I found myself missing Gordon again. I wondered what had become of him. Likely dead. The statistics did not favor him. But he would have come in handy since archeology was one of the perennial academic's fields. I wasn't really up to the task.

I didn't know what to make of the bric-a-brac or the angular, geometric furnishings, or the mono-chromatic clothing. I was, nonetheless, struck by the homogeneity, the sameness of Claimant design and decoration. The uniformity smacked not so much of stagnation as of stasis–a culture that had decided this shall be our existence and no other.

ﻉ✿ﻇ

That evening we convened our council of war after dinner, another masterful repast concocted by Trina. She always shone when we had company (not that our meals alone were ever subject to reproach.)

"So, Cochise, you and your little band of Apaches still plan on taking on the 7th Cavalry?" Trina said, probably trying for playful banter but not quite pulling it off. I think she felt it too, for she quickly appended, "what have you got in mind, and how can I help?"

"Right," I said, "we can't draw up a detailed plan tonight. We need to perform some reconnaissance first, gather what information we can on the enemy."

That sounded good, I thought. Encouraging and professional. Jim, at least, was nodding his head and he'd been in the service.

"But," I said, "in broad brush strokes, we need to make the Claimant soldiers afraid to hit the streets. Now maybe I'm wrong, but to me those big ziggurats appear to be barracks."

"At the least," said Jim. "Forts of some kind too, not just cannon fodder housing."

"So we hit them when they come out," said Luisa.

"Yeah," said Tonio, failing to conceal his excitement, "make them scared to stick their fucking heads out again. What are we waiting for? We've got the guns, let's go to the pyramid at Mt. Tabor and start the killing."

"That one's just as good as any other, I suppose," I said. When confronting civilians try to find common ground before addressing the dispute. "But like I said, let's take a look around first. We're not planning a drive-by. We need to find a good spot to attack from and make sure we have a clear path to withdraw afterward. Besides, you said you've never fired a gun. Maybe Jim ought to make sure you are more of a danger to the Claimants than you are to us before we go in for real."

Tonio bristled for a moment, but I think he was fundamentally a smart kid. He was just overshadowed by a cleverer girlfriend.

"Yeah, OK. You are right. I just want to get back at those..." he paused for a moment, then ran off a rapid-fire string of Spanish profanities. "You know?"

We all nodded. Yeah, we knew. Even Trina the Understanding, who was always conscientious about looking at the other guy's viewpoint before forming her judgment, nodded her agreement, apparently feeling that some recompense was due for the devastation we'd suffered.

"When do we start?" asked Luisa.

"Tonight? Scout them out in the dark?" Tonio asked, all eagerness again.

"Not in the dark," said Jim. "Night recon is for pros, which we ain't."

"Also I wouldn't be able to see shit," I said. "Remember we want to hit them from a distance and run away. In the dark I wouldn't be able to figure out lines of sight, which way to skedaddle, places the Claimants might be holed up along our line of skedaddling. That sort of thing. I think we should start tomorrow. Jim can start basic training while I go take a look."

We left it there for the night, going our separate ways. Jim headed to the spare bedroom, Trina and I to our room, and Tonio and Luisa downstairs–Luisa keeping Tonio in perpetual giggles by whispering "skedaddle" in his ear every time his chuckles threatened to subside.

"Jesus, Nick, you almost sounded like you knew what you were talking about," Trina said as we walked down the hall.

"C'mon Trina. I read. I watch the History Channel."

"Great. Try to remember you're not a soldier." She left it there for awhile. Then, later, when we climbed into bed, "I'm coming with you tomorrow."

I didn't even attempt to argue.

ꙮ

I'm not a particularly light sleeper. Then again I don't enter some sort of semi-coma. The noise I heard was faint, but sufficient to rouse me. It was regular, rhythmic, and growing louder.

I eased out from between the sheets and snatched up my shotgun. I crept out to the front room, only to find Jim's hearing was keener than mine, or he *was* a light sleeper. I could just make him out in the darkness–a red-tinged silhouette, rifle in hand, a crutch under the opposite arm. He was behind a curtain, peaking out the window through a gap in the house's camouflaging outworks.

"What is it?" I whispered.

"Take a look," he whispered back.

So I did. Reddish circles of torchlight bobbed up and down in unison, illuminating a marching column of soldiers. Their disciplined tramp-tramp-tramp produced the sound that had disturbed me. I estimated about fifty of them as I watched the company gradually ascend the hill.

I shared a glance with Jim. Night patrol. Was it random? Were they looking for us? Were they coming *here*?

"Do we have any lights burning?" I asked.

I hadn't yet powered up the generator I'd looted. The noise would have been a dangerous beacon. We'd rigged up some lights to car batteries and we had a couple of kerosene lanterns, but I didn't recall using any light this night.

"Don't think so. Maybe the kids downstairs needed a night light?"

"Check it out, but don't wake them yet."

He leaned his crutch against the wall, placed some weight on the leg experimentally, and seemed satisfied. He padded away with just a slight limp and I turned back to watch the steadily approaching Claimants.

The crimson reflections from spear points and the shifting, rippling red gleam off of the lacquered armor brought back intense memories of the first night of blood and fire. And they tramped inexorably nearer. Nearer to my house. To my wife.

I racked a shell into the riot gun's chamber.

The head of the column was level with the Martens place now, pacing past the idol bedecked fountain. Getting closer.

Jim's footsteps creaked behind me. "No lights." He took up position looking over my shoulder.

They moved beyond the Marten's property line, onto mine. Marching, menacing, by the mail-box. Even with the driveway... and still marching.

I let out a breath I'd been unaware of holding. Just a random patrol after all.

"They're getting bold," said Jim.

"We need to do something about that. Once they get comfortable and methodical..." I didn't need to finish. We were running out of time.

Chapter 5

I GOT AN EARLY START. NOT EARLY ENOUGH TO LEAVE A SLEEPING WIFE behind, but early enough. We did make time for a shower, taking turns pouring water (heated over a battery-powered hot plate) into a large stainless-steel colander hung from the shower head with a twisted wire coat hanger. It was neither a luxurious nor a lengthy procedure, but a bit of warmth and cleanliness can go a long way.

We left Jim explaining firearms safety to Luisa and Tonio, and rolled, unpowered, down the hill.

"We'll find a place to stash the cruiser, then walk the last couple of miles," I said, trying to sound calm, as if bringing my wife along to scout the defenses of an alien, occupying army was unremarkable.

She nodded, tentatively prodding the grip of the little thirty-eight caliber pistol I'd insisted she carry along. She looked unseeing, through the windshield at the transformed Portland we traversed.

"What do you think happened to the electricity?" she asked, dropping the .38 with a grimace of distaste into the glove-box. "Too many power lines turned into something else?"

"Maybe," I said. "Enough transformer-station poles disappear and the grid just can't cope. But I think it was even more than that. I think something happened to Bonneville. I think the dam was compromised. When I crossed the river that night I noticed that the water level was rising. So if the turbines at Bonneville are gone—that's all she wrote for power."

"What about cell phones? I mean, I can see the telephone not working. No power, lines gone. But the cell phones run on batteries. Shouldn't they have worked for a while?"

"Well, sweetheart, cell phones route through local mini-towers that service a small area—a 'cell.' When you leave one cell the mini-tower in the next cell takes over. So it isn't really a question of the phone having power, it's a question of the tower having power—or actually still existing. Maybe the towers have backup generators. I don't know. Cell tower power systems are way out of my comfort zone, baby. Could be some people had cell phone communication within a cell. I really don't know. Did you check yours?"

"Of course, Nick. Didn't you? No, of course you didn't. The police radio stopped working so you stopped caring about talking with anyone."

"Anyone except you."

"Anyone except me. That's what I meant." She leaned her head on my shoulder, silently apologizing for the comment. She was my life and she knew it well enough. She was quiet for a moment. Then she asked, "Are we going to survive this, Nick? Even if we don't get murdered by the Claimants, are we going to survive? I don't know if I'm the pioneer type."

I had my doubts. About survival that is, not about Trina's capacity to rough it. I'd asked myself the same question. But I knew my duty. "We'll get through it Trina. We're not the only survivors. We just need to hold out until the army gets here. Or maybe the navy. Most of those ships at sea must have come through the transformation untouched. Once we deal with the Claimant threat, we can start to rebuild. Enough of the infrastructure remains. And I'm sure there are survivors with more practical skills than cops and cooks."

She nodded. "My dad was in the navy, you know. I remember all of his service buddies were electricians and boiler-fitters and mechanics. I think you're right."

Maybe she did. Or maybe we were just comforting each other.

I parked in a side street off of Stark. The neighborhood, with its houses from the middle of the last century, was interlocked with buildings of an undifferentiated, ageless sameness. A plunging driveway cut through a formerly well-maintained front lawn to what had once been a single-car garage with a ground-level roof. Behind and above the garage had risen a modest two-story home. The front of these structures still existed, like a theme-park facade. A few feet back the wood switched abruptly to the rose-hued stone of a Claimant building. I couldn't make out its purpose, but the other bits of Claimant construction in this amalgam of a neighborhood looked similar.

We left the car in the shade of the narrow driveway's retaining walls and hoofed it south, skirting the western edge of Mount Tabor.

We skulked, moving from cover to cover like a couple of kids playing soldier. Which is what I was doing—playing soldier. Trina was right; I was a cop, not a soldier. I'd never served. I didn't know the first thing about setting up an ambush. But here I was, an untutored amateur, sneaking with my wife through what was for all practical purposes enemy held territory. This was not a childish lark, this was deadly serious.

But other than imitating hunted animals—rabbit, mouse, ostrich, take your pick—what alternative did we have? Besides, I wasn't planning a battle. I didn't need to plan troop movements for an army. I just needed to pick a spot where four people could shoot unsuspecting men who didn't even have guns. And then run away.

"I'm lousy at self-motivation," I muttered.

"What?" whispered Trina.

I just shook my head and we carried on.

The quiet desolation remained eerie. Now and again something hinted at a surviving populace: a peripheral glimpse of light from a window, but when I turned to face it, showed empty, unlit. Imagination, or was someone avoiding notice? The distant thrum of a car engine. Barking dogs. Cooking smells. But we saw no one.

To the east, the rising hillside began to interrupt the changed urban landscape with the patchy forested parcels that climbed up Mount Tabor. We kept west, feeling more sheltered by buildings—unfamiliar though they might be—than by the trees. City folk, the both of us.

The ziggurat grew as we neared. As it came more fully in sight I noticed its ideal location—for the Claimants—between two of Portland's reservoirs. Even a neophyte, armchair soldier like myself recognized the value of water supply. Next I noticed the missing trees, or, rather, noticed the lack of trees. A vast plaza surrounded the ziggurat, about a third of it disappearing back into the hillside, and it was strewn with fallen tree trunks. The arrival of the ziggurat had apparently acted as a gargantuan chain saw, scything through a vast swath of pines.

All the ziggurats I'd seen seemed to have come through with more structural integrity than the common run of Claimant buildings. Curious, that.

"Clean field of fire for them and no hiding place for us to ambush them coming out the front door," I said.

"So ambush them somewhere else," Trina said. "They send out patrols. Find a spot near here and wait for one to come by."

"Aye aye, Admiral," I said, saluting. So we hunted around some more, looking for a promising site for a bushwhacking.

We had a brief scare that forced us to hide behind a topiary hedge. A party of workmen–shirtless, kilt-clad Claimants–trooped by carrying two-handled, cross-cut saws. And later the ziggurat disgorged a patrol, but it marched to the south and west of us so we were in no danger of being spotted.

"That was strangely exhilarating," Trina said when we'd regained the patrol car. "But I think I'll let you go by yourself next time. The high isn't worth that kind of constant tension."

"Want to loot a liquor store on the way home?" I asked, starting the engine. "We can snag a bottle of lemon vodka to take your edge off."

"I'm not drinking warm vodka," she said. Then, a few minutes later, "Maybe a bottle of wine, though."

Chapter 6

THE CLAIMANT SOLDIERS DID NOT SCHEDULE THEIR PATROL PATTERN TO conveniently fit our battle plan. We set the ambush about a half a mile west of the ziggurat. If we'd had a week to observe times and directions we could have discovered their time-table (assuming they had one) and planned accordingly. We did not have that luxury. We needed to start impacting their confidence and hampering their movements as soon as possible.

And so we waited. The campus of a small seminary had once occupied a few square blocks near Mount Tabor. Mostly it still did. It had merged with a collection of utility structures–small, uninhabited storage dumps of dull gray stone. The arrangement of the Claimant outbuildings and the collapsed, sooty remains of the administration building had left a clean lane of fire. It stretched from the groundfloor of a brick edifice that had once been the seminary's lecture hall to the west where the street doglegged around the campus.

We had plenty of time to go over and over the plan. Plenty of time to sip water and take nervous trips to piss. Plenty of time because, while we occasionally heard the rhythmic tramp of boots in the distance, they did not come our way until about three in the afternoon, eight hours after we'd arrived.

It was late summer. Hours of daylight remained and the air was still warm, though the relatively low afternoon heat hinted at the autumn to come.

Again, the steady marching beat announced a Claimant patrol. This time the sound grew louder, more distinct. And then they came into view, the glittering points and edges of their wicked pole arms first, then the elongated helmets, and finally the glossy sheen of orange-and-black hued armor. They came on at an easy pace, four abreast, led by an officer whose armor was covered by a black and orange striped surcoat. His helmet was less lofty, but fronted with a visor bearing the visage of one of the Claimant gods.

I estimated forty soldiers as they neared. So, ten-to-one odds. A company of professional myrmidons against a cop, an ex-tank repairman, and a couple of kids. Yeah.

They marched by, our hiding spots unnoticed. They approached the dogleg and I held my breath. A street branched off southward just before the first angle of the dogleg. If they turned left they wouldn't enter the fire zone.

The officer's stride brought him even with the branching street... and he kept on striding without a pause. I exhaled in relief, and then immediately sucked in another nervous lungful because now he was turning north, into the kill zone. People were about to start dying.

Then he was in the field of fire Jim and I had plotted. In, and marching through. Jim had suggested taking out the officer first, but I had other ideas. So he passed unharmed and unknowing beneath our guns, the soldiers following close behind.

One rank...two...three...four...now!

Jim's rifle boomed, the 30.-06 round flinging a Claimant soldier against the man next to him. Both fell to the pavement in a clatter of lacquered armor and tumbling spears.

The second soldier staggered to his feet a moment later, dripping gore. Even as he rose, another soldier jerked as a round from Luisa's rifle tore through his upper arm. It was her first shot at a living target, and a human one at that. Hell, other than dry firing, it was her first time squeezing the trigger. Hitting anything was a wonder.

The wounded Claimant dropped his weapon, clutching at his spurting wound. Tonio's shotgun bellowed, the decibels eclipsing the startled cries of the Claimants. The big twelve-gauge slug tore up the turf two yards shy of the targets. Not a precision weapon, the Mossberg.

The two rifles sounded again, killing one man and incapacitating another. Leaving them living didn't bother me, the wounded were little threat to us and a burden to the Claimants. Let them live.

But now their discipline began to show. The officer shouted commands, and before we took more than four of them out of the fight, the Claimants lowered the points of their weapons and lumbered towards our ambush.

Tonio fired again and a soldier tumbled flat on his face, a red mist erupting from the gaping hole in his back. It was an odd thing–a lifetime of action movies had conditioned me to expect the soldier to be flung back, like a recalcitrant Chihuahua brought to heel by a vicious tug at the leash. The sprawling collapse, like a dropped sack of dog food, came as a surprise.

The rifles barked again and again. Soldiers jerked at the impact, tumbling to the grass, now just suits of armor stuffed with the wreckage of men.

Still the company advanced, picking up speed. They were a tough, armored mass tipped with gleaming blades, little less deadly for the loss of a few sharp points.

The leading Claimants, now at a sprint, reached–then passed–a dreary looking storage shed of gray masonry that was stocked with leather tack and harness. The shed was about a dozen yards shy of the doorway where Jim, Luisa, and Tonio were blazing away, taking a steady toll.

From the concealing darkness of the shed I stepped into the doorway as the first three soldiers hurtled past me and began pumping buck shot into the following soldiers at point-blank range. I held the Remington tucked tightly against my shoulder, picking targets with a speed and precision that I could only credit to the Portland Police Department's tactical shotgun training course.

I fired off five rounds in rapid succession. The ball bearings punched through armor and meat, ripping open hideous, instantly lethal wounds in each man they hit. The recoil was brutal. The sledge hammer blows grew worse with repetition as the recoil and the action of my off hand to quickly rack each new shell conspired to tug the butt of the weapon further and further from its initial snug seat.

My opening fire was the signal for the other three to break cover and run like hell to the rally point. I stepped out of the cover of the door frame, lowered the riot gun to my hip, and–wrists fighting to hold down the bucking muzzle–fired off the last three shells from the tube. The spreading cones of shot killed two and gashed open the legs of a pair of adjacent Claimants.

And that was enough to break even the impressive discipline of these soldiers. We'd demolished about a third of the company in under a minute. It was too sudden and too devastating. The survivors of the ambush scattered, some discarding their weapons as they ran.

I ran too. That had been a closer thing than I'd anticipated. The last four I'd gunned down had been mere feet away, near enough to gut me like a wild pig. Near enough for me to notice the identical blue tattoos on their faces.

It appeared they'd all fled, but I wasn't risking the possibility of one or two of them possessing cojones of more than standard-issue diameter. In any case, I had no idea how quickly they might regroup. Every second available for flight might be critical.

As it happened, we escaped without incident. We met up at the car, panting from the run, and grinning grins that could indicate anything from exhilaration to hysteria. We piled in and, with a chirp of spinning tires, drove away. For the first mile I drove with less than my usual caution, my heart a six-year-old on a sugar binge.

Tonio jabbered away, sometimes slipping into Spanish, still on a combat high. I wondered how long this would last, and what the crash would be like. If he was going to puke, I hoped he'd wait until he got out of the cruiser.

Luisa had lost her grin at some point. In the rear-view mirror I could see that the tight smile had been replaced by a grim stare, her eyes focused on some point in the cabin but seeing something else entirely. Jim sat beside me up front. He was half turned, trying to converse with Tonio, to calm him down.

I was curious to observe them, and wanted to get back to the house quickly so I could give a greater deal of attention to their behavior. At the same time, I found it mildly amusing that I now fancied myself a combat psychologist. It was odd: I felt a detached interest in the detached interest I felt in the reactions of the other three to the killing—I was clinically interested in my clinical interest. I fought down a rising chuckle.

ಬಲ

Trina greeted us at the door, anxiously. The house was filled with the smells of cooking—an elaborate meal made with professional skill and nervous energy. Not to mention ingenuity, given our lack of refrigeration. I'm sure the food was terrific, but I can't recall a single bite. We sat at the dinner table, shoveling forkfuls into our mouths and recounting the ambush.

Tonio ate as fast as he talked, and I once again feared the potential regurgitative consequences. He occasionally rolled his right shoulder, trying to ease the bruising caused by the Mossberg's recoil. He tried out different phrases to describe to Trina the falling bodies of Claimant soldiers, finally settling on "fucking piñatas," an expression he liked so much that he repeated it over and over once we moved from food to liquor. He did end up sacrificing to the porcelain idol that night, but whether it was from the stress of the afternoon's killing or from over consumption, I'll never know.

Luisa said little. But the grim set of her mouth slipped slowly into a contented smile over the course of the evening. She tried to start a drinking game later on–taking a shot every time Tonio said "fucking piñatas." I stopped worrying about her ability to carry on our little insurgency and started worrying about the aftermath. Did we have a budding sociopath on our hands?

Jim said, "Like I said, it ain't like shooting mule-deer at all." That was the sum total of his personal spoken response to the fight. He wasn't withdrawn. In fact he was the most communicative of us, continuing to try to moderate Tonio and trying to draw out Luisa. To employ a somewhat uncertain cliché, he was a rock. I mean, he provided a certain calm, conversational anchor. At the same time, it was difficult to ascertain what was going on internally.

Like Jim, I'd already had my first combat experience that first bloody, fiery, chaotic night. To a lessened extent I felt the same reaction again–a twinge of delayed guilt, a prickling at the back of the scalp and a tightening of the stomach.

It went away after the first taste of bourbon. If you're going to the trouble of looting a liquor store, you might as well snag the good stuff. And I had.

Later, in our room, Trina cried.

ꕤ

I went to sleep with the fuzzy notion that breakfast would double as a planning session for the next ambush. A pandemic of hangovers postponed the powwow until dinner. I felt relatively chipper and spent a good portion of the day watching out the window with the riot gun in my lap.

Trina stood behind me, rubbing my shoulders after a sandwich lunch of canned tuna-fish. "I won't say I've never been so scared in my life," she said. "Maybe I'm growing emotional calluses, but it is a little bit easier for me every time you risk your stupid neck. So I wasn't a complete wreck yesterday. But I couldn't sit down for more than two minutes at a time. This is hard, Nick."

"I know, sweetheart." I stood up and pulled her into an embrace. "I know it's hard for you. If we can just hit them a few more times, really bloody the Claimants' noses, maybe then we can go to ground, wait for help."

"You don't think this was enough?'

"No. Remember these ziggurats are all over. And one time wasn't enough to hinder even a single base. Word needs to get around that any Claimant fortress or outpost can be hit any time. Look, I'd rather stay here with you. I want to come back safe to you. I mean to come back safe to you."

"This is where I'm supposed to say that I'll try to be strong for you, keep the home-fires burning." She sighed. "Fine. OK. Everything else has changed. I can become a good soldier's wife."

ᘓᘐ

"Thumbs up, attaboys, and gold stars for everyone," I said after a curried rice dish cooked over a propane-fired stove. "Now we plan our next move."

"Do we hit a different base?" Jim asked.

"No, the same one. They have to learn this wasn't an aberration. We ambush another patrol, they'll worry. Maybe beef-up the size and limit the area and duration. Then we can start going after the other ziggurats. Randomly. Fix up a map downstairs with their locations and chuck a dart at it."

"So, we going back to that school?" asked Tonio.

"No, we need to scout another ambush site tomorrow. Damn, we're going to need to do a lot of scouting. I hate to say it, but we're probably going to need to grab a couple of cars, split up, and start mapping the city. Find out where all the ziggurats are."

Tonio stirred excitedly. "But not yet. One job at a time, and right now the priority is the second ambush."

"I don't like the idea of all of us driving around alone," Trina said. "You know what it's like out there. The roads aren't always roads anymore, the Claimants could be anywhere, and even their civilians could be aggressive. A car can't provide certainty of outrunning trouble."

"You're right. It is risky. Maybe we partner up. I can be the odd-man out, go it alone." I raised my hand to forestall Trina's objection. "Just thinking out loud right now. We can make a decision later, after the next ambush."

"Let me come scout with you," said Tonio. "Like you said, it is risky. We should partner up."

"I was thinking maybe Jim–" I began before Tonio interrupted.

"Jim needs to rest that leg after all that running."

"It's still a bit sore," Jim said, an indulgent smile brightening the mottled purple of his still bruised face.

"What about Luisa?" I asked. "Not that I don't want you along, Tonio. It's just that I've got to ask or Trina will call me sexist." It was a feeble lie, but Tonio seemed to buy it. I didn't want to hurt his feelings, but both Jim and Luisa inspired more confidence. I wanted this quiet sneak-and-peak to stay quiet.

"I could use Luisa's help reloading cartridges," Jim said. "She's got the steady hands for the work."

"Go on, Tonio," said Luisa. "Find us a spot to kill some Claimants.

ぷの

So it was Tonio seated next to me as the cruiser glided silently down the hill. I took a different route, intending to approach the ziggurat from the south this time. I didn't want to provide any clues to our whereabouts, and it gave me an opportunity to add to the mental map of this new Portland.

Once again I marveled at the reconfigured town, at the devastation. I thought about death, and then I raised the windows because I realized what the abandoned dumpster odor I was smelling was actually from. I'd been a first responder on body calls before. The stench arose from all the dead. Thousands, hundreds of thousands. Unburied.

I began to worry about disease. Maybe the fires had done some good, cremating a substantial portion of the corpses.

There would be more. Damn, but I was in a grim mood all of a sudden, but there it was. There would be more dead soon. I knew we couldn't be the only survivors. I'd seen too many signs. The jet flyovers, the actual survivors I'd met, distant sounds, Tonio and Luisa's narrative—at least a few of us had come through the change unharmed. A great number of the Claimants had also, though that in itself wasn't particularly compelling evidence that a great number of us had. The whys and wherefores of the change remained a complete mystery.

Still, I'd seen that the Claimants suffered from the change, so maybe if large groups of them had escaped instant death embedded in a wall, maybe entire neighborhoods had been unhurt. Of course the only large groups of Claimants I'd seen had emerged from the ziggurats. The four Trina and I'd seen lounging by the side of the street were just that—only four.

Whatever. Some of us were alive. And now, without our accustomed conveniences, we'd begin to die. Discovered by Claimants and put to the sword. Starved. Carbon-monoxide poison from a generator in an improperly ventilated basement. Killing each other over a can of beans. As a cop I'd seen an inexhaustible variety of unseemly exits from the stage. Without a steady food supply, a regular flow of electricity, and access to hospitals—all of the fundamentals we relied on—the remainder would begin to dwindle. It would happen slowly if the Claimants stayed their hand, rapidly if they secured the city.

Unless we had help. That was what I was trying to do—buy enough time for help to arrive—and moping about Necropolis Portland wasn't going to help.

"Let's find a spot to hide the car, Tonio. We'll walk in the rest of the way."

We parked in an underground lot that was now also a storage cave for cured meats and sausages. We slipped out of the car, closing the doors silently, Tonio's sheathed machete slapping against his thigh. He slid free the blade and cut loose a hanging salami, or whatever the Claimant equivalent was called.

"Why do you carry that brush clearer?" I asked. "I think the Mossberg is your better option."

"I know, man. But I'm still a little uncomfortable with it. It makes me feel better to have something, you know, familiar with me." He cut us each a slice as he spoke, and we began our hike, munching the enemy's food. It wasn't bad.

"Let's remember to load up the trunk when we get back," I said.

We'd driven around to the east slope of Mount Tabor, and the view from the hillside to the city sprawling eastward towards I-205 was just as depressing as that covering the descent westwards toward the Willamette. As far as the eye could see lay the twisted shapes of merged buildings and the wide black streaks of fire-devastated neighborhoods.

"Where do you think everyone is?" I asked, giving voice to my thoughts from earlier. "I mean, those who survived."

"Hiding, man. That's what me and Luisa was doing–hiding and looking for food. Anyone still alive is scared shitless."

"I don't know, Tonio. We can't be that unique. It's a big city. I've heard gunfire, and it can't all just be us shooting each other over a looted bag of chips. Somewhere other people are fighting the Claimants. I saw some of it that first night. If we ever get out of this and rebuild, there are going to be a lot of stories to tell."

"Yeah, people will be buying me beers for the rest of my life." He cut us each another slice of sausage with the satisfied air of a man already enjoying the cold-one due a tale spinner.

ꙮꙮ

We were still a couple miles away from the ziggurat, threading our way through a hopelessly jumbled neighborhood like the handiwork of an insane god playing with mismatched sets of building blocks, when Tonio hissed, "I hear something."

I motioned us to cover, and we flattened ourselves in the shade of Claimant masonry overhung by the top third of an apartment building. A few seconds later I caught it too—the almost musical rhythm of marching soldiers. About a minute later they began to tramp by, a company roughly the same size as the one we'd jumped the other day.

I felt a bit disappointed at first. I don't know what I was expecting—double the troops, advance scouts, flankers, *something* different. I suppose I shouldn't have been surprised. The Claimants didn't show much evidence of being an innovative people and the military is generally assumed to be the most hidebound of a society's institutions. And our plan anticipated that it would take several ambushes to begin to have an effect. Still, I was a little disappointed.

Then I saw it. There, bringing up the rear amidst a bodyguard of four soldiers, was an unarmored Claimant wearing a three-lobed head piece—one of Trina's 'hat and robe' guys. Maybe this wasn't a regular patrol. Maybe they were escorting this priest somewhere else. Or maybe he was escorting them. Maybe we'd made an impression already.

Tonio may have sensed my building ebullience. He looked at me quizzically. I wondered what he saw. Was I quivering like an excited puppy? Grinning like a drunken fool? Pick your cliché; I don't know. But I didn't want to get into it now, raising expectations that might be dashed.

When they'd passed safely out of earshot I said, "Come on. Let's keep going. We have an idea of this patrol route. Let's see if we can find a good spot for an ambush closer to their base."

We ground down some shoe rubber that morning, still hoofing it the long way around. We could have cut across the top of the hill, still mostly wooded and undeveloped. But we stuck to the streets, guessing the backtrack of the patrol route from the width of the streets and the degree to which they remained unobstructed.

As we rounded the far end of our looping path, I noted that the road surface of Division looked relatively pristine as far as I could see.

If I could find a spot to stash the car just off the road Division would make an ideal high-speed escape route. We might be able to set up our ambush in sight of the ziggurat and then high tail it a few blocks to the car. Chancy, but it would sure make the Claimants think twice about sticking their heads out the front door.

We worked our way back north toward the ziggurat that had been serving as a landmark for the last couple of miles. Once again Tonio cautioned that Claimants were nearby. We took cover again, and I scanned the area. There, closer to the towering step-pyramid, were drifting clouds of dust, suggesting construction.

"Let's check it out," I whispered. We slunk forward. Behind a block of single-family homes interlocked with Claimant buildings we saw a gang of shirtless, kilted men constructing the foundation of a new structure from salvaged masonry.

"Shit," I hissed. "They're starting to consolidate around the ziggurats."

"What do you mean?" Tonio whispered back. He was staring intently and I doubt he'd paid much attention to what I'd said.

"Like villagers building close to a castle for protection, back in medieval times. We don't want construction. It smacks of stability. We want things chaotic. Keep them scared and off balance. Next ambush has to be here, where they're starting to feel safe."

So we looked around until we were satisfied, then took the long hike back to the car. And yes, we did remember to fill up the trunk with sausage.

ஐ

"So they've got a construction gang putting up new buildings?" asked Jim, taking a swig from a bottle of beer. One of the advantages I'd enjoyed living in Portland was the access to an embarrassment of craft-beer riches. You couldn't swing a beaver without hitting a brewpub. And good beer, beer with flavor and character, doesn't need to be ice cold to drink. In fact cold masks the full flavor, diminishing the totality of the experience. So, having no refrigeration, it was just as well that we were pushing through the Apocalypse in Portland.

"Yeah," I said. "I don't like it. Shows confidence."

"But I thought you said you'd seen a priest with the soldiers," said Trina, ladling a portion of mashed potatoes on my plate, a boxed concoction she would have turned her nose up at a week ago. "Doesn't that mean you've worried them, because they've changed their behavior?"

"Maybe," I said, digging in. It may have come from a box, but the meal had Trina's touch and was, therefore, delicious. "Or maybe they're confident that simply having a man of the cloth along is enough to thwart the next ambush. The whole Claimant society strikes me as very theocratic. They may well believe it."

"Well," said Luisa, sharing a conspiratorial glance with Jim, "after dinner we've got something to show you that will really put the fear of God into the sons-of-bitches."

I raised an eyebrow. That was the sort of intriguing statement that will make a man hurry through even one of Trina's dinners. And that's what we all did, any pretense to the contrary playing unconvincing and awkward.

We all rattled out to the back yard after a quick scrape and cleansing of the dishes. There Luisa proudly unveiled a five-gallon can of gasoline, every square-inch of which was beaded with ball-bearings, stuck to the aluminum exterior with glue. A rag dangled from the spout.

"Me and Jim were out today too," said Luisa. "We scrounged up five of these and siphoned off gas from about ten cars."

"Home-made claymore mines," said Jim. "Of course not really mines, no sophisticated detonators. Just light, throw, and run."

"How about that?" I said, beginning to adjust the battle plan in my mind. "But maybe we should store them a bit farther from the house."

We each picked one up and made our way next door with the intention of stashing the jury-rigged bombs behind the Claimant fountain. Jim walked beside me, his limp only noticeable if you were looking for it.

"Did you mean all that you said the other day?" he asked.

"All what? I said a lot of things," I answered.

"About buying time until the army can get here. Do you believe that? Or are you just blowing smoke, trying to give the others a bit of hope? 'Cause that's what I think. The bastards are going to nail us eventually, so let's get some payback while the getting's still good. That talk about a holding action is to keep our minds off the inevitable, right?"

"Hell, Jim, I'm not that devious. I do believe it."

"Come on, Nick. We've seen hundreds of Claimants. How many of us have you seen? The change decimated us. What makes you think anyone was spared?"

I started rambling, trying to put my half-formed notions into words. Again I wished Gordon were here. This sort of thinking was his bread-and-butter, not mine. "Building patterns, geography. Similar ideas of where to build based on—on terrain and topography. Most places we put a building, they put a building. So, splat. Everyone is dead. The difference is those ziggurats. Think about it. We keep our military kind of spread out. With guns and bombs you don't need everybody crammed into a small space behind thick walls. You don't *want* everybody like that, like one big target. So our troops are kept spread out. But the Claimants are at a pre-gunpowder technology level, so they can hide safe behind walls. They rely on what are basically castles to hold territory. So while our buildings and their buildings here in the city may, for the most part, be all mashed together, they might not have buildings out in the boonies where we house our big military bases because they wouldn't have use for that land."

"I'd say that sounded almost reasonable, Nick, if reason hadn't taken a powder the night *they* came. The whole thing sounds crazy. If I'm following, your theory is that the Claimants built on the same spots we did—meaning they are from here, from the same place. That makes no kind of sense at all. But if that is true pretty much any damn thing could be true, including something that wiped out every base from Fort Bragg to Fort Lewis. You don't know."

"You're right, I don't know," I said, stooping to store the gas can out of sight of the street. "But I do have hope. I'm not planning some doomed killing-spree like something from a John Woo movie."

"A what, now?" Jim asked, placing his gas can next to mine.

"Never mind. The point is, don't give up. We might still pull through this. Nothing is ever going to be the same, but maybe we can rebuild something worth living for."

"Well, if we can get a brewery up and running again, that'd be worthwhile."

"Amen, Brother Jim," I said, heading back to the house.

ഌഗ

So the next day we left home early to kill a bunch of Claimants in the name of civilization and beer. I kissed Trina goodbye, and she handed me a basket filled with sausage, dry, crumbly cheese, and bread nearing the end of its useful existence.

"Come home safe," she whispered.

I answered with what I hoped was a confident smile, then turned to join the others piling into the cruiser. I placed the basket in the trunk next to the orderly row of gasoline bombs, closed the lid and climbed into the driver's seat.

Chapter 7

THERE IS A HEIGHTENED INTENSITY OF SENSATION DURING COMBAT, though queerly enough it is often either forgotten after the fact or unnoticed as it occurs. The report of a firearm near the ear is the slamming of a heavy, solid-core door. And the repeated, irregular, but rapid shots of even so few as four people in a firing line can begin to mingle into a single note, like the horn section of a symphony orchestra. The nose-hair-curling tang of gunpowder permeates the nostrils, as if one wore insubstantial sulfur nose-plugs. The tumbling trajectory of hot, spent brass is uncertain. The scorching empty casings can bounce off of a bare arm, or drop down the neck of a shirt, leaving behind little burn-mark mementos. And all the time the brain is furiously compiling sensory data, demanding more, selecting and tracking targets, coordinating and directing so that the target dies and the brain lives. Still, given all this, the sound, smell, and feel can completely slip the mind, each sensation discarded once it's experienced. Or by some lucky SOBs it can be utterly ignored.

I did not ignore, and will never forget, the concussive wall of sound and pressure that immediately succeeded the brilliant red burst of a detonating five-gallon can of gasoline.

But the day was some hours old before all that occurred, and was preceded by periods of tension and boredom.

ꕤ

We drove a circuitous loop around Mount Tabor and down Division, concealing the car in the open garage bay of a gas station, the front of which was now blended with what we guessed was the workshop of a Claimant jeweler. Luisa found a loose strand of square-cut amber beads strung on a silver wire and looped it around her neck. The smell of gasoline indicated that the tanks were still available, somewhere beneath the neat stonework.

We skulked northwards, as stealthily as four people can while toting long guns and five sloshing cans of high-octane fuel. Both rifles were equipped with slings. We'd fashioned makeshift slings for the big-bore slug guns. I'm not sure it made the trek that much easier.

When we reached the vantage point from which Tonio and I had observed the construction gang, they were at it again. We crept and low crawled by, dreading detection with every cautious movement, coming to a stop at last where the merged native and Claimant housing gave way to the open land surrounding the ziggurat.

I saw no soldiers guarding the work crew or standing sentinel, but any one of the kilted workmen could have raised the alarm if an accidentally dropped gasoline bomb or similar mishap had caught his attention. I doubt, in retrospect, that we were ever in much danger. The builders were a couple hundred yards from us at all times and we had plenty of cover. After the fact rationalizations don't provide timely comfort, however, and we were all glad to give our frazzled nerves a chance to recover.

We took up our positions and settled in to wait. Gradually, nervousness succumbed to boredom. We still had no idea of the Claimants' patrol schedule, or even if they had a schedule. So there was no telling when a company would depart. It wasn't immediately, it wasn't soon. Staring at the towering slopes of the Claimant fortress was only distracting for so long. We couldn't hazard talk above a whisper, so conversation provided no antidote to rising tedium. I was left, for better or worse, with only my own thoughts for diversion. And even those were disrupted by the soft slither and click of Tonio sliding the blade of the machete an inch free of the sheath and letting it drop back.

Tonio and I were paired up, sheltered by the remnants of a pickup-truck bed, the cab and engine compartment encased in the exterior of the Claimant building that had merged with the house on the corner of 64th and Lincoln. Jim and Luisa composed the other 'fire team', to employ Jim's jargon. They were stationed to our left and forward a few yards in the deep, shaded entry way of another Claimant building. The entry way terminated against the left rear fender and body panel of a Toyota Camry and a section of a fire hydrant.

I could have issued a citation for that.

The idea was that each pair would alternate in the role of grenadier. One team member would light the fuse and the other would hurl the makeshift grenade while the second team continued to lay down small arms fire. All a bit elaborate for just the four of us, but a formulated strategy gave everyone something to concentrate on while we waited, instead of each of us just stewing in our individual nervous juices.

It didn't work.

I sat fretting as another late summer day heated up, watching a drifting band of clouds creep eastward toward the Cascades. I worried about Trina. I worried that something would go wrong. I worried that we couldn't out-run the Claimants back to the car once we'd finished killing. I even worried about the big picture, that Jim was right and our civilization had just been unceremoniously flushed down the cosmic shitter. And, as beads of sweat began to pearl up on my brow and nose, I worried that the soldiers weren't going to patrol today, perhaps celebrating some Claimant day off.

But they did. The massive gate at the base of the ziggurat lifted upwards into the canary-and-buff hued lower tier, the whole process announced and accompanied by a tympani of heavy chain clanking as hidden ratcheting mechanisms labored. A Claimant company began to troop out, preceded by an orange-and-black kitted officer.

Tonio tensed up beside me, slamming the machete home one final time.

"Easy," I said. "Let Luisa and Jim open fire first. Remember the rifles out range our shotguns. We'll get our turn."

I spoke to settle my own jitters as well. There wasn't any point in getting worked up yet. They were out of range and they might not even come in our direction.

Tonio nodded, and busied himself checking our gear: shotguns loaded, spare shells stuffed in our pockets, two gasoline cans with fuses fashioned of strips torn from one of my old t-shirts, a battery-powered propane grill-lighter. We had two of the bombs, Jim and Luisa had three. A friendly competition the previous night had determined that Jim and Tonio possessed the best throwing arms, and Jim, with his lanky frame, edged Tonio for distance.

They did come our way, keeping in step across the broad flagstones paving the vast apron that circled the looming step-pyramid. They seemed to grow larger as they neared, the usual perspective trick enhanced by the dominating backdrop of the towering ziggurat.

My body clenched and tightened inside and out, as if a series of internal vises simultaneously began to clamp down. I picked up the lighter and needlessly performed another test. Tonio had checked its functioning enough that the concern was no longer the mechanism but the fuel. Tonio wrapped his hand around the handle of the gasoline can, adjusting and readjusting his grip.

And still the Claimants marched, getting closer. Closer. They were well within rifle shot. What was Jim waiting for? I glanced over at the other ambush point, despite knowing that I wouldn't be able to see either Jim or Luisa.

Just then a stabbing orange finger flared from the shadows of their shelter, followed by another and the *crack crack* of consecutive rifle shots.

I brought my gaze back on target and saw the officer spin to the paving stones and the soldier behind him double over, his pole arm slipping from his grasp. The soldier tottered for a moment, then dropped to his knees as the formation behind him, seemingly without hesitation, opened and the entire company began double timing it in our direction.

The rifles continued to speak a staccato dialog. Claimants sprawled, thinning the onrush.

Tonio was in a crouch, flexing his legs.

"Ready?" I asked.

He shook his head. "Not yet. Little more. Little more. Now, light me."

I thumbed the barbecue-lighter's safety and clicked the trigger. The tiny blue flame licked at the gasoline soaked strip of T-shirt and the fuse flared up. Tonio stood, moved free from our cover, took a couple momentum building strides forward, and hurled the grenade.

It was a good throw, high arcing, the fuse a streaming tail of fire that shortened rapidly. The can never did hit the ground intact. As Tonio dove back to join me, the burning fuse reached the fuel inside the canister and ignited explosively about ten yards shy of the leading soldiers.

The thin aluminum panels shredded before a blossoming hell-flower firing off the sheathing of ball-bearings in all directions, driving gaping, bloody holes through about ten Claimants, opening a gap in the skirmish line. A couple of ball-bearings whined over head at the same time as the concussive waves of compressed air assaulted our ears and ruffled our hair as they passed beneath the bed of the pickup truck.

Another detonation followed as Jim, not waiting for covering fire, flung a bomb, just clearing the heads of the oncoming soldiers. The explosion tossed a dozen soldiers forward, punctured, scorched and limp, loose limbed like so many sock monkeys.

We'd halved the company's strength. The remainder were well within shotgun range. Tonio and I stood and fired. Tonio had learned from his first combat. He was methodical. He took his time, aiming center mass.

Heavy loads of buck shot crumpled soldier after soldier, none quite coming within spear reach. These were brave men, sprinting as fast as their heavy armor would allow, into the deadly hail of twelve-gauge spread patterns. Ten 00-pellets hurtled through an expanding volume of space to puncture laminate armor, skin, muscle, and vital organs.

I squeezed the trigger, leaning forward against the recoil. Then I racked the slide to eject the spent shell and seat another round. Tracking the next closest target, I fired again. Every sound, smell, and feeling was heightened, enhanced, vibrant, and yet paradoxically second-hand, as if experienced through some ineffable filter.

What drove them on? Was it discipline or a suicidal fanaticism that carried them unflinching into what they must realize was certain death?

I shot down the last solder two yards short of the pickup truck.

An ululation of triumph emanated from Jim and Luisa's firing point as we observed the carnage. The dead, the writhing and moaning living, the quiet and disbelieving living, and the still burning, scattered across the plaza.

But that wasn't all. Partially concealed behind the dissipating curtain of smoke there remained a grouping that hadn't charged, hadn't come within the killing field. I focused, taking in what I guessed might be a priest and a bodyguard detachment. And...

"What the hell is that?" asked Tonio, pointing with the Mossberg.

What the hell was right. Edging from behind the cluster of standing soldiers was...something. It looked like a cartoon tank from some cute Japanese video game. It was about four or five feet tall, rounded like a Volkswagen Bug. But there were legs at the bottom, a head poking out the front, and a long tail terminating in a wrecking ball-like club. It looked like some mutant armadillo/turtle hybrid, like something that had died out long before man first crossed the Bering Strait. But there it was, strapped with tack and harness and with a saddle perched ludicrously atop its round, armored back.

"Whatever it is, it's going to barbecue," Tonio said, snatching up the lighter and our remaining bomb.

"Wait," I said, but he ignored me, starting at a jog for the Claimant squad, leaping over or skirting the fallen soldiers.

I slipped the sling of the riot gun over my head and settled it across my shoulders, muttering, "Shit, shit, shit." I thumbed fresh shells into the tube as fast as I could, glancing up now and then to observe Tonio's progress.

"Go back, Tonio," I heard Luisa cry. But he was a man pumped full of confidence, or adrenaline, and he was in no mood to heed anyone. He just kept moving unhesitatingly into grenade range.

The group of soldiers–my presumed protection detail–split open, allowing someone to step free of its shielding presence, and I saw that my guess was correct. A priest strode clear of his bodyguard and viewed the battlefield. Calmly, as near as I could tell from this distance.

Tonio began triggering the lighter, trying to ignite the fuse as he went. I came around the back of the pickup truck bed, beginning to follow, intending to cover Tonio's retreat.

The priest had apparently seen all he needed to because his head stopped swiveling and locked straight ahead. He raised his arms to shoulder height, cruciform. He allowed his head to flop back, his body went rigid, and I could hear a stream of chanted gabble issue from him.

Tonio had slowed his pace somewhat so he could steady his hand and bring flame to fuse.

And then I began to feel warm. Warmer than the September afternoon warranted. Sweat beaded up on my forehead and began to trickle. The shotgun barrel resting against my chest began to radiate an increasingly uncomfortable heat. A shimmer in the air flickered into existence, distorting my view of the drama before me.

"Damn it Tonio, get out of there!" I yelled through a suddenly parched throat.

But it was far too late for that.

The gasoline bomb in his hand erupted. In a blazing instant Tonio was explosively mulched into scorched rags.

I heard a *crump, crump* behind me and to my left. A wave of heat and sound hurled me to the paving stones. From my ground level vantage I watched a ball bearing roll by. And then body parts began to drop from the sky, as the remains of Tonio, Luisa, and Jim completed their ballistic arcs.

My ears rang. My vision blurred, than refocused. The barrel of my shotgun was blistering my lower chest through the fabric of my shirt. I could feel a skinned knee, and could see one abraded palm stretched out before me on the smoothly worn flagstone. I was alive. But those three explosions meant my three companions were not. That priest, somehow, had detonated the gasoline. How, I had no idea.

Why had the gas cans combusted but my ammunition hadn't cooked off? Maybe the fuel soaked fuses reached ignition point before the sealed gunpowder charges. I didn't know how to apply logic to this new reality. But like Jim had said, after the change, pretty much any damn thing could be true.

I didn't have time to speculate about it anyhow. I was lying prone and defenseless. A squad and a mystically lethal priest represented a clear and present danger. And not far behind them was a pyramid housing who knew how many more Claimants. I had to move to save my own bacon. I could mourn later.

But first, and most important, I needed some payback.

I surged to my feet, staggering into a tottering run, woozy and still a trifle disoriented. I got my feet beneath me as I ran and adjusted the sling on my shotgun, dropping the barrel into firing position. The Claimant bodyguard was advancing, with the exception of one soldier who was scrambling up the side of the bulbous behemoth–an apparently troublesome undertaking as the beast had been spooked by the explosions and was shuffling a slow circle on its own axis.

The Claimants jogged toward me, our closing distance likely to bring us to spear point in seconds. I didn't wait. I fired from the hip as I advanced, spinning a soldier to the paving as the shot tore through his articulated shoulder armor. The next shot struck low in the belly of the adjacent soldier, and he dropped to his knees clutching uselessly at the gushing hole in his bowels.

I gunned down the others without hesitation or remorse, sending the last pitching off his hard-won perch atop the astounding creature. The animal had had enough, and it lumbered back toward the ziggurat. The bodyguard, hanging by one heel from a stirrup, bounced along behind, his helmet ringing and sparking off the paving stones.

Only the priest remained standing, though behind him I could see movement through the distant gate. I took deliberate aim and squeezed off a round. The priest staggered back a step, wobbled, and regained his balance.

He looked down at the shredded front of his tunic–shredded but unbloodied. He looked up at me and grinned. Then he plucked a short, curved dagger from an ornate sheath at his belt and came at me.

I fired again, once more with no effect other than to stop him briefly in his tracks. I let the shotgun dangle from its sling and drew my service pistol, opening up with flurry of double taps. Nothing.

He was getting closer and that knife no longer appeared quite so short to me. This was too much. Huge beasts, fucking bullet-proof wizards. I needed simplicity. I looked around. The fallen Claimants' pole arms were scattered where they'd dropped, none close enough to grasp. But there, within arm's reach, lay Tonio's machete, still cased in its smoldering leather sheath, spattered with blood.

I stooped to snatch up the weapon. I suppose I could have just run. I should have just run. Trina was waiting for me at home. And I'd promised I'd come home safe. But at the moment I wanted only to kill or go down fighting. Jim, Luisa, Tonio—they'd all been under my care, or so I'd seen it. And I had failed them. I had to take out the mad on someone. This someone in particular.

I slid the machete free and tossed the ruined sheath aside. Beneath his three-lobed hat I saw the priest's eyes widen and his smirk disappeared.

My half-formed fear that he was as blade proof as he was bullet proof vanished, and I stepped forward to meet him, grabbing his descending knife arm, and ramming Tonio's machete deep into his gut, feeling the hot blood spill out over my hand and wrist.

As if my thirst for blood had actually been slaked, my rage was shunted to the back of my brain and survival regained the fore. I turned and bolted.

Chapter 8

I POURED OUT THE STORY AND MY GRIEF UPON TRINA'S SHOULDER. THEN I poured myself into a bottle.

I stuck my head out the next day, didn't like the view, and slipped back in. Trina said nothing, making only cooing noises and coaxing me to eat. I felt numb and compliant, the key condition being numbness. The bourbon was fulfilling its purpose.

I must have been fussing that night for I woke with my head cradled on Trina's breast being rocked gently like a choleric infant.

"I got them all killed," I said.

"No, Nick. It wasn't your fault," Trina said, her voice low, soothing like a mug of honeyed tea on a cold day. But I was still far from ready to be soothed, if I even could be.

"My plan. My idea to take the fight to the Claimants. My...hubris. Who the hell do I think I am? I'm just an out-of-work cop. We should have just kept our heads down and waited."

"Waited for what? For how long? No, Nick, you're just repeating my arguments, and I was wrong. This wasn't your fault. Everyone knew the risk."

I started to reply, wanting to feel the rhetorical scourge flensing my back. But Trina cut me off with, "Go back to sleep, Nick. We can argue about what a bastard you are tomorrow."

Oddly enough, that was enough to get me through the night. Barely. The next afternoon I resorted again to my friend Smooth Brown Liquor, and that got me through the day.

Trina and I talked some more, never really arguing. Trina offered up perfectly logical points. An awful lot of people had died already and more would before this thing ended. None of that was, or would be, my fault. I hadn't started this, I couldn't be expected to finish it, all I'd done was my best. And so had the other three. It could just as easily have been me that died. And so on, and so on.

I couldn't rationally dispute any of it, but I remained unconvinced. Part of me was still a cop, sworn to protect the community. And I'd just allowed most of my community to die.

Trina continued trying gamely to haul me free of the murky depths of despondency. "We're starting to run short of food," she announced.

I doubted that, we'd stockpiled aggressively. But I could use an opportunity to replenish our store of high-end booze. Why settle?

I crossed over to the fireplace and retrieved the saber from its mounting. "Do you have a shopping list?" I asked.

ꟸ

Here's the thing about a quiet post-apocalyptic environment: it's boring. At first the experience is akin to vacationing in a secluded cabin in the wilderness. Preparations keep you busy. You enjoy the feeling of self-sufficiency, of partaking of the pioneer life. Once the wood box is filled and the groceries put away you can relax, read, and daydream.

At some point, however, you begin to miss television, the internet, telephone calls, and even traffic noise. Bare survival—once you've passed the tipping point when you're pretty sure you're not going to starve, and you're no longer in imminent mortal peril—grows tedious.

Then add to the boredom the oppressive knowledge of the collapse of civilization. That sort of contemplation plays havoc with your motivation to get out of bed in the morning. Existential crises are easier to avoid when you can look out the window and see actual existence. Meaninglessness is a crushingly omnipresent concept when you are driving through an apparently deserted, practically demolished city, your car the only thing moving except for the increasingly numerous packs of wild dogs.

Add to that the memory of three friends erupting into fireballs and knowing it was your fault.

So I was a little disappointed to find the remains of the nearest liquor store already cleaned out. Just a quarter of the storefront was still accessible, the rest was a Claimant structure that I took to be a holding tank or reservoir, though I wasn't all that curious. I suppose the evidence of survivors was a cheerful bit of news, but I'd been looking forward to another bottle of Maker's Mark.

I drove on, skirting a blackened stretch of the city. Charred timbers thrust skyward like skeletal giants clawing free from the grave, soot covered Claimant buildings serving as headstones. A partially destroyed convenience store marked the end of this burned section. Most of the mini-mart's roof was lost, and all of one wall.

I got out of the cruiser and poked through the shelves, finding more evidence of survivors. I sent an un-looted can skittering across the filthy tile floor, but felt no inclination to retrieve it. A malaise was rooting itself deeper in my brain and the chance to pursue a stray can of chili-mac–last tin in the store or not–was hardly sufficient stimulation to rip it loose.

I climbed back into the cruiser and drove off, spurred into continued movement only by inertia, a hankering for bourbon, and a vague hope of encountering a squadron of Claimant troops to plow through at fifty miles per hour, damn the risk.

I tacked roughly northwards, recollecting a liquor store about twenty blocks or so from where Trina and I had encountered the priest and the other three Claimants. I wondered if they were still there. I didn't have any particular urge to slay the three civilians, but if I happened to run across the other fellow with the hat and robe... It was something to do. Besides I might stumble across an intact grocery store or restaurant, giving Trina reason to believe I was mission focused.

My zigzag navigation brought me at length to an open stretch of road, unimpeded by Claimant buildings, affording me a view of downtown across the Willamette. The skyline was no longer recognizable. Familiar towers had toppled. Few bridges remained standing. A couple of ziggurats climbed skyward, now the highest visible landmarks. I sat and stared until the mounting urge for a drink goaded me on.

ഌ൫

The liquor store still stood, bracketed and partially obscured by a pair of Claimant tenements–three-story affairs of chunky, uninspiring architecture, brightened only by the Claimant penchant for color.

I caught signs of a struggle in the vicinity, perhaps a small-scale pitched battle. Spent cartridges glittered from the gutter. Bloody streaks described where people had fallen and where the corpses had been dragged away.

The clean up bothered me. It spoke of organization. If Portlanders had won this fight and were organized enough to police up the aftermath, where were they? No, this had the earmarks of a Claimant victory, the new residents consolidating and settling in.

I got out of the car nonetheless, carrying a duffel bag in one hand and my drawn pistol in the other. I stood for a moment, listening and taking a slow turn about one heel. Nothing. Quiet and inactive.

I started towards the store. As I reached to push open the door, I caught a burst of movement out of the corner of my eye. I pivoted my head and saw a shirtless, kilted Claimant sprinting away, no doubt to report my presence.

I didn't know how much time I had before a reaction force could respond, but I pushed open the door. I'd better loot as efficiently as possible.

I grazed rapidly, filling the gym bag with small-batch, numbered bottles of bourbon. As I plundered, I worked out what was nagging me. I grabbed a cordial at random (in the hope that Trina might enjoy it) when it hit me–the absence of the chime from the motion detector. How odd to not have your presence announced by that ubiquitous electronic tinkle. I'd noticed it that first night as well. Funny how people can handle major upheaval with equanimity, but get spooked over trifles.

I was out within five minutes. I turned when I reached the car and saw a dozen incurious Claimant faces staring at me from the tenement windows. I placed the bag in the back seat, liberated a bottle of Bullet, and saluted the onlookers. "You poor ignorant bastards, living over all that booze and too stupid to enjoy a drop. Here's to you."

I pried free the top and took a swig, feeling the sweet warmth glide through my insides. Then, obeying my ebbing good sense, I drove off.

I made my way back east, following the gradual rise of Broadway. I recognized the back of a decent restaurant thrusting from the side of a low, blockish Claimant building. Again not bothering to conceal the cruiser, I hopped out and tried the back door. It was locked.

I returned to the cruiser, retrieved my baton and smashed in the small rectangular window set in the door. I scraped free the remaining shards of glass, then reached in and unlocked the door.

It smelled none too good inside. I was in a combination kitchen and pantry where the perishables had, in fact, begun to perish. I declined to open the walk-in freezer. The odor of rancid meat and spoiled dairy had already filtered through the seals, and I had no intention of enjoying the full effect. I selected a few institutional-sized cans of assorted food stuffs, not bothering to be selective. I found unopened boxes of pasta and a twenty-pound sack of rice. Loading the trunk with food, I figured, would suffice to justify the trip to Trina and smooth over any discontent my haul of alcohol might engender.

I rewarded myself with another slug from the open bottle and rumbled on up Broadway. I wove around a massive stone water trough, a looming statue of one of the more gruesome Claimant deities, and a porphyry obelisk some forty feet tall. The obelisk was etched with the indecipherable Claimant script, each letter inlaid with copper.

Further up the variegated road surface I reached the stretch of buildings–perhaps the homes and workhouses of tradesmen or craftsmen–where Trina and I had seen the three Claimants and the priest. I slowed, just creeping by, looking for some sign of life.

I spotted another runner bearing news of my whereabouts. He shot away, hoofing it fast for a man in sandals. I guessed these automatons had been instructed to report to higher authority upon glimpsing living Portlanders. The early lack of reaction, the incurious, dull inertness, was apparently unsatisfactory. It seems the Claimant powers-that-be were experiencing the downside of a submissive population devoid of initiative and were doing their best to issue anticipatory instructions.

Well, fine. I was mildly interested in who or what would respond to the summons. I didn't feel like going home quite yet anyway. I shifted into park and took up the bottle to have another pull or two while I waited.

I was not obliged to wait long. No ziggurat peeked over the nearby roofs, so I wasn't surprised that the first responder was no soldier. It was, I was tickled to see, my old friend the hat-and-robe. He emerged from around the same corner the runner had disappeared behind, approaching with a confident stride. He drew up about a dozen paces short of the cruiser and raised his arms in a fashion reminiscent of the pyromantic priest before the ziggurat.

I stepped free of the cruiser, snatching up the shotgun as I exited. I didn't know if the buckshot would take him down–it hadn't put down the last hat-and-robe, so this would be an experiment of sorts–but I figured it would at least prevent him from blowing up my car. The hairs on my knuckles were, in fact, beginning to curl, as I brought the butt stock to my shoulder and pumped a round directly into his chest. The force of the blow knocked him onto his ass, but other than that, and a somewhat satisfying look of astonishment, the shotgun blast provided no other results. Except...the rising heat immediately dissipated.

"How'd you like that, huh? Courtesy of the Portland PD." I tossed the riot gun back onto the front seat, and leaned in to retrieve the antique cavalry saber. I scraped it free of its metal scabbard and stood up, a curving length of slightly tarnished, age-blunted steel in hand.

The priest's bugged eyes focused on the sword and grew, if anything, wider. He crabbed backwards, scrambled to his feet, and shot up a short flight of stairs into the nearest building, shouting.

I began to follow, but had not yet built up a head of steam when three Claimants emerged from the doorway the priest had entered. They were armed, in a fashion: a chunk of wood, a mallet, and straight edged kitchen knife. Not particularly menacing, but there were three of them, and death by bludgeoning was still death. The sword in my hand no longer inspired a martial ardor. It wasn't sharp and I had no idea how to use it.

I eyed the distance. The three were just starting down the stairs. Academy self-defense theory dictated that an officer could draw and fire his weapon if the action was initiated while the closing target was still at least fifteen yards distant. That appeared to be roughly the spread here, but I was beginning to regret the last couple sips of bourbon. My spatial assessments were, perhaps, a trifle unreliable at the moment, and not un-coincidentally, my reflexes might just be a wee bit impaired. But I no longer had a choice. I had to test the praxis.

I let the saber clang to the road at my feet, and clawed at the Glock at my hip. My hand fumbled, slipping off the rear of the slide. Shit!

The first Claimant was already at the bottom of the stairs. I reached again, grasped the pebbled grip, and dragged the weapon free. There he was, filling my vision, heavy length of firewood upraised. I had no time to adopt a proper firing stance or take a two-handed grip. My hand came up as his started its descent. My finger squeezed, the Glock bucked once, twice, and the Claimant collapsed against me. The impact drove me reeling backwards, the club falling past my shoulder, free of his dead hand. I toppled to the ground beneath his weight.

The other two were right on his heels. I jerked my shooting hand free of the heavy corpse and fired off five rounds as fast as I could pull the trigger, missing at least twice.

It wasn't a clinic in marksmanship, but it served. Barely.

The last round took the knife-man through the wind-pipe as he stooped over me. He fell to his knees, dropping the knife to clutch at his ruined, spurting throat, before keeling over on his side.

I rolled the body off of me, holstered the pistol, and snatched up the saber. A rational man would have gotten back into the car and driven away. But I think I had given rationality the day off. Its usefulness had been in question for some days now.

I staggered toward the stairs before getting my feet firmly beneath me. Then I plunged into the building in pursuit of hat-and-robe.

This was my first opportunity to inspect a complete, unmerged, occupied Claimant structure. I am afraid, however, that I gave it only a cursory viewing, intent as I was on the chase. The interior was warm in russets, yellows, and ochers. A niche near the entry enshrined household gods, or some such Claimant iconography. They were a collection in miniature of the usual ugly buggers, like Hummel figurines for the Goth set. The wall frescoes were geometric, less ornate than the partial images I'd viewed in the remnants of the Claimant homes in my neighborhood. Because the building was narrow it was laid out in a linear fashion, room following room. Exactly that in fact–two rooms. The front was perhaps intended as the formal chamber, since the back room appeared more utilitarian, the walls lined with work benches. A stairway led up and a rear door gaped open, giving me a glimpse of a robe billowing out from behind a running figure.

I dashed after him, sparing little attention for the contents of the back room, so I remain unable to report what exactly the structure's inhabitant made, sold, or repaired. Gold gleamed in small piles, and in discrete pieces. Amber colored plaques on the walls threw off a warm, reflected light.

But I wasn't here as a tourist. A three-step stair gave access up to and down from the rear door. I ignored it, my stride carrying me over and down the yard or so to the ground.

The priest was pacing for all he was worth, but I gained steadily. He didn't strike me as the sort who frequented the gymnasium diligently.

He rounded a corner, momentarily out of view. I was nearly on his heels and saw him brought up short by the plate-glass front of a beauty parlor, the interior now lined with dull orange stone walls entombing the barber chairs.

He spun to face me and was tugging free his half-crescent knife when I caught him. I gave him no time to employ the shiv. I barely slowed my stride. I brought the saber down, taking advantage of my momentum.

Whatever protection he'd invoked against firearms had no apparent effect on swords, for the blade hacked through his three-lobed cap and his skull, the dull length of steel burying itself to the bridge of his nose. The blow flung his corpse back against the plate glass with enough force to create a spreading mandala of lightning bolt cracks before he slumped to the ground, his weight dragging his cloven skull free of the embedded saber with the sound of a shoe drawn clear of a sucking mud puddle.

I stood over him for a moment, panting. I felt no better. I'd exorcised no demons of despondency. He'd been more than eager to kill me, so I felt some satisfaction at beating him to the punch, but that was it. There was no catharsis in this ugly mess of violence.

I wanted another drink. So I went back to the car and took another swallow as I drove home, not blind to the incongruity, the hypocrisy of a police officer drinking and driving in his patrol car. But who was there to care?

Chapter 9

TRINA WAS NOT, I THINK, HOODWINKED BY MY HAUL FROM THE RESTAURANT. But she said nothing when she watched me unload the trove of hooch. And I had returned with a respectable stock of vittles. We bunkered down for the better part of two weeks, eating–and for my part, drinking–through a good chunk of our supplies, all thought of taking the fight to the enemy abandoned. Trina and I weren't going to tackle the nascent Claimant empire on our own, and I wouldn't have taken her into a fight even had she expressed a desire. I wasn't about to risk anyone else, let alone my wife.

She was something to behold, when I was sober enough to notice: patient, stoic, uncomplaining. For a while at least. A booze hound for a husband is trying for any woman. This–this invasion, this calamity, this global-scale applecart upsetting–had to be an assault on every survivor's sanity.

And once Claimant patrols resumed, as they inevitably would, rising tension would pile on top of despair and the growing sense of confinement. It would be enough to batter down the steeliest self-possession.

༄༅

"You know what I think I miss the most?" I was sprawled on the couch before the blank, useless television set pouring three fingers of eighty-proof anodyne. "College football. We should be over a month into the season. I'd really like to see a game."

I heard something drop heavily to the floor in the kitchen, where Trina had been taking refuge more and more consistently. Silence followed, then a sob. Trina emerged, holding to her eyes a dish towel which she proceeded to fling at me.

"You know what I'd really like to see?" she asked, her voice quavering. "My husband. A man, not some drunken quitter."

"Whoa, hey!" The human capacity to feel wronged even when completely culpable is boundless. And I felt wronged. I'd tried. What had I to show for it? Three dead friends. What else could we do? "What do you want from me? What can I do? Either help will arrive, or we'll be found and killed. That's what we have to face and you begrudge me the occasional drink?"

She ignored both the absurdity and the actual hint of reality contained therein. She laid into me, her voice ascending in pitch and volume as she went. "I've put up with it. This whole nightmare has been hard, and it has been harder on you than me. Going out there, seeing Jim, and Tonio and Luisa killed. I understand. You needed some time. Well you've had time. At this point, if there was anywhere to go, I'd go. And maybe I should just try. I don't see how it could be any more dangerous out there since my only protection here is a lush who is usually passed out on the couch." She was nearly screaming by the end.

"What do you mean 'go'? Go where?"

"Hell, Nick, I don't know. I can't exactly run to my mother, or make an appointment with a marriage counselor. Just, go. Take a car and go. See what else is out there. Maybe I'd just find death, but that's all I have here, watching you drink yourself to death. How long do you think I'll last after that?"

"Come on baby, it's under control. I mean, I've been on a bender, true. But I don't think I have what it takes to become a bona fide wino. I just don't think I've got the stomach for it." I patted my stomach gingerly. There was some basis for my assertion. I was feeling none too good. I doubt that under normal circumstances I had the constitution of an alcoholic. But part of me was thinking that if I could just power through this weak moment–say another three or four days of sustained drinking–my body might surrender to the permanent occupation of the bourbon army and I could stumble blissfully through my remaining existence in a golden haze.

"It is way too late for bullshit, Nick. You could never pull it off even when you had all your wits about you. It certainly won't work now. I've had it. You pull yourself together or I'm trying my luck out there."

The enormity of what she was suggesting began to sink into my booze sodden brain. She wasn't bluffing. We'd been married long enough–going on seven years–to recognize each others' tells, and she was neither playing with her hair nor failing to meet my eyes. She was serious. It was tantamount to suicide, but she meant it.

I wobbled to my feet. I looked at the bottle in my hand, considering the grand gesture of emptying the contents down the kitchen sink. No, there was no reason to be wasteful. I thought for awhile, capped the bottle and set it on the coffee table.

"Maybe you're on to something," I said. "Maybe leaving is not such a bad idea."

A stricken look of sadness crossed her face, and I hurriedly followed up. "Not just you, sweetheart. I mean us."

"What do you mean?"

"I mean, let's load up the car and get out of Dodge. Could be things are better beyond the city. We don't know."

"You're serious?" she said, eyes on the half-empty bottle on the table.

"Look, I'm not having the proverbial moment of clarity. Quitting ain't easy, and to be up front with you, I've got no intention of quitting. Maybe ease up on the throttle. I'm still going to, what do you call it, seek refuge in the bottle sometimes. I'm still pretty tore up. But yes, I am serious about this road trip. What do we have to lose?"

I'm not sure what she expected to happen after her outburst, but it certainly wasn't this. Probably the whole thing had been spontaneous, so she'd had no expectations. Whatever the case, my proposal left her bereft of a coherent rejoinder for some minutes. But only minutes. Trina was resilient.

ꕥ

So we stuffed the cruiser to the limits of its reinforced windows. I will aver that I had zero hopes for our little jaunt. All evidence pointed to a large scale, if not worldwide, phenomenon. The prospects of improved conditions beyond the city limits seemed dubious. But if my theory of a liberating troop movement possibly rolling south from Fort Lewis was accurate, maybe we could meet it halfway.

Maybe.

Primarily I wanted to make Trina happy. Even at my most heavily medicated I had a nebulous notion of what I was putting her through.

I owed her, and if I were to avoid breaking through the wall into full-fledged alcoholism I needed a chance to dry out.

And if the whole thing was hopeless, if the Claimants were destined to complete our extermination, I'd just as soon fall on the open road as I would in a desperate last stand here, surrounded by the familiar trappings of domesticity. Something about bleeding out beneath the IKEA bookshelves and the still well-maintained houseplants made the thought of a violent death that much worse.

It was, then, the morning after our confrontation, with the trunk filled with spare canisters of fuel and drinking water, and the cabin packed with food and ammunition, that we set forth on our expedition.

We made our way eastward, toward I-5 northbound. I-84, we noticed, was still a canal. It emptied into the Willamette, which showed no signs of receding to its pre-calamity level. If anything it had risen higher, lifting tugs, barges, and pleasure craft onto flooded streets.

I half expected I-5 to be impassible, jammed with the abandoned vehicles of all the others trying to flee town. But that was absurd. The death toll had been both overwhelming and sudden. There weren't enough left alive to create a traffic hazard. No, the calamity itself created the traffic hazard. The freeway had not been spared the alterations the surface streets had suffered. I couldn't even begin to guess what conditions might prevail. I hadn't been aware of holding my breath until I saw that the overpass leading to the nearest freeway on-ramp was still intact. We motored down onto the highway, pointing the cruiser's nose towards Seattle.

But after that first lucky break, things failed to go uniformly our way. Vast sections of the roadbed were simply missing. The manufactured geologic strata of the freeway were laid bare across the raw faces of each gap.

At the first such check I stopped, puffing out my cheeks in exasperation.

"Don't give up so easily, Nick. That's not like you," said Trina.

I looked around. The pitch of the shoulder rose at varying angles to the sound-proofing walls that diminished the highway noise for the adjacent residences. The grade didn't look too steep here, so I cranked the steering wheel to the right, bumped up onto the grass-sided embankment and eased around the missing section of highway.

The angle was precarious. I felt my way up, letting the car tell me how much it could take before rolling onto its side and dropping us into a pit.

We crept around that obstacle and regained the road. The next gap in the freeway, however, was hemmed in by retaining walls, leaving no room to drive around.

This time I just chuckled. "Don't worry, Trina. I'm not giving up." We were forced to backtrack and find an exit leading to an even longer detour. I shifted into reverse to give myself some room, pulled a U-turn, and drove back down the freeway to the nearest off-ramp. There I turned around again and exited the freeway.

The slow crawling detour through this northeastern Portland neighborhood revealed nothing new. The sprawl of Claimant settlement had fundamentally altered the makeup of the city here as well. We saw the lofty reach of two more ziggurats. Thus far, not promising.

We continued on as best we could, navigating for a freeway entrance beyond the last encountered gap. We drove through another section of the city destroyed by fire, crossing over heat-warped asphalt and blackened cobbles. We passed another stretch of pristine Claimant buildings. A half-dozen or so men in colorful tunics watched us go by. One of their number turned to leave.

"Off to report us, I guess," I said to Trina. "Not quite the urgency here as nearer to home. I guess my infamy really only stretched a few miles." It was a rueful statement, and I didn't bother to conceal my despondency.

"Where are all the women?" asked Trina, I guess both curious and desirous of leading my thoughts away from my failures. She was snuggled up next to me, seat-belt law be damned, picking unconsciously at a half -healed scab on my neck. It was a souvenir–I think–of that last battle in the ziggurat plaza.

"I don't know. We saw the one old farmer's wife. But in the more urban sections...you're right, it's no girls allowed."

"Well, they've got to be somewhere. The Claimants are human too. Physically anyway."

I had no reply. We lacked answers to even these fundamental questions about the interlopers. It was frustrating. The itch for a drink crawled at the back of my brain.

We kept on until we found a freeway entrance. Then it was more of the same—detour after meandering detour.

As we neared the northern reaches of the city, approaching the Columbia River, the situation grew increasingly hazardous. The bypasses through side streets became more treacherous as intact streets were increasingly slick with water, and the damp flagstones of Claimant roadbeds shifted as moisture undermined their grounding. Farther north puddles of standing water obscured the streets, and the Claimant roads, when paved, were hopelessly awash. The unpaved sections were near bogs.

At last the freeway came to a breach too far. We could see I-5 continue at the far end of the break, beginning to rise toward the distant river crossing. But looking down we saw a slough, flowing sluggishly around the lower levels of buildings—Claimant, Portland, and amalgamated. The slough deposited a layer of slime and detritus on the upstream walls.

I turned off the engine, got out, and walked to the edge, gazing into the murky water below. Trina came to stand at my side.

"I don't think that's just the result of Bonneville dam disappearing," I said.

"Why not?" she asked.

"It's been too long. Pent up water would raise the river level, then subside. And if it was still just the backed up Columbia pushing through, the water would be moving faster."

"Then what's causing it?"

"I wish I knew, baby."

We fetched lunch from the car and ate our sandwiches there, sitting on the snapped off section of freeway, our feet dangling over the edge. A breeze picked up from the west, presaging inclement weather from the Pacific. Maybe the first big storm of the fall. We munched in silence, watching heavy gray clouds mount.

"What now?" Trina asked, tossing the wrappings into the muck below, Miss Recycling no longer quite as wound up about the environment. A gust of wind sent a drizzle slanting from the vanguard of sodden cloud banks.

"I don't know. If the water level is high here, it's probably worse around Puget Sound. I don't think help is going to come from the north."

"So we go back home?" She sounded both disappointed and relieved, if such a thing is possible.

"Well, for now. Let's re-think. Take a look at the map. Maybe we can try south, or east."

"Try it again?" She brightened, and she turned to look at me. She searched my face, hoping to see signs of a new-born optimism, a shrugging off of guilt and despair.

I'm not sure what she saw. I wasn't about to break out into a medley from "Little Orphan Annie." It was just that I'd embarked on a new project and I hate giving up. I've stayed up until dawn to finish a jigsaw puzzle, and I hate jigsaw puzzles.

I gave her the best smile I could manage. "Yes, try it again. But we need to plan it a little better. A four-wheel drive. Maybe two, with winches and a come-along. I don't know. Let's just try to get home in one piece first."

That didn't prove much of a challenge. I knew the obstacles now, and just had to clear them in reverse. The only hang-up was that little enclave of Claimants we'd driven through earlier. I didn't want to hazard a welcoming committee gambling on my returning the way I'd come. So I embarked on a lengthy circumnavigation of that neighborhood, a bypass that grew longer and longer as impassable roads and fallen buildings forced even lengthier detours.

But as the early sun began to dip behind the cloud-shadowed West Hills, we rolled up the last hill to home, a steady rain imitating the first day of Intro-to-Tap-Dance on the car roof. Visibility was so poor that I had to turn on my headlights, hoping that the weather would keep any unfriendly watchers indoors.

If not for those twin cones of light I wouldn't have noticed the figure sheltering under the peaked portico of our entryway. The false front I'd built from blocks of stone commandeered from surrounding Claimant buildings aided his concealment. We could have easily walked within two yards of him, unaware, if not for the beams sweeping across him for an instant.

"Shit!" I hissed, braking hard.

"What?" asked Trina, who had apparently not caught sight of our visitor.

"Stay here. Keep your head down," I said, as I threw the transmission into park and reached for the twelve-gauge.

"What..." began Trina again, but I didn't hear the follow up. I was out the door, and trotting in a crouch–not an easy thing to do–towards the house.

I dropped to one knee behind a square-cut hunk of masonry. "Hands where I can see them!"

"Civilization collapses, and the first thing to go is common courtesy. No wonder it takes man so long to clamber up from dark ages." The voice was droll, precise, and familiar.

Chapter 10

Gordon, Trina, and me. Candles and kerosene lanterns provided a cheery glow. Trina labored in the kitchen, cooking over a hotplate powered by a car battery. We could, it is true, have powered the entire house with the gasoline fueled generator in the basement. But even though the depth of the room, the thickness of the walls, and the camouflaging stone blocks would probably muffle the noise, it just wasn't worth risking a stray decibel catching the attention of a passing Claimant ear.

So it wasn't precisely like old times, but what ever would be now?

ᘓᘐ

Once I gave Trina the all clear and she approached close enough to see Gordon, she squealed–an honest to God squeal of delight–and rushed to embrace our dripping wet friend. We ushered him in, got a kettle of water boiling for a shower, and then got him a warm blanket for the wait.

I went back out in the rain and darkness to move the cruiser into concealment and unload a few essentials. I could finish unpacking tomorrow.

Now the two of us sat across the dining room table, grinning inanely, enjoying the aroma of the cooking odors drifting in. We each clutched a tumbler of bourbon.

Trina frowned when I fetched the bottle, but it was a fleeting displeasure. The advent of Gordon overrode any concern about me taking a tumble off the wagon. As it happened I merely sipped, the soothing warmth enhancing the pleasure of unexpected company. Gulping the stuff down, I hoped, was a thing of the past.

"It's damn good to see you, Gordon," I said. "I mean, it's good to see anyone, but I didn't expect...I mean I didn't hold out much hope that you'd survived."

"Never lose hope, Nick. Here I am, in the flesh, larger than life and even better looking." Gordon was a bespectacled, skinny little dink whose head always appeared just a touch large for his slender shoulders. My terrycloth bathrobe looked ridiculously oversized on his spare frame. We'd been tight in college and never lost touch. He'd been my best man at the wedding, probably would have come along on the honeymoon if asked. He'd been a frequent visitor, beneficiary of Trina's culinary skill, and victim of her attempts to set him up on dates.

"It's good to see the two of you also," he continued. "As you can see, I didn't lose hope. I took a risk, I know, but I think it was worth it."

I raised an eyebrow. The tone of his voice betokened something more than just happiness in finding a friend in the midst of chaos. But a heavy waft of steam, redolent of spice, announced the arrival of dinner, and questions were set aside to concentrate on yet another of Trina's miracles.

"Was that..?" Gordon asked, leaving the question hanging.

"Spam? Yes it was," said Trina, smiling broadly like an amateur conjurer pulling off a successful trick.

"You are a wonder. What you ever saw in this flatfoot, I'll never know." The rug had been pulled from beneath the planet's feet, yet the customary Trina and Gordon repartee, with only minor variations, remained constant.

Gordon and I helped Trina with the dishes. I'd taken a dishwasher for granted. Roughing it, even in my own kitchen, was irksome. Chalk up another on my list of grievances with the Claimants.

That done and fresh drinks in hand (including a glass of pinot noir for Trina, preempting a little moue of disapproval at my going back to the well for a second bucket), we retired to the sitting room. I liked the sound of that–retired to the sitting room–a small touch of class in a world of chaos.

"To survival against the odds," said Gordon, raising his glass for a ritual clink, clink, clink. "I am glad. I'd hoped, but it was a desperate optimism." He sipped, his mind somewhere else. Then, "How was it for you? How was your apocalypse?"

"You want to sit on your mystery? Withhold your story until the end? Heighten the drama?" Trina asked. "Fine. I'm in the mood for conversation." She tossed off her glass, left the room, and returned with the open bottle of wine. "There I was, asleep..." she said, pouring her second glass. "Go on, Nick, tell the story."

So I did. Unsparing.

"Still," I said, when I'd brought the tale up to finding Gordon on the front porch, "we're alive. There's that."

"Bullet-proof priests, huh?" said Gordon. "I'd an inkling."

Trina and I traded raised eyebrows. But we knew better than to rush Gordon through a story.

Gordon fetched the Maker's Mark for his third. I held my hand over my glass–still about a third full–and was rewarded by a beam of affirmation from Trina.

Gordon leaned back in the overstuffed easy chair, embracing the role of a man enjoying a well-deserved drink. "Having run of the library after hours saved my life. I was down in the stacks, searching for a volume listing production output from the Venetian Arsenal during the sixteenth century. The shelves sort of quivered for a moment, and when I looked around, the doorway was now blocked off by a stone wall. Of course you know what happened, a building of what you call the Claimants now overlapped the same spatial coordinates as the library."

He took a drink, his eyes narrowing behind his spectacles. I could imagine him reliving the terror, the shock and growing claustrophobic horror.

"I found an exit eventually. A crawl space led to a disused storage room that led to a boiler room that led to the lower levels of our new neighbor's building. I was out, but into enemy territory, so to speak. It had taken me the better part of a day to get this far so I was pretty hungry. I wasn't too hesitant about exploring.

"I found massive stone corridors, gigantic chambers, side passages, room after room. I also found any number of hiding places of the nook-and-cranny variety, which was a good thing as this enormous pile of masonry wasn't entirely unoccupied. The soldiers weren't too troubling. They tended to travel in groups, marching, so they announced their presence long before coming into sight. It was the priests that gave me the most scares–last minute escapes with my heart in my throat, that sort of thing.

"But I found pantries and kitchens at last–big, institutional-sized refectories. I nested in the stacks, where I'd been when the change occurred, and the entry was pretty well concealed, so I stopped worrying too much about my immediate survival. No, there were two really interesting discoveries, one you've probably already figured out: What was left of the library was engulfed by a Claimant ziggurat. That gives you an idea of what I was wandering through. The other discovery was a private study or library."

Gordon emitted a leonine, jaw-cracking yawn. Behind his spectacles his eyelids were fighting a losing battle against gravity, but he struggled on. "I filched a couple of volumes or scrolls–seriously, scrolls. The Claimants appear to have been using bound books for millennia, but they stubbornly stick with scrolls as well. It was a generously stocked library, so I hazarded that a couple items at a time wouldn't be missed. So I spent my hours that weren't occupied by pilfering food in attempting to decipher the Claimant's written language."

Gordon perked up, momentarily driving back fatigue. "And I did it! Certain stem repetitions reminded me of the Sumerian cuneiform from the original 'Gilgamesh' tablets. I wasn't able to power the microfiche machine, so I couldn't view clean copies of the tablet fragments, but I tracked down a magazine article with good reproductions of a small proportion. That was enough to get me started. The Claimant language seems to be related to Sumerian. Or, more precisely, Sumerian seems to be related to the Claimant language–a debased, vastly simplified version."

His excitement faded. Another yawn threatened to bifurcate his face. So I held back the questions clamoring for answers and just pointed toward the guest bedroom. Gordon knew the gesture well enough. As did Trina, who disappeared for a moment, returning with a packaged toothbrush (courtesy of one of our looting excursions) and a water glass. Gordon nodded, levered himself free of the chair, and tottered away to the bathroom.

I could only imagine how tired Gordon was. He hadn't finished his story, but the ending must include his making his way, on foot, a dozen miles or so through a now unfamiliar city to our house. He'd have been frightened and never entirely sure of his bearings. After our day's outing, Trina and I were none too chipper either, though we hadn't done nearly so much of the lifting-them-up and putting-them-down. But we were happy enough to call it a day and put off questions until the morning.

"Poor Gordon," said Trina as we put ourselves down for the night. "All alone, hiding for weeks. I can't even begin to imagine what it must have been like."

"Yeah," I said. "But Gordon's always been tougher than he looks. You know we met in college, but I never told you how."

"That's right, you never did. I guess intellectually I knew that, but somehow it felt like you'd always known each other." Trina rested her head on my shoulder, raising a questioning eyebrow and a listening ear. Then, finding a half-formed pimple on the back of my left arm, she absently began picking at it while she listened.

"We were both rushing the same fraternity. Gordon left the rush table in the student center with a brochure and party invitation before we had a chance to meet, but I recognized him outside a few minutes later, near the music building. It seems a couple of students who really resented the whole Greek system had found a non-stereotypical frat guy to explain their socio-economic worldview to. The lecture apparently consisted of pounding on a little guy that each of them outweighed by at least thirty pounds. The thing is, Gordon was handling it. I mean, they were beating him, sure, but he was hanging in, taking every punch and kick and not going down. He even got in a couple of licks of his own. I was pretty impressed."

"Then you jumped in and saved him," said Trina, "and he's been your faithful sidekick ever since."

"Well, it didn't take much to convince these two that their lapse from pacifism was a mistake. It required no heroics."

"Whatever you say. Go to sleep, hero."

ജ്ജ

We spent the morning unloading the cruiser. Gordon was stiff from his hike, and the shift as a porter was just what he needed to get the muscles loose. Gordon and I pitched in to help Trina prepare lunch, mostly just getting in her way.

"I think your idea of trying eastward next time is a good one," said Gordon, mopping up a puddle of gravy with a crust of bread.

"Why east?" asked Trina.

"Well, you've already figured out that north might lead to just a vast bog."

"Why is that?" I interrupted.

"One thing at a time, Nick," Gordon said. "South will just be congested. The Claimants built up the Willamette valley too. But they didn't seem to have a great interest in the plains and high desert between the Cascades and the Rockies. At least I don't think so. I could only learn so much with my rudimentary grasp of their language and spotty access to their texts."

"Did you learn who they are?" asked Trina at the same time I asked "Did you learn how they got here?"

"Yes, and I think so," Gordon answered us both, laughing. "Damn, it is good to be able talk with someone. I've had to keep my yap sealed tight for so long, avoiding discovery. It's a relief to just let the words spill out without fear of some light-footed priest overhearing. Not that I was ever tempted to start talking to myself."

"Of course not," I reassured him. "But you're stalling."

"Hey, you need to let a fine wine have a chance to breathe. You don't just dive straight in."

"Since when were you an oenophile? I call bullshit on the whole 'need to decant' thing. Dive in already."

"Wine was never your strong subject, honey," said Trina, "so don't be too hasty about asserting an opinion. But he still has a point, Gordon. You're stalling."

"OK, fine," said Gordon, raising his hands in mock surrender. "Look, normally I'd preface this by saying that you're going to find this hard to believe. But given what we've all experienced so far I'll just assume you'll keep open minds.

"The Claimants–they are us. Just human beings like us. From Earth."

That statement stalled the conversation for a good thirty seconds.

"And we just never noticed them before?" I asked at last, drawing out the question to salt it with as much sarcasm as possible. It was a weak effort. Gordon was right–at this point I was willing to consider almost any explanation as plausible.

"From Earth," Gordon repeated, "a long time ago. A *long* time ago."

"Time travel?" asked Trina.

"No. They didn't travel through time. They didn't actually travel anywhere. Let me try to get some of this out without further interruptions, OK? See, Plato and some of the other 'ancient' writers were on the right track when mentioning vanished lands and civilizations. Atlantis, Mu, Lemuria, Hyperborea. Real places, real islands, continents, and subcontinents. The cradles of the earliest human cultures, wellsprings of art and science. Progenitors of a golden age that lasted for ten thousand years."

"What happened?" I asked, remembering too late Gordon's stricture against interruptions.

"They left, and took several land masses with them. Or rather, they didn't leave, they just sort of shifted."

"Huh?" Trina and I harmonized.

"Hard to understand, I know. Hard to explain too. I've only been able to piece together an educated guess. But as near as I can make out, about fifty thousand years ago the greatest priests or wizards–either from the various competing civilizations, or just from Atlantis (I've read conflicting accounts) performed a ritual that created some sort of rift. It bi-located the Earth in parallel dimensions, or duplicated it in an alternate reality. Something like that. Maybe the theoretical physics guys could spin you an explanation, something about M theory and branes. I don't know. But what happened is that one of the Earths was now bereft of a decent chunk of real estate and operating under a different set of physical laws."

"Different physical laws?" I asked.

"Right. You told me about the bulletproof priests. That isn't something that would have been possible before."

"So different physical laws means magic," I said.

"Wait a minute," said Trina. "You said not possible before. So it is possible now. That means the universe is now functioning under a different–an older–set of physical rules? How did that happen? Did the Claimants or Atlanteans, or whatever, perform that ritual again? In reverse or something?"

"Well, now I have to jump from educated guesses to completely unsupported speculation. But I won't let that stop me. You may remember reading about the Chinese rushing through a super collider, one almost half again as big as the Large Hadron Collider in Switzerland?"

"Yeah, I remember something about that," I said. "They were trying to beat the West in locating the Higgs, uh, Higgins..."

Gordon came to my rescue. "Higgs Boson particle. There was press speculation–uninformed, fear-mongering speculation–that the particle experiments would create a black hole and destroy the Earth. Well, the particle experiments didn't destroy the Earth, but they did destroy the barrier between the two dimensions. At least that's what I'm guessing. It wasn't the Atlanteans this time. It was us. Oops."

"So the two Earths merged into one again," said Trina.

"And a couple of new continents displaced a couple billion tons of ocean water," I said.

"Like a fat guy in a bath tub," said Gordon.

"Wow. I mean, wow," I said. That explained the river levels and the unnaturally high water table. "That is a lot to take in. Good work, by the way, Gordon."

"It's just a working hypothesis, but I'm reasonably comfortable with it."

Trina stood, and began clearing the dishes. Gordon and I rose to assist. Trina said, "So if Puget Sound is now twice its usual size, and if the valley south is likely a maze of Atlantean–or Lemurian, or Mu... what would that be, Muvian? Anyways, if the Willamette Valley is a maze of Claimant farming settlements, then that's why you were saying we should try east?"

"Yes. Portland got hit pretty hard, otherwise we'd probably have seen some sort of response by now from the National Guard or local Army Reserve units. Idaho, I'm guessing, won't have suffered as much from the, uh, the reunion. Its Guard and Reserve forces are probably up and functional. And any troops from eastern Washington and Oregon may have headed that way to link up."

"Normally a pretty easy trip, Gordon. Now it could be quite the ride," I said. "Still, if you're right, it promises at least greater safety, and maybe a chance for salvaging some of the good 'ole, U S of A. Not to mention that people will be pretty interested in your information."

"They just might, at that," said Gordon, with a half grin. "What's the next step?"

"Truck shopping," I said.

Chapter 11

Trina volunteered to stay behind and get a start on reassembling the supplies we'd just unloaded for our forthcoming excursion. We were pretty well sorted out from the last attempt, but with an additional participant and the promise of two larger vehicles, we had an opportunity to depart well prepared.

I handed Gordon my service pistol as we walked to the cruiser's hiding place. Both of the nine millimeter pistols had been lost during the battle at the ziggurat. "We'll look to restock the arsenal while we're out. In the meantime, I don't want you unarmed. I have to tell you that I'm impressed you made it all the way here without a run-in."

"I lettered in hide and seek," Gordon said, popping the magazine and checking the load. He knew what he was doing; I'd taken him target shooting often enough. "I wish I'd had this with me, though," he added quietly, and I wondered what narrow encounters had birthed that statement.

"OK," I said, "let's go boost some cars."

We cruised eastwards, looking for the least altered neighborhoods. A recent model Toyota Land Cruiser caught our attention after just a couple of miles.

"Do you know how to hot-wire a car?" asked Gordon.

"No. You?" He shook his head. "Even if either of us did, it's not something we'd want to have to do every single time. The house looks partially intact. Let's see if we can find the keys."

We could not, so we continued on, venturing farther east than I'd dared since the Reunion. We spotted another ziggurat in the distance. It was far enough away that I didn't feel the need to start edging around it yet.

"Pretty impressive, aren't they?" I observed. "You say they serve as both barracks and, what would you call it, monasteries?"

"Yes. They seem to be basically one-stop military, religious, and administrative centers. No real differentiation there, no separation of powers. Its theocratic from the top down."

A passing squall reduced visibility, a shifting gray curtain draped over the patrol car, isolating the two of us from the shadowy world beyond the rain spattered windows. I slowed to a crawl. There was an almost brittle tension about Gordon. He reminded me of some recently released prisoners, nerves tamped down under rigorous self-control, the vast outside world simultaneously frightening and exhilarating. Was that the sort of price Gordon had paid?

He turned my direction and flashed the old mischievous grin. No. Gordon's experience may have left a mark, but it wasn't a debilitating mark. He'd come through it OK.

"What the hell?" I asked, as a naked Canadian Goose caromed off of the cruiser's hood, leaving a saucer-shaped dent. I hit the brakes and sat dumbfounded as the remainder of a migrating vee slammed into the ground around us. Waiting for a moment to make sure the skies were clear of falling birds, we exited the car into the slowly easing precipitation to examine the fowl.

"Hungry?" asked Gordon, hoisting a plump, smoldering goose. "Your goose is cooked."

The smell of scorched feathers permeated the air. Looking closer we could see the lumpen shapes of dead birds dotting the ground in the direction of the ziggurat.

"What do you make of it?" I asked.

"You told me about the priests' pyrokinetics. I'm guessing air defense. Our fly-boys probably took out a few Atlantean strongholds. I bet if it wasn't so cloudy we'd see a heat shimmer overhead."

"They've heated the air hot enough to knock down missiles? That doesn't seem likely. These birds are crispy, but not charred to ash."

"Different physical laws, Nick. Remember that. We can't assume even the most basic facts anymore."

"Well, huh," I said. "Think those different physical laws have something to do with the ziggurats passing through the Reunion mostly intact?"

"Probably. Remember I'm operating from hypotheses based on cursory readings from foreign texts. I've barely scratched the surface weirdness. The deeper mojo remains unplumbed. But I think you've got a sound idea. As we've seen, the ziggurats possess some sort of protection, perhaps some we've not yet seen, protections employed as defense against each other. It is possible those protections inadvertently limited the degree to which the ziggurats suffered from the Reunion."

"So, if I've got this right, when the Reunion occurred, both sides got creamed. Except for the Atlantean soldiers, all nice and cozy inside the ziggurats." Shit, they'd had us outgunned from the word 'go.' Even without guns.

ଈଓ

We found our first vehicle less than a mile from Interstate 205: a long bed Ford F-250 with a quad-cab and a three-inch lift. The keys weren't a problem since they were still clutched in the owner's hand. He was slumped against the front left off-road tire with an arrow protruding from his back, and he smelled none too good.

"One thing I don't miss about the police force is body call," I said as I freed the Playboy key fob and dangling bunch of keys from the corpse's grip.

We checked out our prize. The gas tank was full. The tool box in the bed opened to one of the smaller keys from the ring, and contained both a come-along and a tow line. The winch on the front bumper functioned, and the bank of lights on the roof could freeze an entire herd of deer.

As there remained plenty of daylight, we switched rides, hooking the police cruiser to the rear hitch via the tow line. A shallow step depending from the frame eased the clamber up into the cab. The engine growled to life and we continued our search, I to the throaty reverberations of the big V-8 power plant, Gordon playing brakeman on the police cruiser-cum-caboose.

We passed the limit of the ziggurat's defensive perimeter, or so I guessed. I saw no more dead birds.

I cut north, toward what had been an industrial zone. We passed through a massive construction staging ground, zigzagging between towering piles of cut stone. I could make out kilted figures at work.

Here stood one atop a pile affixing a harness about a block of masonry. There two more were encouraging an absolutely enormous ox as it dragged a laden sledge through the muck. Another was maneuvering what I took to be a crane: a contraption of poles, pulleys, and ropes. It was likely powered by yet another of the huge bovines standing idle nearby.

Off to one side I saw another pair of workmen unloading stacked corpses from a cart. They were dumping the bodies into a shallow trench grave. Atlantean sanitation services? Civic pride? Welcome to Portland, we have fewer bloated corpses than San Francisco. Whatever, it was yet another sign of organization and that wasn't good.

We left the Atlantean industrial park and entered one of our own, transitioning from a clayey mud to asphalt. The rain began to let up as I drove into the parking lot, passing a cement mixer and a pair of earth movers.

We got out to confer in the drizzle, talking in hushed voices.

"They just watched us drive by," said Gordon. "Displayed no initiative."

"They may have sent a runner to report us," I said. "If someone like me has been giving the local troops a hard time, the priests have probably issued standing orders to send a message. If not, then they are just so many cattle in a field, watching the traffic pass."

"Completely docile. Tens of thousands of years of cultural stratification. It makes the Indian caste system pale to insignificance."

I smiled at that. I could see Gordon already composing mental notes for a research paper. I wasn't concerned so much with ingrained cultural attitudes as with the fact that building was evidently under way.

With Gordon's arrival I'd experienced a new sense of hope. Maybe we could still win. Maybe our civilization still had a chance. But if the enemy was already entrenched and rebuilding, the odds were lessened if we were still scattered and disorganized.

"Over there, near the flagpole," said Gordon, pointing towards a low, single-story brick administrative building with Old Glory still depending soddenly from a fifty-foot shaft. There, parked near the main entrance, squatted a Hummer–the type manufactured with a slightly smaller cab to allow space for a short cargo bed at the rear.

"That just might do," I said. "Let's see about the keys."

The glass of the front door was shattered, spilling into the lobby. Chairs resting askew and an overturned potted plant suggested a rush of men, either panicked or with a purpose. I switched on my flashlight as the fading light from the gray skies outside grew ineffective. I picked out droplets and streaks of blood.

We continued on, reaching an inner office. Blood splatters had soaked the carpet. Behind an overturned desk lay the hacked remains of a paunchy man in charcoal slacks and a white short-sleeved shirt, stained red. An empty, short-barreled .357 rested next to his outstretched, mangled hand.

I took the pistol and shoved it into my waistband. "This will take .38s. I've got a few boxes at home. But we should be able to find some .357 eventually." I was stalling. I didn't really want to rifle through the corpse's pockets for car keys.

Gordon spared me the ordeal. Behind the office door, dangling from a coat hook, hung a rumpled sports coat. Gordon reached into the right front pocket and retrieved a set of keys. He performed a little jangling flourish, then displayed the Hummer key fob.

"I'll drive this one," he said.

We drove back slowly. The sodden skies and growing twilight increased the dangers of an already hazardous drive and I had to worry about an un-piloted car drifting unpredictably from the end of a tow-line. We maintained a snail's pace, so I had plenty of time to think.

My mind segued from one topic to another. For example, why *was* I still towing the police cruiser? Was it a sense of responsibility, a lingering loyalty to the police force? When would I completely accept that I was no longer a cop? Did I actually believe that I would return the car in triumph to the garage and sign in the keys? Why not just ditch it here? All it did was impede Gordon and endanger me. Since we hadn't rigged brake lights or turn signals, he must be having a hard time noticing when I slowed or turned.

He was coping well enough, all thing considered. That was true–he was coping. Trapped in the belly of the beast, alone, and yet he'd escaped. I suppose driving the Hummer in low-visibility conditions didn't provide much of a challenge by comparison.

We parked the vehicles in front of the house. I knew of no concealment nearby for all three, especially nothing the size of the two off-road trucks. We ran a risk of discovery, but anticipated hitting the road by mid-morning. After that it shouldn't matter if an Atlantean patrol stumbled across the cruiser and uncovered the house behind its masking masonry.

Trina came outside to examine our prizes by flashlight. "What, couldn't find anything bigger?" she asked with a smile.

"We were looking for a monster-truck Winnebago and an army bridge-layer, but this is the best we could do," I replied, giving her a peck on the cheek.

"Is that a gun in your pants...oh, yeah, that is a gun." She turned and led the way inside.

"I loaned Gordon the Glock. He's practiced with it. We found this today. It will do me for a backup."

We assembled in the living room, where Trina had a steaming teapot and three mugs dangling tags. I slumped wearily on the couch. "So, I'm thinking you ought to carry my little .38 snubby. Just in case, sweetheart. Just in case."

She masked her discomfort by pouring hot water. "Here you go. Careful, it's still hot."

"I don't want you to shoot anyone, Trina. I'll do my damnedest to keep you from that situation. But you know what it's like out there."

"Here, Gordon. Do you take honey? Lemon?"

"Just keep it with you. I'll feel better knowing you have an option." I sipped at my tea. I hated these conversations. These arguments. Patience remains an elusive virtue, but I try. For Trina, I try.

Trina peered at me intently over the rim of her mug. I took three more sips while she stared. Gordon's gaze was roving over the walls, anywhere but at the two of us. He stopped short of uncomfortable whistling.

At length Trina stood and left the room. Gordon and I competed in the Portland open-class raised eyebrow championship. A minute later Trina returned with her battered winter coat–a lined, knee-length number in leather and plaid wool. She fished the .38 from one pocket and a box of shells from another.

"Show me again how to use it," Trina said, "then stop talking about it, OK?"

"Whenever I think I couldn't love you anymore...."

ꙮ

Dinner was a simple affair: sandwiches and a salad from the last produce of the backyard garden. Trina had been too busy provisioning to indulge herself in the kitchen.

Simplicity didn't seem to dampen Gordon's appetite. He wolfed down the meal, evidently savoring every bite.

"Not exactly what the Atlanteans served, huh Gordon?" I asked.

He snorted. "Imagine eating nothing but fish sticks and macaroni and cheese for every meal, three times a day, seven days a week. Not that they served fish sticks or pasta of any sort. But the staple diet of the soldiers and serving staff lacks variety. Now, the priests seem to eat quite a bit better, but I never did get access to the upper level kitchens. I caught a glimpse of a few serving trays and managed a whiff now and then, that's all, but it was easy enough to deduce who the indulged gourmands were. Man, I wanted to get out of there. If I never have another bowl of gruel I'll die...slightly more content than if I'd died having had another bowl of gruel. And let's not get into boiled goat."

"Boiled goat?" asked Trina, curious, at the same time I asked, "Tough to find an escape route?"

"Aficionados of the goat, the Atlanteans," Gordon said. "Or, at least they find it an efficient source of protein. It can be fed on pretty much anything and raised pretty much anywhere.

"Escape wasn't really a problem. I found a way out within the first week. The ziggurat had absorbed much of the campus, not just the library, but I found a gap leading out. I could have waltzed–well, crawled–out any time I wanted."

"Then why did you stay?" asked Trina.

"Well, like I told you, I had access to a library. When would I find a better chance to study them?"

"Always the academic," I said.

"Yes, not a practical bone in my body," he said. "I can't imagine how figuring out the cause of the initial split or subsequent Reunion could be remotely useful."

"Wait, that sounds remarkably like sarcasm," I said. "You're not trying to imply...."

"That there could be a way to split the two Earths again? Might be I'm implying that."

Chapter 12

GORDON KNEW A GOOD EXIT LINE WHEN HE SAID ONE, SO HE REFUSED TO elaborate until the next morning at breakfast, smugly resisting our entreaties. He was more forthcoming over pancakes. We had a full day ahead of us and Trina was abandoning her kitchen (possibly forever), so she laid out quite a spread, using up what remaining perishables we couldn't bring with us.

Powering through a second stack smeared with strawberry preserves, Gordon said, "I wish I could tell you I'd uncovered a magic incantation that would send the Atlanteans back home and restore the Earth to its previous condition. But I can't. I don't know the secrets of this new–or old–paradigm. What I know is that it is possible. I know the story, filtered through fifty millennia, and copied and re-copied from original texts that crumbled to dust ages ago. Despite the antiquity it is a consistent story, remarkably similar, point by important point, in all the sources I found. A convincing story. It was done before and the Atlanteans can do it again. They're constitutionally stuck in a rut, incapable of change or advancement. But they don't throw anything away, and that includes knowledge and methods."

"They can do it," said Trina, doling out slices of fried potted meat (something she'd have turned up her professional nose at not too long ago), "but we can't. How does that help us?"

"We can't, if by we, you mean the three of us," said Gordon, sipping his coffee. "We haven't spent decades studying and practicing Atlantean physics–we aren't wizards. But *they* can do it–the more practiced, powerful practitioners–the Atlantean high priests. It's just a matter of convincing them to do it."

"And how do we do that?" asked Trina again, frustrated, obviously feeling a letdown from the euphoria Gordon had instilled the previous night.

"We don't, sweetheart," I said, understanding Gordon's intent. "The three of us can't waltz into a ziggurat, kidnap Pope Atlantis, and force him to work his mojo. But the United States Army can make a pretty convincing argument."

"Precisely," said Gordon. "The army–whatever bit of it we can find functioning–just needs to know what I know. With sufficient manpower, they can capture some top magi to do the job. The story indicates that it might take more than just Pope Atlantis, to employ Nick's not particularly accurate phrase. We just need to get this information to a sufficiently sizable, functioning armed authority. Army, Marines, Air Force, doesn't matter."

"That's the plan?" asked Trina. "Let me see if I have this straight. We need to travel blindly across the country to find the army. Then we need to convince the army to kidnap Atlantean priests. The army then needs to torture the priests into casting a magic spell to reverse the reunion of parallel Earths, a reunion that we apparently caused, by the way, with the new Chinese atom smashing ring. Have I summed up these multiple absurdities and ethically questionable actions fairly enough?"

"Precisely," said Gordon again, grinning imperturbably into the face of Trina's sarcasm.

"Trina," I said, keeping my voice as level and non-confrontational as six-plus years of marriage allowed, "if there is any chance of..."

She didn't let me finish. "I know, I know. Damn it. We have to try. And my... qualms... are maybe a bit out of place under the circumstances. Doesn't mean I have to like it, or treat it like some boys' adventure."

"No, you are absolutely right, Trina," I said. "This isn't something to undertake lightly."

"But we have to do it," said Gordon, "and we might as well get to it." He got to his feet, picking up his emptied plate. "I suppose washing the dishes when we intend to abandon the place is absurd."

"But we're going to do it anyway," said Trina firmly.

And so we did, washing, drying, and placing each plate, fork, pot, and pan in its proper place before turning to the task of loading for the trek.

The load out was a trek in itself. We weren't sure how far we'd have to go or even where. We might encounter anything. Anything at all. Maps were of questionable use. The upshot was we provisioned like a family of pioneers about to set out on the Oregon trail. We packed camping gear, tools, cases of food, and jugs of water. From the basement we retrieved the car batteries that showed the least sign of corrosion. The truck bed was laden with cans full of gasoline, plastic quart bottles of motor oil, an inflatable mattress, suitcases stuffed full of clothing, and the personal items Trina couldn't bring herself to leave behind.

We ran out of space for the kitchen sink.

ཀྵ

It was approaching noon when we finally pulled out, bidding our house a last adieu. Trina rode in the pickup with me. Gordon followed in the Hummer, driving with the maniacal glee of a teenager.

We had nearly reached the bottom of the hill when the Atlanteans sprang their ambush.

The *spang* and *click* of arrowheads and wooden shafts glancing off the truck hood announced the attack. The Atlanteans hadn't yet stumbled upon the breakthrough concept of aiming for the tires. Still, they drove the iron wedges with enough force to be a credible threat. Any single arrow could punch through glass and flesh. I was terrified about what havoc the impact of arrowheads and wooden splinters could work inside the engine compartment.

Tok. Tok. Scrrritch. Spang. Feathered shafts whistled by horizontally–misses. Or crossed my vision diagonally–non-lethal hits.

"Shit!" My foot ground into the accelerator. "Get down!" I yelled, pushing down on Trina's shoulder.

My peripheral vision caught something large coming fast from the same direction as the arrows. It was like seeing a car in an intersection the instant before getting t-boned. Impact crumpled the sheet metal of the passenger door, bowing in the interior panel, dislodging the armrest, and knocking Trina against the center console. The Ford rocked on its suspension, threatening to tip. Then it righted and kept moving.

In the miraculously undamaged passenger side mirror I saw another of those oversized, armored armadillos staggering on wobbly legs and the Hummer–rear passenger window shattered–swerving to avoid it.

I looked forward again. There was a bend in the road at the bottom of the hill. Just beyond it lay a barricade of stone blocks manned by a platoon of spear-wielding Atlantean soldiers.

"Nick!" Trina screamed. She'd popped up again after the impact. "Look out!"

I cranked the wheel to the right and stomped down on the brake pedal, throwing the truck into a shuddering, rubber-smearing slide. As we came to a stop I stabbed the button to automatically lower all the windows, jammed down the emergency brake, and fumbled the .357 free from my waistband.

"Trina," I said with a laborious, patently false calm, "find something to shoot and start shooting."

I practiced my own preaching and opened up at the soldiers behind the hip-high wall. At the same time, they surged over the top, amazingly lithe and dexterous considering the encumbrance of head-to-toe armor and heavy pole arms.

The *pop pop* behind me told me Trina was engaging as well. Who or what I didn't know.

I put five of them down before dropping the pistol on the seat and reaching for the shotgun. It hadn't been enough. A surviving Atlantean was rumbling on at full charge, his thick-bladed spear point looming like the foreshortening in a comic book panel.

With my right hand I reached blindly for Trina, and forced her back hard against her seat. With my left I found a grip on the Remington, just behind the trigger guard. I hurled myself back against the seat as the wavy-edged blade plunged by, almost grazing my nose. The soldier smacked against the side of the truck, fully committed to his attack. I raised the elbow of my left arm and delivered a backhand to his face with the shotgun's butt stock. It wasn't much of a blow, one-handed and short-armed, but it sent him back a step, blood leaking from his newly askew nose.

I flung open the door, knocking him off balance, and followed, dropping from the cab. I shot him point blank from the hip, my jeans absorbing a spattering of blood. Two of his comrades were not far behind him, coming fast. I took them both down, both shells delivering a tight spread, center mass.

That did for the barricade. Four of the five I'd taken out with the pistol were still moving; the thirty-eight caliber slugs pushed through the .357 were not quite equal to the task of penetrating armor and man as powerfully as I could have wished. Still, those four were out of the fight just as effectively as the fifth.

I spun on my heel to see Trina, hands shaking, fumbling open a box of .38s, the snub nose open in her lap. The Hummer blocked my vision beyond her. Gordon was leaning across the passenger seat, sending controlled double taps out the window.

"You're doing great, sweetheart," I said, leaning in to grab a box of twelve-gauge shells.

I sprinted around the back of the truck to join Gordon. What Trina had been shooting at remained uncertain. If any of the Atlanteans had been in her line of fire, they'd apparently been in no real danger of getting hit.

As I cleared the truck's bumper I turned my head to catch a glimpse of Trina, contorting my neck to get the angle. Her face was pale.

But my baby was in there, swinging.

"Keep it together," I called over the din of the fight. "I'm proud of you."

The archers had regrouped, forming up in the street behind the scaly beast that seemed to have gotten its legs back under it. Six of them lay unmoving on the street, blood pooling beneath each. I made fifteen left standing: fourteen remaining soldiers and one officer goading the beast.

"What the hell is that?" I asked.

"Glyptodon. Been extinct for about ten-thousand years," Gordon said. He opened his mouth again to elaborate. "They–"

"Never mind, tell me later," I interrupted when I realized Gordon would gladly hold forth on paleontology indefinitely. We didn't have time for class. "I'll move the critter then you start taking down the soldiers."

A fine enough plan, in theory. The thick, naturally armor-plated hide rendered the praxis uncertain. This was a job for slugs and I was loaded with buckshot.

"Nothing ventured," I muttered, and leaned across the hood of the Hummer, leveling the shotgun barrel at the beast's head. Aiming at the eyes with a wide-choke smooth-bore wasn't exactly feasible, but the spread of pellets gave me decent odds.

I squeezed the trigger, leaning into the butt stock to reduce the recoil. I don't think I damaged an eye. But one or two of the ball-bearings smacked into, or caromed off of, the relatively tender flesh around the sockets, and that was enough to spook the beast.

It snorted its protest, shaking its pony keg of a head. Veering off sharply, it commenced a waddling stride that built up surprising speed and momentum–away from me and Gordon.

The flight of the beast deprived the archers of their mobile cover. Gordon took full advantage, the plan proving serviceable after all. Firing with both speed and accuracy–Wild Bill Hickok in spectacles and Nikes–Gordon drilled three Atlantean archers through the chest before I was able to join in.

An arrow brushed by my left shoulder, its fletching scratching grooves into my leather jacket, reminding me that this wasn't a shooting gallery. I dropped prone and rolled to my right, protected from arrows by the body of the Hummer and the two front tires.

I began firing at the advancing legs, all I could see from my vantage point. Working the slide of the riot gun was awkward from that position, but not a real hindrance. Shins and knees squirted blood like a tomato forced through a colander and soldiers collapsed, bringing heads and torsos into my sights. Armor chimed against asphalt. I kept shooting at legs until I emptied the tubular magazine. Then I rolled behind the tire to reload.

As I reloaded, Trina, looking as white as a naked mime in a blizzard, lowered herself to the ground next to me and began firing one-handed. Bullets sparked and ricocheted off the road surface, and I experienced a whirling rush of confused emotions.

Up until this moment I'd kept fear at bay. Or rather, I'd simply had no time for fear, simply reacting to the needs of the instant. But with my wife beside me, at risk of the slings and arrows, the specter of my mortality sprang forth to meet the specter of Trina's mortality. The two met in a high-stepping macabre dance to the syncopation of gun fire. Muddling the emotional waters further was a brief surge of pride at the sight of Trina fighting with me, almost literally shoulder-to-shoulder. The potentially noble sentiment was ruined by a wholly uncharitable flash of amusement at the futility of her wildly inaccurate contribution. All this hit me in the time it took her to empty the wheel-gun.

And then—five shots later, to be precise—it was quiet. Except for the moaning of the wounded, that is, and the dwindling sound of retreating boot heels. I stood up to take stock. The beast was vanishing into a clump of trees, its club-like tail whipping in agitation. The officer of the botched ambush was likewise performing a tactical retrograde action, leaving behind his entire *hors de combat* company.

"Why the hell didn't he have a priest in support?" I wondered aloud.

Gordon, a man unwilling to allow any question—even a rhetorical one—to suffer unanswered, emerged from the Hummer. His eyes were wide and bright behind his glasses. "Perhaps a personal vendetta against you? You took a toll on the local Atlanteans. Or maybe the priest is en route and we just happened to arrive before the ambush was completely set."

"In which case we'd better scoot," I said, reaching down to haul Trina to her feet. I pulled her tight, into a fierce, one-armed hug. I put my lips next to her ear and whispered, "My Valkyrie. You were terrific. And you can cry in the truck. Come on."

Gordon hauled himself back into the big 4x4. Trina and I sprinted toward the Ford. Somewhere in the distance I could hear the panicked beast bulling its way through obstacles like a wounded rhino.

Atlantean myrmidons groaned, or screamed maledictions or prayers in their alien tongue.

I tossed the shotgun through the open passenger door and helped Trina up into the cab. I slammed the door, grateful that the battering from the Atlantean beast hadn't damaged the latching mechanism. I hustled around the far side and hoisted myself in. I shifted into low-range four wheel drive, and jounced over the curb, through a low hedge, over a sodden flower bed, and into a shallow ditch to clear the barricade. Gordon followed the trail I blazed.

Back on the street, a soldier, his chest armor a crimson smear, pushed himself to his knees and tried gamely to hurl his clumsy spear at the truck as we drove by. The weapon fell far short, and the soldier followed suit, collapsing face first, unmoving. That was the last blow.

We were clear, but there was no going home now.

Chapter 13

It is—or was—a common misconception that Oregon is a soggy state, awash in precipitation six months a year. The truth is that the bulk of the state, the eastern two-thirds, is dry. High desert and ranching country. The coastal range and the lofty Cascades extend parallel barriers along the length of the state, north to south, taking the brunt of the storms trundling in from the Pacific. Beyond the second mountainous bulwark, relatively little rain falls. To the east lies sage brush plains, vast lava fields, Indian reservations, ranches, and such farms as irrigation can support, including, naturally potato farms along the Idaho border. At least, that used to be the case. We'd find out if it still was.

We'd find out, presupposing we escaped Portland and cleared Mount Hood. That was still far from certain.

Trina sobbed most of the way through the city. I ceased my attempts at consolation once I correctly interpreted her broken responses and hand gestures as "I know, I know." She didn't need me to explain the circumstances, or explicate the morality of her actions. She knew all of that, she just needed to clear the emotional blockage. So I shut up and let her cry.

I was long past the anxiety that had suffused the first six months or so of our marriage—the deep seated dread that each tiff and each minor irritation would lead inexorably to divorce. She had just emerged from what was certainly a traumatic experience. She needed some time to purge the emotions. She'd get over it. She wasn't going to leave me. Besides, where would she go?

I had plenty to keep me occupied in any case. As I drove through the two merged versions of Portland, fighting off the impending shakes, I relived the recent fracas and the reality of the danger truly sank in. I wanted a beer or eight. I wanted a safe place to sit and think.

Gordon's revelations had wrought a profound change to my outlook. No longer was I living an apocalyptic existence, desiring only to stave off a violent death for Trina and myself, counting each day a victory. Hope had reared its dangerously beautiful head. If we died now, the consequences were vastly more significant than the exit of three people from a world no longer their own. If we died now, the chance to rebuild our world might die with us. It was an adjustment. All things considered it was a marvelous change, but still a change. I'd always been a creature of routine and habit.

Working slowly eastward toward Gresham, I felt the need to consult with Gordon on our route. The immutable law that you always forget something when packing blew a derisive raspberry at me. We'd neglected to bring along any mode of communication between vehicles.

I worked over the question while beginning to nudge my zigs and zags a touch more to the north. A single-story Atlantean building stretched across the roadway. It was russet hued and open at frequent, regular intervals by tall, narrow windows. There was enough room to edge around and I slowed to creep through the gap. Rounding the far side, back onto the street, I saw that the rear half of a semi-truck's trailer merged into the side of the building. I pulled to a stop next to the rig and got out.

"What is it?" asked Trina.

"Just an idea," I said. "We don't have any way to talk to Gordon. That truck ought to have a CB radio."

"And you're going to remove it from the big rig and install it in here? Nick the Electrician. This I've got to see." She smiled.

"Feeling a bit better, I see." I'd once attempted to save a few dollars by installing a new radio/CD player in her car and had botched the job soundly. One of the many things I'll never live down. If I live.

Gordon brought the Hummer to a stop nearby. He too climbed out and watched as I scrambled up into the cab of the big eighteen-wheeler.

"Ah. Ten-four good buddy," he said, divining my intent.

He clambered up the other side to join me in the spacious cab and produced a multi-tool from his pocket. We got to work, spelunking the broad dash, tracing wires, and producing a great deal of grunts and profanities. At last our labors bore fruit and we emerged triumphantly with the radio. Gordon brought out another prize as well: a yellow aluminum sign painted with black figures. It parodied the deer-crossing highway signs, in this case a pair of buxom silhouettes, the sort normally seen adorning a truck's mud flaps, strutting arm in arm. While I requisitioned the semi's CB radio antenna, Gordon was patching the smashed window of the Hummer with the sign and a roll of duct tape. Trina provided the sarcastic applause.

We had a powwow before continuing.

"I-84 is a canal where it nears the Willamette," I said. "But I'm guessing that's only for a stretch of it. I don't want to thread the suburbs all the way to Sandy. If 84 is clear, we'll have a straight run past the mountain."

"That's a lot of 'ifs'," said Gordon. "But it's worth trying. The more time we spend in these merged neighborhoods, the more we risk encountering additional troops."

"And we might have a better chance of finding another abandoned semi," said Trina. "One CB isn't much use."

That settled, we mounted up and wended the eerie maze, working gradually north and east.

We drove through another Atlantean enclave, receiving the usual incurious stares from the tradesmen-workers-drones. We now expected the exception of one messenger tasked with sprinting off to alert his betters. The workers were busy. A section of merged housing was in the process of demolition. Aluminum siding and bricks were heaped to one side, the exposed interiors of partial Atlantean structures open to the elements.

These signs of industrious domestication summoned up renewed anxiety. I could only hope that our hypothetical resistance army in Idaho was at least as active.

Interstate 205 provided the first check. It ran north-south across our route. Large sections of it remained intact, which I suppose was positive, but the overpass we'd hoped to use to cross it had not remained intact. Its piers had been undermined by the flattened remains of some unidentifiable Atlantean structure. Still, Trina and I had played this game before. We turned north, following the freeway, looking for an overpass.

"Screw it," I said. I'd wanted to reach I-84 further east, but 205 would take us there as well. We'd just ascertain its status as road or canal a bit earlier than planned, that's all. I used the nearest off-ramp as an on-ramp and drove north in the southbound lane. Even given the doll-like proportions presented by the side mirror, I could see Gordon's grin. He was evidently enjoying the traffic transgression immensely.

We bypassed missing sections of the roadbed and scattered the feathered denizens of what appeared to be a large-scale Atlantean poultry farm that had come through the merger unharmed in the middle of three lanes of traffic. A pair of kilted poultry farmers emerged from the vast, low-roofed main building after we passed, staring hard at our retreating bumpers. More, I guessed, out of indignation than curiosity.

Trina laughed for the next five minutes.

To the east of 205, I-84 was dry, retaining its character as a freeway–that is, to the extent that any of the roads or highways had retained their character. I restrained a whoop. This trip promised a yo-yo aspect of highs and lows. If I celebrated the highs too extravagantly, how could I stomach the lows with equanimity?

Every now and again I managed to give myself good advice.

A ziggurat loomed at the crest of Rocky Butte State Park. I watched warily for any sign of Atlantean soldiers, then huffed a relieved sigh as I watched the ziggurat receding gradually in the rear view mirror. As I-84 edged closer to the Columbia River the gaps in the concrete and the obstructing buildings grew more frequent and more numerous. The noise-baffling wall lining the freeway to the south hadn't fared well, resembling a gigantic row of broken teeth. The overlay of Atlantean buildings creeping northward toward the river was as thick as I'd yet seen, and many had come through the Reunion smack dab in the middle of the highway. It was already mid-afternoon and we weren't making great time.

We came to a halt at yet another gap, practically a fissure this time, with a creek bed at its base. An eighteen-wheeler lay mangled at the bottom, the stream trickling between the tall tires.

"Did we bring a rope?" Trina asked.

ᘓᘐ

Slithering down to the icy water on a chilly fall day wasn't pleasant. Removing the ripe and formerly very rotund cadaver from the driver's seat was even less so. Still, the practice garnered from the previous CB radio extraction sped up at least one portion of the operation considerably. And the rope proved handy in ascending to the highway once again.

Crossing the stream was another matter entirely.

"Pretty high density of structures here along the river," said Gordon. "An extensive fishing industry, judging from the smell and relative frequency of that image." He pointed to the nearest Atlantean building, a squat, pastel blue square. A vaguely amphibian looking member of the Atlantean pantheon hunkered in front of it and a putrid miasma of rotting fish erupted from it. "I know his name from the texts, but I still don't have much of a grasp on the pronunciation."

"Great, professor. Maybe he can swim our rigs over the creek for us."

"Now don't get snippy, Nick. I'm just suggesting that since this looks to be a high traffic area, there's probably a way over the creek somewhere nearby."

Right. The Atlanteans would have needed to traverse the creek too. I wasn't processing information rapidly, logically, or even intuitively.

"Of course," I said, conceding the point. "Sorry, it's been a tough day. Let's find a way over, and then start hunting up a place to spend the night. I don't want to risk travel in the dark."

The shoulder flanking the north side of the highway near the fissure dropped a yard to a narrow cobblestone pathway that almost seemed to spring from the side of I-84, like a pedestrian byway planned and financed by the local Parks and Recreation Department, instead of what it was–an artifact of the Reunion. A pathway for Atlantean workers. Our vehicles wheelbases were just narrow enough to fit.

We followed the narrow street along the fissure as far as we could, until a gas station brought us up short. Its garage blocked the route, and its partially exposed fuel tanks hung precariously in midair halfway down the fissure. Another powder blue building reeking of fish abutted the garage, blocking our way around. And past that building the maze of merged buildings lay thick and un-navigable.

"What do we do? Over," came Gordon's voice, testing his newly installed CB.

That was a really good question. This little detour hadn't restored my wits to high-level functioning. I still felt tired and stupid.

"Can we just drive through the walls?" Trina asked. "That garage doesn't look all that sturdy and we've got these two big trucks."

That didn't strike me as a workable solution. We could probably bash through, but flimsy or not, those walls could easily disable one or both of our vehicles. Still, the suggestion was enough to give me an idea.

I keyed the handset. "Think we can winch down the wall?"

There was a delay before, "Huh. Maybe. Why are we talking on the CB?"

Another good question. I climbed out of the cab. Gordon clambered out of the Hummer and together we went to inspect the garage wall with its corrugated aluminum siding.

"Whack it with an axe?" I was at the point where my best ideas seemed to involve hitting things, or yanking them down. But it seemed the best way to see if there was another layer of construction that we'd need to breach, and create punctures to grapple with the winches.

Gordon shrugged and returned to the Hummer for his pioneer kit. I stepped aside to allow him room to wind up and swing. The axe hacked through the siding and into a layer of plywood beyond. Nothing more, no brick to worry about. Nodding his satisfaction, Gordon delivered a couple more strategically placed whacks.

After that it was a simple matter of employing the winches. Neither Gordon nor I had ever used a winch before, and we hadn't bothered testing them. That simple matter turned into an hour-long project as the sun began to sink, and worries about Atlantean soldiers rose.

At length, sweating from exertion despite the bitter Columbia River Gorge wind and the autumn afternoon chill, two ten-thousand pound capacity electric winches working in tandem ripped down a section of wall. The horrendous growling sound of straining electrical motors was abruptly drowned out by the screaming of tearing metal.

Which left us with one more wall to go.

At this point I was tempted to employ Trina's suggestion after all. Maybe we could get by with only one truck, and pick up another later on if the opportunity arose. But we knew what we were doing now. We swung axes and deployed the winches again. Familiarity brought our time down to twenty minutes.

We were through. And still on the wrong side of the gully.

ꙮ

A dozen pairs of eyes stared blankly at our creeping caravan from the shelter of a portico. Square pillars painted a soft orange supported the overhang of the two-story Atlantean building. Industrial-size spools of cord and piles of fish netting provided a good clue as to the building's purpose. I shook my head at the docility of the onlookers, not in bafflement but in response to a sudden wash of pity. Human lives rendered no more meaningful than that of domesticated animals. All ambition, all creativity crushed by the weight of a theocratic culture, its sheer stagnation stifling any prospect of progress, any thought of change.

I pitied them, yes. But even more I feared the remainder of humanity falling under the same thrall, the same unquestioning obedience of ancient writ and the blind acquiescence to the whims of the interpreters of that writ. If I had to blast, carve, or drive through a thousand of the poor bastards in order to give humanity a chance, I would do so unhesitatingly.

First, however, we needed to find a crossing.

We did. Eventually. It was probably under a mile from the garage, though it took the better part of two miles driving to reach due to the chaotic warren we were forced to negotiate. A stretch of scorched earth helped. With all of the wooden structures burnt to the ground it was easier to maneuver between and around the blackened stone buildings.

The bridge was located just a few hundred yards from the river's edge. A chunky stone hut, practically identical to the little Atlantean farm houses I'd seen near home (as I still thought of it), hunkered like a brooding troll near the bridge. A woman of indeterminate age—anywhere from thirty to sixty, if her caste lived that long—sat on a three-legged stool in front of the door. A girl of about eight sat cross-legged in the dirt next to her. They appeared to be mending a net, a task the woman continued as we approached. The girl looked up from her needle to inspect us with eyes of prodigious hopelessness, but a back-handed cuff from her mother returned her attention to her labor.

Given its importance to us, the bridge was a disappointingly unprepossessing affair, even pedestrian—very nearly so in the practical sense of the word. I had to pull the side mirrors in to squeeze between the guard rails, and the squeal of metal on stone from the Hummer was piercing even through closed windows. But we were through, and we turned south again, working our way back to the freeway.

We were in a race now with the sun. A slow, frustrating race.

"I don't think we're going to get too far, Gordon," I called over the radio. "If we can get across the freeway let's just call it good. Find a spot to conceal the rigs and just sleep inside 'em."

"Balance of risks," Gordon's voice replied through the speaker. "No option is a safe option."

Risk was right. I took several of them in the course of regaining the freeway. The truck lost a bit of paint, but we arrived unscathed. We were still a mile or so from the next off-ramp, but a gap in the sound-baffling wall that corresponded with a flagstoned boulevard bisecting the freeway gave us an exit. The Atlantean road lay about a yard below the surface of the freeway, the constituent layers of I-84 revealed in cross-section to either side.

I got out of the truck and fetched a pair of four-inch by six-inch planks from the bed. These I lowered at a diagonal, creating a ramp. Trina slid over to the driver's seat and followed my hand signals to drive the truck down to the lower roadbed. Gordon followed, stopping to retrieve the boards, and then we worked our way south. We passed an apartment complex bearing the signs of a fight: broken windows, spent brass glittering on the ground, scorch marks on the walls, and–most tellingly–an upper torso dangling lifelessly from an upstairs window, the point of an arrow protruding from the spine.

We drove through another burnt over section, then back into a labyrinth of amalgamated structures, and kept cruising until we found a likely hiding spot. An Atlantean villa had combined with a sprawling brick home on a corner lot and the Craftsman-style house next door. A two-car garage cut into one arm of the box-like villa. The garage door was open and empty of cars. We could just fit the truck and Hummer inside. A side door led from the garage into the wild tangle of merged walls, meeting and crossing impenetrably. A back door led to the villa's peristyle, its orderly garden with its ugly Atlantean pantheon-themed fountain incongruously adorned with a rusting child's swing set.

I lowered the garage door. Any nearby residents might notice this alteration of the neighborhood landscape, but the alternative was even more risky.

ꙮ

I was exhausted. I'm pretty sure we all were feeling done in, with shadowy phantoms of weariness floating just at the cusp of peripheral vision.

"We need a watch schedule," I said, the statement broken in the middle by a yawn. "Trina, you take first watch. Wake me at–" I checked my watch "– ten o'clock. You get the dawn patrol, Gordon. I'll wake you at three."

Trina looked as cranky and tired as I felt. But she thought it through and seemed to realize that the first watch was the easiest. Not easy, but better than the other two options. After enough time together, two people can decipher the semiotics of each other's brow-furrows, lip-pursings, and jaw-tightenings with a scary degree of accuracy. So next I read her deciding whether or not to be offended that I'd dealt her the easy shift. Finally a shrug.

Good. I do worry about her feelings. At the moment, however, I was smothering beneath an Everest of worry, and an ephemeral wifely irk was a relative pebble of concern.

I stretched out on a blanket on the garage floor in front of the truck, cradling the riot gun, and climbed Everest. I wanted to sleep. I badly needed sleep. But worry wouldn't allow it.

The morning's battle had been nip and tuck. How many more of those could I scrape through? Was there an Atlantean halberd with my name on it? Trina was no Amazon. Nothing in her life had prepared her for this sort of violence. I'd have to watch her back as well as covering my own ass. How was she coping with the day's events? She'd seemed to have come through the immediate emotional aftermath. She was always pretty tough minded underneath that wonderful, soft layer of compassion. Still, this was unprecedented.

What about Gordon? Maybe the political infighting gets vicious in the Archeology and History departments of the university. Even so I doubt it had trained Gordon for this. He could handle firearms, and he was no shrinking violet. He'd held up his end quite well, all things considered. Even seemed to be enjoying himself at times during the day. Maybe that's what I should be worrying about–the development of an adrenaline craving violence-junkie. He'd been imprisoned in the ziggurat for a long time. Maybe he was just exhilarated by this freedom. On the other hand, maybe he was exacting a messy revenge and might sacrifice safety and good sense for the opportunity to keep killing.

No, let that one go. Gordon's mental state is just another pebble on the mountain. Stick to the boulders.

For all this fighting and driving and labor, we'd yet to clear the borders of Portland. We remained within the eastern fringes of the city where Portland blended seamlessly into Gresham. Was the entire trip going to be like this? It would be January before we reached Troutdale at this rate, assuming we ever got out of Portland.

Plenty of Atlanteans had watched our painfully slow trek toward this far Northeastern Portland neighborhood. A squad of soldiers could be searching for us right now. We hadn't exactly left ourselves an escape route. Was this garage going to turn into our Alamo? All it would take is enough manpower to keep us pinned down long enough for a priest to arrive, and that'd be all she wrote. Death and a Viking funeral in one neat package.

The mountain contained a great deal more to fret about, but whether I did or not I can't recall. I do recall Trina shaking me awake at 10:30.

"I wanted to give you another hour, Nick," she whispered, "but I can't keep my eyes open any longer."

So she crawled into the blanket, still warm from my body heat, and I woke to pace and worry some more. I even found time to gnaw at my guilt over the deaths of Jim, and Tonio and Luisa. It was cold, so the pacing served a bigger purpose than maintaining alertness.

This trip was going to seriously try my nerves. I badly wanted a drink. I've spent more pleasant hours than the hours I passed in that cold garage, senses on edge, listening for the approach of marching feet, stressed and trouble worn. Even bad hours pass, however, and eventually I woke Gordon to spell me. Then I snuggled in next to Trina for forty more uncomfortable winks.

ജ്ജ

No soldiers arrived to kill us in our sleep. That was about the only pleasant aspect to waking from a night spent on a concrete garage floor.

"God, my back," I said, trying to contort my vertebrae into some imagined anodyne alignment.

"My neck," said Trina, twisting about as if endeavoring to unscrew her head.

"My stomach," said Gordon. "I've been hungry since you woke me. What's for breakfast?"

We sat in amiable proximity on the lowered tailgate of the Ford, munching a meal of granola bars and canned fruit-cocktail. While it was a slightly claustrophobic dining room it had a certain comforting familiarity, a garage lined with the quotidian bric-a-brac of the American family home: aluminum and woven-plastic folding chairs hanging from nails, bicycles propped against a wall, the smell of spilled automotive fluids permeating the floor, a tool-strewn workbench.

Trina looked pensive, her hair tucked under a green bandanna, one stray lock escaping to brush across a lined brow. "What I've been wondering," she said, "is how come we seem to see so many Atlanteans but so few of us? I mean, we met a few survivors before you showed up, Gordon, but since then we've just encountered Claimants. Excuse me, I meant to say 'Atlanteans.' Do they just have a higher population than we do?"

Gordon spooned in a chunk of pineapple before assuming his didactic expression. "I don't know for certain, Trina. I do, however, have a hypothesis."

"Of course you do," I said.

"Stick a spoon in it," said Trina. "I'm trying to learn something here."

Gordon continued, rambling somewhat, his lecture notes not yet in order. "The Atlantean society–and in our case I do mean 'Atlantean' proper given the limits of my observations. The inhabitants of Mu, Lemuria and Hyperborea spread to the equivalents of, respectively, Africa, Australasia, and Europe. The Atlanteans expanded into the Americas. As I was saying, the Atlantean society is regimented, highly disciplined. The military comprises a percentage of their population (and what that might have been prior to the Reunion, I couldn't say) vastly higher than ours. And those troops seem primarily barracked in the ziggurats, which seem to have come through the Reunion more complete than other buildings. We've seen the protections the priests throw up against aircraft. Perhaps they maintained other defenses that just happened to be efficacious during the transition. The point being, Trina, that when two cultures meet unexpectedly, the more militant and organized culture has an advantage."

"The Atlanteans just sent out a bunch of troops with no compunction about slaughtering every one they met," I said. "We were a disorganized, scattered mess of individuals–scared, confused, and mostly unarmed."

Trina nodded. "We see more of them because they killed more of us. OK, I can see that. But, why such a big military?"

"I believe there are at least three reasons," said Gordon. "One, Atlantean society–and here I'm using the term loosely to include all the Claimants, based on my reading of their texts–is rigidly traditional. Soldiers are thirty percent, or whatever, of the population because they've always been so.

"Two, I mentioned the distribution of the cultures–Mu here, Atlantis there. That wasn't a simple organic drift. They've been fighting each other for fifty thousand years. Peace might break out for a century now and again, but eventually new alliances, new treachery, and new affronts get the war drums beating again. And when they are not fighting each other they are jockeying for political position, often leading to bloody internecine feuding. So they have so many soldiers because they need them.

"And three, maybe just speculation on my part, but maybe so many soldiers can keep the remainder–the serfs, the downtrodden castes–docile. Millennia of servitude has probably beaten any gumption out of them, but a company of heavily armored myrmidons is pretty good insurance against some peasant having a subversive idea once every couple of generations."

I think Gordon missed teaching, same as I missed policing.

ꕥ

I tossed my empty fruit-cocktail tin in a plastic recycling bin with a wry smile at the futility. It was about time to get moving again. While Trina and Gordon were finishing their speculative history lesson I prowled around the garage, idly searching for anything useful to add to our load. I glanced through the window set in the back door of the garage as I ambled past. The morning light showed something that had been hidden in the shadows of the cloistered peristyle the night before–a door leading into a section of the villa.

I checked the load in the .357 and opened the door.

The formal, almost sterile seeming garden had not seen tending in some time. Of course autumn in Portland wasn't a friend to decorative verdure.

I passed under the colonnade and stopped before the door. It was not locked. The handle was a simple bracket of a reddish stone. I pulled and the door swung open noiselessly to reveal the maze of conjoined structures I'd expected. Yet not entirely so. Between a stretch of drywall and a length of whitewashed and frescoed stone was a space wide enough for me to edge through sideways. I followed this as far as I could. The passage ended at the wood-paneled wall of a rec room. Who still used wood paneling? But at my back the stone wall terminated, leaving an open space that I pivoted into. The space proved to be an ascending stairwell, or at least the left half of a stairwell. I climbed up sideways, an awkward, crab-like ascent.

The stairs led to a portion of what had probably been the master bedroom of this Portland house. A section of king-size bed was visible, the remainder buried inside a stone wall plastered in light green, over which spread a partial fresco in black and red depicting some scene from Atlantean mythology. I poked around a bit, hoping to find something useful, like a box of .357 ammunition. I didn't find any.

I did, however, see a rectangular section of window, about a foot long and six inches wide. Tiny shards of glass clung to the edges. The rest crunched beneath my feet.

"Nick, where are you?" I heard Trina's voice behind me.

"Don't run off alone, damn it," followed Gordon's voice.

"Come on up," I said, not turning my gaze from the scene beyond the smashed window pane. "Trina, I think I can answer your question about why we don't see more women."

I felt Trina come up behind me. She rested a hand on my shoulder. "My God," she said, raising her other hand in front of her face.

The window granted us a view into a lengthy chamber, much of it having escaped merger with the local subdivision during the Reunion. The walls were painted a delicate lilac. Numerous pieces of furniture, blockish and geometrical like all Atlantean craft (but executed with more grace and elegance than any I'd seen to date), indicated a high level of comfort. An open wardrobe or armoire near the far end of the chamber revealed a heap of garments in multiple hues.

A foot stool, one leg snapped off, lay just below the broken window. Slight concave bulges and a pattern of cracks around the window indicated a vigorous, but futile assault on the wall separating the chamber from the vestigial room we stood in.

And slumped on the floor, singly or huddled together, were the corpses of seven women. No, four women and three girls.

"Poor things must have starved to death," said Trina at last.

"Dehydration, more likely," said Gordon. "Without food, humans can last for–" he cut the lecture short when Trina glared at him.

We stood there for a minute, allowing the evidence and our imaginations to relate the gruesome tale of slow death: the initial shock, the cries for help, the dawning recognition, the frantic attempts to batter through the wall. The search for human contact and comfort during the final moments.

"You'll notice three of the women are from the serving class," Gordon said.

I hadn't, actually. But now that he'd pointed it out, the difference in clothing, hairstyle, and adornment was obvious. So an Atlantean mother, her three daughters and three servants.

"Separate living quarters," I said. "A, what do you call it, seraglio? That's why we saw no women. They live segregated from the men."

"Except for the poor women," Trina said. "If we had traveled more through the farming sections, or along the river, we might have seen some more of them."

Gordon had his lower lip gripped between his teeth. He looked as if he were taking notes. Trina was still a bit misty eyed. My curiosity, however, had been satisfied, and, as interesting as this look into Atlantean anthropology might be, I wanted to make tracks. We'd pushed our luck far enough.

"Let's get out of here before we join these ladies' permanent slumber party," I said. The callow remark had its intended effect; Trina's attention switched away from the tragic scene to my vulgar lack of respect and she followed me back to the garage, explaining in detail my lapses of etiquette, taste, and good breeding.

Chapter 14

The local troops had not, it appeared, tracked us down. Yet. We backed out of the garage and were on our way again without facing a hostile farewell.

Out of sheer paranoia, we found a new route back to the freeway instead of backtracking the way we'd come. Once there we made good time. The Atlanteans appeared to have surveyed nearly the same roadbed, and for several miles we encountered few serious breaks. Where gaps appeared in the freeway there was usually a stone paved roadway that we could ease down onto, often without the use of ramps.

Thus we reached Troutdale a couple of hours after lunch. And there we ran into trouble. The bridge spanning the mouth of the Sandy river no longer existed. The Sandy itself now appeared to be as much a canal as a river at this point, widened, smooth sided, and lined with towpaths. Solidly constructed stone abutments hinted at an Atlantean bridge that had been built at the same point. The two crossings had apparently canceled each other out.

We all got out for a bit of palaver.

"Now what?" asked Trina.

"Bound to be another bridge further south," I said. "We drive south until we find one."

"We're going to run into the same problem again," said Gordon. "I should have thought of this earlier. We're dealing with a pre-industrial society. They have no railways. Of course they are going to rely on waterways for commerce. Any number of canals are going to connect agricultural land to the Columbia River."

"We'll cross that canal when we get to it," said Trina. "Let's cross this one first. Once we get across do we head back this way, toward the highway? It looks like there used to be an Atlantean bridge here. So if the road keeps paralleling the Columbia, doesn't that mean the other canals are likely to have bridges at roughly the same point? I mean, near the intersection of road, canal, and river?"

"It makes sense," I answered. "But, on second thought, maybe we don't want to pass the mountain to the north. Natural choke point between the river and the mountain."

"Right," said Gordon. "That's likely to be the most heavily fortified area between Portland and, I don't know, the Idaho border. Unless the Atlanteans have built up a city somewhere we never considered advantageous.

"Remember we're dealing with a civilization that is constantly ready for war. The Atlanteans don't just see a convenient passage from one area to another, they see a defensive position. Due consideration tells us that following I-84 all the way to Idaho might not be such a good idea after all."

"So we go over the mountain?" asked Trina.

"I don't trust the roads," I said. "In the city we can always find another street if one is blocked—or gone. If the highway over the pass isn't intact we'd be hosed. Can't cut through the forest, not even with a Hummer." I added the last to forestall Gordon who looked aggrieved. Jesus, a couple of days driving the Hummer and he was taking any questioning of its prowess as a personal affront.

"OK, south of the mountain it is," said Trina. "Then we hope we don't run short of bridges."

That seemed to sum it up well enough.

ĐŊ

We mounted up and drove south into Troutdale. The percentage of Atlantean buildings diminished. Signs of conflict increased. We passed burnt-out hulks of automobiles, charred fences, and a gutted city hall. Entire neighborhoods had been razed by fire, but they lacked the scorched stone remnants of Atlantean construction. These fires weren't the result of the Reunion. They'd occurred later. Deliberately.

On the credit side of the ledger, it was easier to navigate. We headed south, creeping westward away from the river. We continued passing evidence of systematic violence. Front doors had been battered in, windows smashed. The more obvious rallying points—churches, schools—were either fire damaged or reduced to cinders.

"These people put up a fight," said Trina.

"Yeah, but individually, and in dribs and drabs. Looks like the Atlanteans cut them down one house at a time, or burned them out when they did concentrate."

A flicker of motion caught my eye.

We were passing by the community college, most of it the worse for wear from smoke damage, broken down doors, and shattered windows. A few cars lined the streets, some occupying nearly empty parking lots. Some of the vehicles squatted on shredded tires. Others had been reduced to burnt hulks. Caved-in doors suggested massive blunt force damage. My imagination supplied the culprit: Atlantean living mobile armor, the should-be-extinct beast.

A form sprinted from one of the less damaged buildings, the motion that had drawn my attention.

"Stop!" shrilled Trina who'd caught sight of her too. It was a girl who couldn't have been more than five years old, in a short, yellow Sesame Street frock and bright orange sneakers. She was running that heedless stride of childhood–full-out, waving both arms.

I braked. The girl was still a good fifty yards away as I brought the truck to a halt. The door from which the girl had come opened again and a woman emerged, breaking immediately into pursuit. I thought I glimpsed another figure in the doorway, but the door swung shut before I could be sure.

Trina dropped from the cab even before I came to a complete stop. She was around the front of the truck and on her knees to welcome the girl while the other woman still had twenty yards to go.

"Help us help us help us!" the little girl was repeating in the staccato of a piccolo trumpet.

"It's OK. We're here," said Trina, gathering the onrushing form into an embrace.

I got out to stand next to the pair, keeping an eye on the woman as she decelerated to a jog. The mother? What story had we just stumbled into?

"Brittney! We don't leave the library!" She was in full scold before she reached us. But the lines on her face formed a worry pattern, not an anger pattern, and she fell to her knees facing Trina. She placed one gentle hand on the girl's head, her own head swiveling to take in me and Trina and the arriving Gordon. More than that, she was taking in the horizon, the thousand-yard stare incongruous from a Troutdale mom.

"Are you Brittney's mom?" I asked. What I did not want was small get-to-know-you chit-chat. I felt as nervous out in the open as the frazzled looking woman apparently did. I wanted an info-dump forthwith.

"Yes. Cynthia. But we need to get back inside. And you'd best come in too." She spoke fast, fear in every rapid-fire word. There was fear, yes, but also a shrewd caution. "If you're coming, best hide the cars. We can't have *them* seeing something new." She stopped, reflecting, then said, "Maybe best if you just drove off."

She pried the little girl from Trina's grasp. The little girl looked bewildered. Didn't her mother want our help?

"You and Gordon hide the trucks," said Trina. "I'll go with them and wait for you."

I hesitated. I didn't want to split up. This was too out of the blue. What sort of post-apocalyptic lunacy might Trina be walking into alone? But I recognized that determined set of her jaw. I wasn't going to get her away without a long argument, and delay was our greatest enemy.

I gestured to Gordon. He returned to the Hummer. I spoke to Trina as I climbed back up into the cab. "OK, sweetheart. Be careful. You have your little friend with you?"

She patted her waistband surreptitiously. Good. At least she would be walking into any potential trap with her eyes open.

Gordon and I stashed the trucks between a recreational vehicle up on blocks and a blue tarp-covered woodpile. The house next to the woodpile had been reduced to three precariously leaning fire-charred walls, yet the woodpile remained unscathed. Weird, but a comfortingly mundane variety of weird.

We hoofed it the half mile back to the college. I was just considering whether to knock when the door opened enough to allow entrance one at a time.

Trina sat sipping a cup of tea in a library-cum-refugee camp. Sheets, hung between rows of shelving, created private apartments. Hotplates and microwave ovens powered by a series of car batteries helped convert the librarian's station into a kitchen. Mismatched plates and silverware filled the niches and cubbyholes behind the appliance-lined counter. I saw, in addition to Trina, around a dozen people, all sitting quietly.

Cynthia and Brittney sat at a reading table on either side of Trina. Opposite her sat a man in late middle-age, his thin blonde hair gone considerably gray.

He stood as we approached. "You can't stay," he said. "Get back in your cars and keep going."

"OK," I said as Gordon asked, "What happened here?" My voice conveyed bemused acceptance, Gordon's plain curiosity. Curiosity was bad news for cats like us.

"Look, he doesn't want us," I said. "Let's go while we've still got daylight."

"We can't just leave these people," Trina said.

"We can if they want to stay."

Gordon snatched a nearby chair and plopped himself down onto it. "What happened here?" he repeated.

The man sighed, then sat down again. "If telling you will hurry you away, then I'll give you a brief account."

I sat down too, exasperated at being ignored.

"The local yokels fought the invaders," he began after taking time to compose his narrative. He obviously didn't consider introductions a necessary antecedent, hoping we'd be gone so soon that such pleasantries would prove irrelevant. "Rednecks with deer-rifles and shotguns. They thought they were successful. The invaders kept away for a couple of days and these delusional Daniel Boones clapped each other on the back and hunted down any civilian invaders they could find. They even tried to organize, held a meeting to appoint an emergency interim government. I attended that meeting."

He paused, I guess reliving the experience before continuing. "I spoke, pointing out that all they were going to accomplish was to attract attention. Our duly elected authorities will resolve the matter, and send legitimately armed forces in to rout the invaders. Gun-happy civilian vigilantes would just make matters worse.

"They didn't listen. Of course.

"I foresaw what would result and collected as many as I could who would listen to reason. We stockpiled supplies and took refuge here in my library, causing a bit of cosmetic damage to the exterior to make the building appear already swept. And then we waited. The invaders came in force as I knew they would. They came with beasts–glyptodonts I believe–and several individuals capable of pyrokinesis. The local militia morons never had a chance. The invaders systematically cornered and killed all of them. They'd just trap one or two in a house, take a few casualties to assure it was occupied, then burn the place to the ground, waiting to cut down any who tried to make a run for it.

"We kept our heads down and stayed quiet. And we've done so since. We have enough food to wait out the winter. I'm positive a government response team will arrive by spring."

He withdrew a hip flask from a jacket pocket and took a self-congratulatory pull. He did not offer the rest of us a snort.

I rose to my feet. "Right then. We'll get going and let you carry on."

"Nick," hissed Trina.

"OK, fine. Look, we're on our way to meet with the, uh, legitimately armed forces. Why don't you come with us? We can scrounge up a few more trucks, maybe a fifth-wheel with a kitchen and a bathroom. Let's meet that government response team halfway, what do you say?"

I knew what he was going to say. And I felt bad for the folks who'd bought his go-to-ground solution. The Atlanteans were methodical. Conquered territory is secured and occupied. Once the workers arrived to begin construction, this band of ostriches would have their heads unceremoniously yanked first from the sand and second from their bodies. Still, I had to try. For Trina. And, well, hadn't I been pursuing the same course before Trina's exasperation and Gordon's timely arrival revived a sense of purpose? Pay it forward, right? Or at least give it a shot before vamoosing.

"No, we're not going to join you fighting your way through enemy territory, Rambo," the librarian said. "We'll come through this ordeal. Peacefully."

"I sympathize with your position," I said. I'd been trained, as a police officer, to avoid arguing a specific point. It wasn't my job to win debates. Ethical and legal conflicts I could leave for shrinks and shysters. I was trained to find points of agreement and use those as levers for peaceful conflict resolution. So, I tried. "I had much the same idea: bunker down, wait it out. My house was unscathed. I stocked up on food, camouflaged the exterior. Like you. But the–invaders–are relentless."

I lowered my voice, not wanting to put a scare in his flock of sheep, though perhaps that's exactly what they needed. "They...will...find you."

"Then we will surrender," he said with a benign smile.

Trina released an exasperated growl. "They are not concerned with surrender. Don't you understand? If they find you they will kill you."

"We always transfer our fears and aggression to the 'other,' don't we?" he said

"OK, Trina, I think it's time to go, before he asks us to hand out flowers at the airport." I raised my voice loud enough to be heard clearly. "If anyone is interested in making a break for it, we're leaving now. Grab your gear and join us at the door."

Brittney looked up at her mother expectantly. I don't know what she'd understood of the conversation, but she seemed to want to come with us. Anyway, with Trina. Cynthia frowned. But it was easier to stay put than to pull up roots, even shallow roots in barren soil. She held her daughter close and shook her head.

Gordon opened, then shut his mouth. This was not an academic colleague with whom he could reason. He sighed, then led our way to the door.

Trina muttered exasperated profanities beneath her breath during the walk to the truck, her eyes glistening with the tears she fought back. I knew that she was using the exasperation to mask her fear for the doomed little girl.

Chapter 15

THE NEXT FEW MILES SOUTHWARD WERE MORE OF THE SAME: A GRAND-scale forensic record of struggle and slaughter. Again we made good time. As the afternoon drew on and we reached the vicinity of Boring and Estacada, the character of the surroundings shifted. It had been rural to begin with, but post-Reunion the countryside appeared to be on almost an entirely agricultural footing. Atlantean farmland dominated as far as I could see. Undamaged houses still stood, but most complete buildings were the ugly, bunker-like Atlantean farm houses. The ground was leveled and terraced and had apparently scythed through much of the existing construction.

The Atlanteans had been busy demolishing and collecting the constituent pieces of the ruined houses and storefronts, churches and barns. Vast repositories had been created, the enormous piles of plank, brick, and steel creating convenient depots of building material (assuming the Atlanteans ever gained enough architectural and engineering flexibility to use anything other than stone.)

The roads disappeared and reappeared in the fallow loam, but four-wheel drive allowed us to plow a more or less straight line. The autumn rains had transformed sections of field into gooey bogs that sent us slithering and slinging mud in arcing muck rainbows. Soon enough the vehicles were plastered with a layer of mud that would have, in happier times, signified the drivers having a grand old time. Instead we just cursed the delays. We were making for Highway 26, intending to pass south of Mount Hood in hopes of then trending eastward to meet Highway 84 and follow it in to Boise.

We'd see.

ണ്ട

We pitched camp as dusk descended, finding a flat stretch of grass out of sight of any farm house or of the few ziggurats we'd seen perched atop high ground. In the distance they appeared like so many gargoyles or stone vultures.

I had enough sense to stretch a tarp over the load in the truck bed, so our tent and other camping gear remained essentially mud free.

We set up a tent and sat cross-legged and cramped around a battery-powered hotplate. No one said much.

We all knew that the Reunion was a global phenomenon. But to experience it, mile after slogging mile, hammered home the bitter reality with the casual strength of a seasoned roustabout.

We held to the same watch schedule that night, and again the next as we performed the long, gradual turn east.

We had our first scare the next day, running the Santiam Pass beneath a ziggurat that sat glowering over the highway. Surprise was a neutral factor; we didn't see the hulking fortress until we'd driven within bow shot range, and the Atlanteans had no lookout set. The road wasn't blockaded either. Perhaps the Atlanteans found it too convenient to impede, or perhaps they were just too confident that the countryside had been subdued. We passed beneath with only a belated scattering of arrows to send us on our way.

Sisters was a ghost town. Blackened houses and the stench of decaying bodies informed us why no curious heads peeked out of windows to watch us drive through. Any curious heads still alive had already got the hell out of town.

The bridge across the Deschutes was our next major concern. If no Atlantean analog existed we'd have to try further south, and I worried that Bend would be as infested as Portland. Of course I had no way of knowing. Geography would generally indicate where major population centers should arise, but it wasn't an imperative.

I think I actually held my breath as the land dipped and I caught a glint of sun reflecting off of water in a river bend to the north. And there it was, still standing, still spanning the rapid waters of the Deschutes.

"We've been too lucky," I declared over the CB. "Bound to turn on us soon."

Gordon delivered a theatrical sigh, deliberately loud enough to come through the radio speaker. "Save your superstition. Luck has no pattern. Otherwise it wouldn't be chance."

"That does it," said Trina, grabbing the handset from me. "We're doomed."

It felt good to laugh, but it wasn't truly cathartic. A hint of hysteria underlay the merriment.

ꙮ

The winches proved useful later that day. At least one of the dams in the Redmond area no longer existed and a swath of mud swaddled debris–everything from tree trunks to sections of pre-fab homes–buried a mile-long stretch of the road. We picked our way through, as gracefully as a couple of water buffalo in a rice paddy, but about halfway across the Ford became mired hub deep in the muck. It took about an hour for Gordon to tug me free. Ultimately, in fact, it required both winches working in tandem to break free of the suction.

We carried on, passing flooded Atlantean farm houses, the surrounding fields washed clean of topsoil by the sudden deluge.

It was the next day that the half-feared, half-expected problem arose. Canals. Or one at least.

"Oh, hell," I said without much heat, getting out of the cab to confront the obstacle.

We were well east and south of Mount Hood by now, the last tracts of ruined farmland behind us, crossing high sagebrush desert uninhabited by either us or the Atlanteans. Here, stretching in an undeviating line south to north, flowed a canal. It was at least five yards across. It might as well have been a hundred.

"North or south?" asked Trina. No anger in her voice, no resigned sigh. The question sounded calm and matter of fact. She took my hand and gave it a squeeze, before beginning to pick at a partially healed scab on the back of my thumb.

"South, I think. It's a good guess that there's a bridge to the north, but it's also a good guess that the Atlanteans are in strength that way. Let's try south."

Gordon approached as I spoke. "I agree. Maybe there is no bridge to the south, but while we know this will eventually empty into the Columbia, or some tributary that empties into the Columbia, we also know that this canal has to begin somewhere. Maybe we can just go around."

I didn't like the sound of that at all. I wanted a bridge. Close. A detour of unknown duration was a disheartening prospect.

I walked to the edge and looked down into the water. The back end of a rusting Chevy pickup truck thrust up from the canal, creating a slowly swirling eddy around the sunken chassis. I tried to imagine the shock of the driver when his headlights abruptly revealed water in place of asphalt, so suddenly that he had no time to avert the plunge. Had he even had time for panic, or had death followed surprise almost instantaneously?

The truck's fuel-cap cover was missing, but the fuel cap itself was still visible and dry.

"Hand me the siphon," I said to Trina. Then, to Gordon, "Let's fix a safety harness to me. I want to get in and see if there's any fuel left in that tank."

Gas stations were in short supply, and without electricity the pumps weren't of much use anyhow. We had to take advantage of every opportunity to top off our jerry cans.

With one end of a rope hooked to me and the other to the bumper of the Ford, and with Trina and Gordon paying out the length, I lowered myself into the chill waters. I clung to the angled bed of the pickup and pulled myself forward to the gas cap to begin the fumbling task of unscrewing it with cold fingers. The water was dark, conveying bits of vegetation and a solution of soil and minerals, but I could just make out the cab of the truck. A corpse bobbed and swayed in the current, still held in place by a seat belt.

A capricious eddy swirled through the cab, catching and shifting the body. The head swiveled, the face resolving in the murk. It was Jim, his decaying features twisted in reproach. "Your fault," he mouthed.

I blinked away the phantasm and shivered, but not from the cold alone. A wave of despair seemed to flow over me along with the waters of the canal. A despondent notion tried to take root. *Let go. Surrender.*

A desire to abandon hope and my wife and friend, to float off into the cold and dark. Or simply to find a quiet place somewhere with a supply of liquid essence of oblivion and drink until the Atlanteans found me, alive or dead. But the roots could not find purchase. A policeman deals everyday with the worst of humanity. He looks into the grim face of misery, meaningless pain, and shallowly buried savagery. If he's promising soil for burnout, chronic dejection, or clinical depression, he doesn't usually last long.

I'd already lived through the temptation. When Trina called down, "Everything OK, Nick?" I fought off the mood and got busy siphoning out four gallons of gasoline. Despondency was a luxury and I was on a budget. I clambered back up the bank, dripping filthy water and shivering. I presented my prize to my wife.

"God, I miss hot showers," said Trina, looking up and down my sodden frame as she took the proffered jerry can.

ꙮ

No road paralleled the canal. A tow path was visible–on the other side, of course. For us the journey was a pure off-road excursion. It was disappointing that so many aspects of the trip would have been riotous good fun under different circumstances. Instead we were just concerned with keeping the trucks in working order. A snapped axle or a punctured fuel tank could leave us at the mercy of the elements or the Atlanteans, whichever got to us first.

We found no crossing that day, and we drifted out of visual range of the canal to pitch camp. Travel the next day proved more arduous as the canal cut undeviatingly through increasingly rough and hilly country. I doubt we covered more than fifteen miles of straight-line distance, though we spooled up at least twice that on the odometers. The camp that night was low-spirited and quiet, the downbeat mood enhanced by a steady rain provided by that cliché mongering dramatist–Mother Nature.

The following day the terrain leveled out for an easier haul. Easier, but not trouble free. A near blinding squall led to an unnoticed sharp rock puncturing a tire. After a stint in the mud with a jack and a tire iron, we continued our trip. And we began to garner a hint as to why a canal led this direction, some reason for this particular Atlantean aquatic-highway's existence. The rocky ground began to give way to cultivated fields, and we could see houses in the distance, like neatly ordered rows of childrens' blocks.

About that time we caught sight of an Atlantean busily herding those oversized cattle Trina and I had seen milling through Lloyd Center.

"Aurochs!" Gordon declared delightedly over the CB.

We caught distant glimpses of two other noteworthy items: the top of a ziggurat, and the arch of a bridge over the canal.

"Veer west!" I said over the radio, after performing the same maneuver myself.

Maybe the Atlantean peon hadn't spotted us. Maybe if he had spotted us, his ingrained incuriosity and lack of initiative would prevent him from reporting the sighting. The point was that we needed solid intelligence prior to making an attempt at the bridge. Only luck had kept us unscathed the last time we came within close proximity of a ziggurat.

Gordon followed me for about a mile until the fields petered out into stony, rising ground. We sheltered the trucks in a copse of low scrub trees that ringed a low, rocky hillock. A dented aluminum sign atop a bent pole announced that we were on Bureau of Land Management acreage. I wished the BLM would appear to deal with trespassers.

"So they heavily farm this side of the Cascades as well," said Trina. "I suppose I assumed they'd limit themselves to ranching. God, can you imagine what the Willamette Valley must look like?"

"Well, it stands to reason, I suppose," Gordon said. "The Atlanteans don't have the capacity for commercial-scale farming like we do, or our technology for food preservation. Most of their population, continent wide, is probably involved in agriculture, barging a constant stream of food up canals to the urban centers. If they can irrigate an area, they'll farm it."

"I'm sure that will be fascinating information for the research paper," I said. "More immediately, how does it alter our theory that we'll find the army, or at least some organized resistance, in Boise?"

"I still think the theory is sound. I don't think the Atlanteans possess the social foundation to have achieved a population density as high as ours. I think food supply, infant mortality, and disease, in concert, imposed a population ceiling. And at this point, what have we got to lose?"

"Well argued," I said. "So I suppose now we'd better go have a look at what we're up against. Hope you brought your hiking shoes."

We fished out a pair of binoculars from our stores of gear. I checked the load in the pistol, still wishing I'd been able to rustle up some proper rounds for it instead of feeding it the anemic .38 loads.

"I'm leaving the shotgun with you, sweetheart," I said. "Gordon and I are just going on a scout. If we encounter any hostiles, we'll run. If you have any problems, shoot once to alert us, then take the truck and drive off."

From the look she gave me, Trina wasn't keen on being left behind. "If I'm not supposed to stay behind to guard the trucks, why shouldn't I just come with you?"

I opened my mouth to explain my flawlessly logical rationale, then snapped it shut. "OK, anyone else want to whip my ass in a debate? No? Then give me the shotgun. Let's go."

So we scouted, keeping low and staying alert. We were beyond harvest season so the fields we crossed weren't in need of tending. Nonetheless we spotted plenty of kilted agricultural types going about their appointed routines with bovine placidity. Plenty left to do in preparation for the winter, I supposed. None appeared to notice us. Maybe we were stealthy enough to avoid attention. Maybe we were perfectly visible, but this far out in the sticks no altercations had occurred, so no instructions to report strangers had been issued. I was inclined to believe the latter theory. The Atlantean peasants in Portland had proven remarkably incurious until some time after I'd begun racking up a body count.

The ziggurat stepped up from its base on a rise about a quarter mile west of the canal. It struck me as a substantially smaller version of the Atlantean standard fortress, more ziggurette than ziggurat.

Maybe the powers-that-be considered a smaller garrison sufficient for the mud-heels this far out in the hinterland.

A loading dock and three small buildings–maybe a storehouse, an administration office, and a load master's house–lay just to the south of the bridge on the near side. A barge was tied up to a pair of the bollards that lined that section of canal. Through the binoculars, I could see a bit of to and fro-ing between the theorized storehouse and one of the two smaller buildings.

The bridge, a solidly buttressed, high-arched span of stone blocks, crossed the canal like a taunting promise of freedom. A cart path led from the ziggurat to the bridge and continued on the other side, dwindling to an insignificant ribbon in the distance. Each end of the bridge was barred by a heavy timber. One end of each barrier was set on a swivel embedded in the railing, the other end resting in a squared-off niche in the opposite railing.

It appeared each could be swung outward easily enough. But making that prospect less likely was the pair of guards standing at each barrier, beehive helmets on, laminar armor gleaming, pole-arms at attention.

"Maybe a small garrison, but still an Atlantean garrison," I said. If I sounded like I was petulant and grumbling, that's only because I was. "They're just goddamned biological robots. Why can't they slough off, like normal people? We're out here in the boondocks. Take your helmets off, sit down. What have you got to guard against out here?"

"Other than us," said Trina.

"Right, other than little 'ol us. And all we want to do is pass by."

"So, what's the plan?" asked Gordon. "Ramming speed?"

"No," I said, handing him the binoculars. "Those beams look solid. I don't think we can smash our way through. We need to move them out of the way."

"OK, we drive up, shoot the guards, move the first barrier, shoot the other guards, move the second barrier, and we're through."

"Well, professor, if there were no more variables, I'd say your working hypothesis was viable."

"Enlighten me, Hannibal. What variables am I overlooking?"

"Noise. The garrison in the ziggurat will hear us long before we reach the bridge. They'll have a rapid reaction platoon out before we arrive. I'm not sure we can shoot our way through before reinforcements hit us from behind."

"Come on, we're in trucks with big damn V-8s. They're on foot. We can beat them to the bridge."

"If we were driving on a road, yeah. What part of our trip so far makes you think we can cross these fields at sustained high speed?" From the look on Gordon's face I'd just improved my debating win-loss record.

"So what do we do then?" Trina asked.

"We shoot the guards and move the barriers," I said, then held up my hand to forestall objections. "Or rather, I shoot the guards and move the barriers while the two of you are driving. If the guards are down and both gates swung open by the time you arrive, maybe we can cross before any soldiers can double time it down from the fortress."

"Tricky timing," said Gordon. "We can't wait until we hear the gunfire. And you can't wait until you hear the engines. Either way we're back to the scenario of a platoon reaching the bridge before we do."

"Except we're not. I *can* wait until I hear the engines. Driving, taking out the guards, stopping for the gates—all of that would take too long. But like I said, I'll have the bridge open by the time you arrive. With luck I can just hop in the truck bed. You'll barely have to slow down. And if there's a delay, or this ziggurat houses the Atlantean sprint team, I'll already be in place to hit that platoon as they come."

"Nick, I don't like this," said Trina. "You out here alone, I mean. What if one of the trucks breaks down? What if your 'rapid reaction force' theory is wrong and they send everybody at you in a wave?"

"No army is that efficient, Trina, not even these Atlantean guys. Look, we have to take a risk if we're going to cross. Tell you what, if you get a flat tire right out of the gate or if it just gets too hot, I'll jump in the canal. You can pick me up a mile downstream." She wasn't buying it, so I tried again. "What choice do we have? We can't go back to Portland. I don't like this stunt any better than you do, but remember what we're trying to accomplish. It isn't just our lives at stake. We've got to get Gordon and his big brain across this bridge."

"Damn it, Nick! OK, fine. You be Nick the Wonder Cop. But if you let them kill you, you're off my Christmas-gift list." She kissed me long and completely enough that Gordon turned away to allow us an illusion of privacy. "I love you," she whispered.

"Love you too, sweetheart. Chin up, right? We'll compare stories tonight when we camp."

She was reluctant to release me from her embrace, but at last she turned and joined Gordon on the hike back to the trucks. That left me alone to wonder what I'd volunteered for.

Solitude and trepidation are a toxic mixture. So I did my best to counteract it with activity. I began stalking carefully towards the bridge, employing what concealment was available. The bridge held my attention, and the two guards facing this side of the canal were the focus of my worry, though the growing shadow of the ziggurat gradually vied with them for bugaboo primacy.

When I'd crept as close as I dared on two feet I lowered myself into the damp loam and commenced a low crawl, concentrating on keeping the barrel of the riot gun unfouled. I skirted around a lone farmer working a section of ground with a manure rake. Another, canal-side, was tinkering with what appeared to be a simple irrigation pump. Still others were visible across the canal performing tasks that remained mysterious to this city boy.

I kept low, worming through the filth, closer and closer to the bridge. It was a pity the dockside buildings were on the opposite side of the cart path. I could have used them for cover. I thought briefly of risking a scamper across the track but quickly discarded the notion as too risky. Such a move would have put me directly in the line of sight of the guards and exposed me to any sharp-eyed watcher from the ziggurat.

The fields petered out in stony soil that created a sort of buffer zone between canal and cropland, an undulating barrier averaging about ten yards in width. Rocky hummocks and tussocks of sage promised at least a hope of approaching to within gunshot unobserved. The problem–OK, one of the myriad problems–was that my plan ideally called for taking down the guards on the far side of the bridge first in case they possessed some method of hardening the barrier or damaging the bridge, or some other unforeseeable contingency.

I dragged myself from brush to boulder, realizing that I'd just have to rely on speed, accuracy, and luck. Damn, I wished I had a rifle with a scope.

The activity did, as a matter of fact, serve to alleviate my nerves. I never got the chance to sit and stew in my fears because, just as I crept as far as I dared, within tolerably lethal range of buckshot, I heard the distant grumble of engines. The belly crawl must have taken longer than I'd thought.

The head of the nearest guard shifted, as if his sound baffling casque allowed a barely audible hint of danger to filter through. The other soldier hadn't yet caught the noise. I did not intend to wait until he did.

I pushed myself up to a kneeling position. The first guard–head already turned a few degrees to his right–saw the motion. He must have earned Bridge Guard of the Month honors nine times running, for he showed no hesitation, transitioning from sentry-duty-erect to a spear-lowered-lope in an instant. Just about the same instant it took me to swing the butt stock of the shotgun to my shoulder and slam a swarm of steel ball-bearings through his chest armor.

His partner stumbled and tumbled backwards over the low stone parapet into the canal as my second shot drifted a bit high. It perforated neck and head, catching the guard in mid-turn and off balance.

I scrambled up, trying to reach full sprint before my feet were solidly beneath me. I landed face-first in a tangle of sage, tore myself free, and this time maintained my balance as I heel-and-toed it full-out to the bridge.

The other two guards were not, in fact, dragging battleship anchor chains across the bridge roadway. Nor were they strewing it with caltrops, nor pulling a hidden lever dropping the middle section into the canal. They were, however, charging over the span, those big, intimidating spear points leading the way.

I hurtled up from the fields to the raised cart path as the two soldiers neared the end of their sprint. I had no time to bring the shotgun to my shoulder again, and only just enough time to level it at the belly of the nearest guard, squeeze the trigger, fight the recoil, chamber another round, shift my aim a couple of inches, and fire again. The last guard clattered to the hard-packed clay surface a bare yard away, one of the spiky cutting surfaces of his spear gouging a chunk from the front of my boot sole.

The echoes of the gunfire rolled over the open fields, temporarily masking the sound of approaching engines. Only temporarily, for within a moment I heard the bear-with-a-chest-cold rumble of V8s. And a bicycle-chain choir of armored men running... Behind me.

I spun on my heel.

"Shit!" No rapid reaction force was that rapid. Or comprised of so few. The four men pelting down the cart path must have been the scheduled shift change for the bridge guard. And they were getting close. A distant glimpse of an opening gateway at the base of the ziggurat told me that more soldiers would be joining these four soon. And I still hadn't had time to clear the bridge barriers. This plan was in the express lane to hell and accelerating.

I suppose I should have been grateful the Atlanteans didn't employ cavalry. They'd domesticated the glyptodont and the auroch, but hadn't bothered with the horse. If I lived through this, I'd have to remember to ask Gordon's thoughts on parallel social evolution.

I groped in a jacket pocket for shotgun shells, spilling a couple onto the ground in my haste. I still had four rounds in the tube, but I preferred not to rely on flawless marksmanship. I managed to thumb in two fresh loads before my nerve broke. I nestled the Remington tight to my shoulder, bent my knees to a half crouch, leaned forward a hair, and opened fire.

It wasn't precise. It wasn't pretty. It wasn't clean. And it took every round I had in the riot gun. But the four replacement guards went down. Two still moved, rolling and crying in agony to their gods, or cursing my name. I don't know; I don't speak Atlantean. I think one had a chance at surviving if Atlantean medicine was even remotely competent. The other would probably cease bitching soon. Cease doing anything soon.

If I didn't want to join him on that journey I had to move fast, and I was none too sure I could manage. The two trucks were in view, bouncing across muddy, rutted fields. The reinforced squad, or short-handed platoon comprising the Atlantean rapid reaction force was also in view, moving fast while maintaining formation. If I couldn't get the bars removed by the time Trina and Gordon arrived, we'd be trapped between canal and fortress. I doubted we'd be able to shoot our way free. And if the ziggurat housed a priest, our goose was as good as cooked.

I slung the empty shotgun and it banged rhythmically against my back as I dashed to the first barrier. I lifted, tugged, and damn near threw out my back. The thick timber didn't budge.

It couldn't be that heavy. I fought back the threatening panic and took a precious second to simply observe. Basic awareness, the type of thing any rookie cop had to learn. A hefty pin, like a railroad tie with a two-inch loop at the fat end, was thrust through the bar opposite the swivel point, where the bar lay on the niche cut into the railing. Two strides took me there and I yanked out the pin, freeing the bar. Now I could have swung open the barrier with one finger, though of course I used full force and both hands, wasting time restraining the bar as it hurtled back at me on the rebound.

The trucks were fifty yards away now, the soldiers roughly the same distance. Given equivalent surfaces, no contest there. But the soldiers were jogging along a smooth surface while the trucks were chugging along in low-range four-wheel drive, flinging mud behind them as they jounced, swayed, and yawed. I didn't have the luxury of viewing the race, I was too busy sprinting across the bridge to the second barrier.

I tugged loose the retaining pin and shoved open the bar. That's when the first arrow whipped past my ear.

Oh shit. The rapid reaction troops were archers. I dove to the ground, seeking shelter behind the stone railing, as a dozen more arrows winged by, or skipped off the hard-packed cart track. Thank god for Atlantean masonry. I stuck my head out for a peek.

The troop had come to a halt about ten yards short of the bridge, apparently hoping to bring me down with arrows before I'd moved the bar. Too late, bastards.

Trina was nearing the path. I could make out stark terror in her pale, wide-eyed face as she hit the track, the front end of the truck leaping up, right front tire six inches off of the ground. The front end came back to earth hard, compressing, then rebounding. I could see her spinning the wheel, trying to make the sharp turn onto the path. She was moving fast, maybe too fast. The back end slipped, mud-caked wheels throwing off a shroud of accumulated muck, grabbing for traction. The right side of the Ford banged against the inside of the big timber bar, the barrier only about three-quarters open. Trina overcompensated, the left front bumper rebounding off the solid stone railing, but she was safely onto the bridge.

OK, relatively safe. An arrow caromed off the roof of the cab. Two more punctured the tarp, embedding themselves in the supplies or the kitchen sink beneath.

Then Gordon followed, nearly sideswiping the forming skirmish line of archers. They didn't exactly scatter. Those who needed to moved out of the way, the rest held their ground, and more arrows flew.

I couldn't see anymore. Both vehicles blocked my view of the Atlanteans. I stood so that Trina could see me despite her panic. I was on the driver's side, which was fine. I didn't absolutely need to climb into the passenger's seat.

The truck slowed, Trina waved a needless summons, "Come on, you asshole," written across her features as plainly as on an electronic reader-board. I placed both hands on the side rail of the truck bed and heaved myself aboard, rolling painfully over the uneven surfaces and sharp corners of the packed supplies. I snapped two arrow shafts as I did so, my momentum nearly tumbling me off the far side.

She floored it then, and we rocketed over the bridge onto the narrow cart path beyond, with little margin for error on either side. No shoulder indeed. A slip at this speed would likely roll the truck. I grabbed a tie down projecting from the side rail and held on, white-knuckled.

I snuck a peek over my shoulder. Gordon was nearly right on our bumper, wearing either an adrenaline-stoked grin or a grimace of terror. Flip a coin.

We put probably half a mile between us and the bridge before Trina's fear eased and she let up on the accelerator. She let the truck roll to a gentle stop and I hopped out, then opened the driver's side door.

She turned to face me, eyes still rounded. Her hand shook as she fumbled for the seat belt release. I grabbed ahold as she slipped out, and pulled her into a bear hug.

"Ohgodohgodohgodohgod," she said. She trembled, a continuous surge of muscle tremors.

"Are you hurt?" I asked, belatedly feeling for protruding arrows or broken bones.

"I think she has a future racing the Baja 1000," came Gordon's voice. He sounded jaunty.

"I'm OK," Trina said, grabbing the reins of body and mind, getting the team under control. "I'm not hurt. I was just a little scared."

I let the understatement go. "How about you, Gordon?"

"I am intact, thank you Nick," he answered, a model of retrained glee. So, not a grimace of terror then. "I'm afraid the same cannot be said for the Hummer, however."

I released Trina after getting a half-smile of reassurance. Gordon was right. The rear windows at the back of the Hummer had been reduced to shards of safety glass. The right rear tire was hissing air. The arrow shaft emerging from the sidewall was regulating the leak, allowing for a slow, flatulent death rather than a catastrophic blowout.

But we were alive, and across the canal.

ଌଓ

We limped another two miles down the cart path before stopping to change the tire. It was a slow job made slower by our haste. We could not rule out pursuit and that had us on edge.

The path itself petered out another couple of miles further, its useful role terminating as the farmland gave way to rising badlands, sagebrush-stubbled craggy hills rising into a north-south ridge line. We cast around a bit, searching for a route east, and finally stumbled upon Highway 26, the roadway appearing intact and uninterrupted here in the more desolate stretches of country.

We called it an early night. Trina cried silently in my arms until she fell asleep. Crying worked for her. There'd be no judgments or aspersions coming from me.

After that we made good time. We encountered no additional canals. We kept our speed lower than ultimately proved necessary, but we'd had too much experience with abrupt chasms or dangerous shifts of roadway surface to trust the continued integrity of the highway. Still, we moved along at a steady, uninterrupted clip.

The first couple of small towns we passed through told us that the Atlanteans had dispatched patrols covering pretty significant distance, or, alternatively, that there was another ziggurat nearby. These towns hadn't consisted of much to begin with, now they consisted of nothing at all–nothing but a few demolished or burnt buildings and a scattering of corpses well on the road to skeletonization.

The next couple of towns–and there only were a handful between the last canal and the Idaho border–provided more of a mystery. Ghost towns. Empty buildings. Undamaged, but empty of life and much of the stocks from store shelves.

The gas station/grocery/sporting-goods store in Ironside had not been picked completely clean. I scored a box of .357 ammunition while Trina delightedly pounced on a jar of pickles and a tin of sardines. Apparently the last one to clean out the shelves was watching his sodium intake.

"Where do you think everybody went?" Trina asked. "And why leave? I mean we haven't seen sign of the Atlanteans for miles."

"I don't know," I said, "but you'll notice there's no power. I'm beginning to think Gordon is on to something after all. People would seek refuge where they could access electricity. They aren't here. So...there just might be a remnant of our civilization in Boise. "

"Thanks for the vote of confidence," said Gordon, trying on a hunter's orange mesh baseball cap.

Near mid-afternoon I caught sight of the feathery beginning of a contrail, stretching to a vanishing needle point in the east. It was further evidence that Gordon's hypothesis might prove true. It wasn't much, just a wispy collection of hydrocarbons in the air, but it put a smile on my face. Trina's too, when I pointed it out.

I picked up the CB handset. "Mighty funny looking clouds they got in these parts," I drawled. I was answered by a delighted whoop.

ᘓᘏ

The wan rays of the descending sun cast the "Welcome to Idaho" sign in a pinkish glow. We decided against pushing on in the darkness, mistrustful of our own optimism, which was sufficiently buoyed by the fact that the bridge spanning the Oregon-Idaho border stood unbroken. The overconfident make mistakes. We'd curtail our enthusiasm for the night.

We hadn't driven far the next morning when we met our escort. A military truck, a massive green beast with a canvas canopy covering the bed, was parked sideways across the highway's center, obstructing the entirely notional traffic. Four soldiers, M16 rifles held at port arms, stood before it.

One raised a hand, instructing us to halt. He was a clean-shaven kid, not even out of his teens, with a corporal's chevrons on his collar and shoulders. The other three looked similar: young, washed, and pressed. I wondered how we looked–and smelled–to him.

"Welcome to the Unoccupied US of A, sir," he said, flashing a smile. "Glad you made it."

Chapter 16

THE SOLDIER WASN'T AN OPEN AND GIVING DISPENSER OF KNOWLEDGE. "You'll see, sir," or "Someone else can provide you an answer, ma'am," or "That's above my pay grade" was about all our anxious, confused queries could drag loose. He did, however, promise to escort us to headquarters as soon as relief arrived for his sentry post. "Bringing in refugees is a nice change of pace from killing lobsters" was the most Corporal Manse would volunteer.

Within twenty minutes, another truck eased to a halt with a diesel rumble of downshifts and the arthritic complaint of aged brakes. Another quartet of sentries hopped out. Corporal Manse walked us back to our vehicles, delivering a rote, brief explanation of the escort to HQ he was about to provide. His instructions were basic: We were to follow his deuce-and-a-half (as he termed his truck in the soon-to-be familiar military parlance) without deviation until he authorized us to leave our vehicles. At that point he would turn us over to intake officers who would provide us with further instructions.

He lowered his guard enough to hazard the unauthorized observation, "Sweet ride," as we approached the Ford. He and the other soldiers looked askance, however, at the bright yellow Hummer (well, still bright yellow beneath the layers of muck and road grime).

Having learned the futility of questions, we remounted our hard-used trucks and, once the deuce-and-a-half had completed a two point turn, followed in single file.

The first towns we drove through in Idaho looked no different from the last few we'd seen in Oregon. Empty. But soon we entered the outer range of Boise's functional power grid and we saw life. People. People working, people shopping, people smiling. Most, I observed, were armed. A frontier mentality, I supposed, no less real for the diminutive size of the frontier.

Boise levered itself into view like an old man hoisting himself slowly off of the couch, office buildings and apartment towers gaining in size as we neared. It looked unscathed. It looked safe. It looked like the end of a nightmare. It looked wonderful.

Proximity, however, revealed that Boise had not, in fact, come through the transition undamaged. An amalgamated neighborhood lay in ruins on the outskirts of town, so much useless rubble waiting for a bulldozer. A condominium complex was split by one of those Atlantean communal wells/shrines. And then we drove by the remnants of a ziggurat, the wall of its lower tier mostly intact, the rest a bombed out hulk. Heavy equipment was still at work clearing away the wreckage. The bombardment must have been quite a sight.

Uniforms pervaded the city. As we left the outlying suburbs and entered the greater Boise area, traffic picked up. We'd been driving slowly, keeping to a constant 35 mph, but now our speed was regulated by traffic. Actual traffic. It was wonderful. A military policeman stood in each major intersection we crossed, the overhead traffic signals either non-functional or perhaps simply turned off to conserve power. Any given vehicle appeared just as likely to contain military personnel as civilians.

I say 'military personnel' instead of the more specific 'soldiers' because while the Army predominated, I soon caught glimpses of Navy whites. Then alerted to the diversity, I paid greater attention and quickly enough picked out Marines and Airmen as well.

The Airmen, I suppose, were to be expected. Mountain Home Air Force Base was, I remembered, within an hour of Boise. A serendipitous roar of jet engines made me smile.

Our escort drove steadily through the city. The dome of the state capitol rose into view framed by the fawn-colored hills in the background. Emanating from the grounds of the capitol building, and blocking off the surrounding streets, stretched a tent city of army green. Corporal Manse pulled to a stop before a barricade of sandbags and concrete barriers manned by a platoon of soldiers armed with crew-served weapons and M16 rifles.

One of our escorts dropped from the back of the truck and sauntered our way. "Corporal Manse requests that you wait here until he returns," said the young soldier with the thick roux of a New Orleans accent.

We were not required to cool our heels for long. Manse returned within twenty minutes, guiding a blonde and quite pretty Air Force lieutenant.

"Hi," she said, beaming at the three of us. "I'm Lieutenant Ibsen, but you all can call me Vicki. I'm the intake processing officer. I'll see to it that you're properly welcomed into the community, set you up with temporary housing, and get you started looking for work. Welcome to Boise."

It was all so banal, so goddamned comforting. I just burst out laughing. It must have been infectious. One after another, commencing with Trina and Gordon, everyone in our little cluster joined in.

"That is just fantastic, Vicki," I said once I'd regained my composure. "And we're really looking forward to that. But first, can you direct us to whoever is in charge?"

"You want me to take you directly to General Brown?" Her eyes widened. It was cute. I caught Gordon stretching involuntarily to his full five-foot-seven. "We have procedures, sir. I can't just bring every civilian who wanders into the Unoccupied States in to see the General."

"He'll want to see us, Vicki. Specifically, he'll want to see this man," I said grabbing Gordon by the arm. "We know how to beat them. Leastways, he does."

ꕤ

We didn't get in to see the General right away. Bureaucracy is bureaucracy, even after the apocalypse. And, to be fair, it was likely we weren't the first crackpots or wild-eyed prophets to find their way to this bastion of lost civilization. Lieutenant Ibsen was at least willing to take our claim at face value and left to petition an interview. To her further credit, she didn't forget her primary responsibility and arranged for her deputy to take us in hand.

We were whisked away to a school gymnasium sectioned off with privacy screens and evenly spaced cots. It was only about a quarter occupied. We were assigned a cubicle in the gym and locker space in a hallway lined with graduating class photos and sports team awards.

And, most blessed of all, we showered. Long, steaming showers. Even if we utterly failed and the world was ground beneath the Atlantean heel, the trip was still worthwhile.

This day was an embarrassment of riches and I'm not easily chagrined. That night we went out to a restaurant for a leisurely dinner. A fine meal, though I can't recall the particulars, other than the beer. I savored three of them, a quiet smile accompanying each sip. I pondered a fourth, but the reproachful look on Trina's face stayed me.

That is not precisely correct. I knew that if I had the fourth beer I would begin to mistake that look, taking what was in fact concern for my well being for shrewish meddling. It had been too good of a day for me to ruin.

ဢဢ

The very next day, Trina was offered a job as chef de cuisine at an upscale diner. The owners were struggling to maintain their market niche given the narrowed variety of produce coming in to the city. Foi gras and Kobe beef were consigned to fond memories. To compensate, they hoped to employ novel methods of presentation and unexpected combinations of increasingly over-familiar ingredients. Trina was elated, given the opportunity to employ her talents once again. Not to mention that we could begin hunting for an apartment. Racking out in a school gymnasium, while a step above sleeping rough in the Oregon desert, was less than ideal.

Vicki Ibsen swung by the school later that day to inform me and Gordon that she'd secured interviews for us with, respectively, the Boise Police Department and Boise State University. Interviews, not firm offers.

"You're a marvel, Vicki. We really appreciate all you're doing for us," I said. Gordon remained silent while he untangled his tongue. "We just might take you up on it. Later. Thing is, we really, really still need to see the General."

"I cannot overemphasize the importance of the information we are carrying," Gordon added. I was pleased to hear "we," considering that inflating his importance in Lieutenant Ibsen's eyes was to his advantage and now that I'd helped him get here, he didn't actually need me. The seeds of victory were siloed in his noggin, not mine.

Nonetheless, the proffered job interview got me thinking. What did I want to do with the rest of my life, now that the rest of my life could be optimistically calculated in terms of years rather than weeks or months? Did I want to pick up here where I'd left off in Portland? Policing was policing. The transition to Boise was hardly daunting. Maybe, but the prospect felt almost like surrender. I was invested in fighting the Atlanteans. Too many people had died and I'd spilled too much blood to just walk away from the battle. Perhaps I should enlist in the Army. Thing is, they'd probably just place me in the Military Police, figuring it the best use of my skills. And given the reality on the ground–the MPs directing traffic–was there a significant difference between the Boise PD and Army MP? Other than that, I'd be giving up certain freedoms if I enlisted. I wanted to help beat the Atlanteans, not prevent Humvees t-boning pickup trucks at intersections.

No, we had to see General Brown before I could seriously contemplate future employment.

"I have passed your request up the chain," Vicki said. "I should have word soon."

I briefly considered the direct approach: knocking on the door and demanding. But the vivid image that arose in response–grim faced, impassive, and heavily armed sentries–left that idea stillborn.

ꙮ

Word did arrive soon, the next morning in fact. The General requested that Gordon and I attend him at "oh-eight-hundred." Given that this instruction was delivered at 5:30 by a pair of stone-faced, uniformed Airmen, it didn't provide quite the giddy rush it should have. It was too damned early for excitement.

Trina did not join us. Today was her first on the new job.

The state capitol building had undergone a complete makeover. It was now quite obviously the headquarters of an armed camp, the center of a major military operation. State functionaries in business suits still strode the cold marble halls, indicating that civilian law still operated to some extent, but the overwhelming presence of uniformed personnel told the story: the military was running the show.

Bundled wires and power cables were strung along the walls and high ceilings. Officers stalked purposefully by the antechamber where Gordon and I sat, thumbs a-twiddle, watching the clock tick closer and closer to nine o'clock. Several of these purposeful officers entered and exited the office. Behind whose door worked the eminence we impatiently waited to see. "Hurry up and wait" ran the unofficial motto of the armed forces, and I was experiencing the aptness of the expression firsthand.

"The General will see you now," an aide informed us. Tossing paper cups that still contained the last swallows of bad coffee into a waste basket, we at last entered the presence.

The office General Brown occupied was surprisingly small. It wasn't precisely spartan. Relics of the previous tenant remained in evidence, but the room was neatly maintained, uncluttered despite the crowd of maps, charts, and files visible on nearly every available surface. A bay of three windows behind a heavy, hand carved cherrywood desk allowed a view down into a command and control center. A portion of the state capitol building had been transformed into something resembling the tactical operations center of a battleship, or, considering the lack of exterior windows, perhaps of a submarine. A bustle of officers representing every branch of the armed forces, including the Coast Guard, stabbed at computer keyboards, jabbered into handsets, and eyeballed large flat-screen monitors displaying satellite imagery, Doppler radar weather scrolls, and gun-sight camera video that I could only assume was real time.

The General rose to greet us from a short-backed plastic chair. A swiveling, padded leather chair was pushed into one corner where it functioned as an easel propping up a map of the Northwestern United States. General Brown was compact, about Gordon's height. His closely cropped hair was more salt than pepper. A pair of bifocals dangling from a chain rested on the front of his crisply ironed Air Force uniform.

He held out a hand. "Professor Cameron, Officer Gates. Welcome. Please be seated. I'm sorry I can't offer you a great deal of time. I'm sure you can understand I'm up to my crotch in crocodiles at the moment."

We each shook his hand. His grip was as firm as one would expect. There were two guest chairs facing the desk. We sat.

"We appreciate that your time is valuable, sir," I said in my best placate-the-brass voice. "But I think you will consider what Gordon–Professor Cameron–has to say worth sparing a few extra minutes."

"I'm listening," he said. If a man can be both open and guarded he was.

"General Brown, I spent several weeks trapped inside a ziggurat. With full access to one of their libraries. I cracked their written language." No preamble, no lead-in. It was an effective tactic.

The General punched a button on his telephone. "Stillson, push my schedule back an hour." He stood, walked around to the front of the desk, and leaned back against it, hoisting his narrow frame up to half perch on the edge. "You've read their books? You know who they are?"

"I have and I do, sir," said Gordon.

"Well that is, that is...that could be a game changer, Professor." He stood again and began to pace. "Maybe I should brief you before you brief me. Bring you up to speed. I assume you've not had access to any news since Doomsday."

Doomsday. It fit, near enough.

"Well, there is so much it is difficult to decide where to begin," said General Brown. But, being a General and all, he decided swiftly enough. "The Invaders appeared at approximately 0300 hours local time, arriving simultaneously and globally. Their advent was, as you are quite aware, catastrophic. Intel estimates a roughly 75% mortality rate within the first twelve hours of Doomsday. The merger of Invader structures with ours accounted only for about a third of the deaths. I call it a merger. The science dinks have hung multisyllabic tags on it. Co-location, spatial displacement, quantum something or other. I think they're making it up as they go. Give something a name and people think you understand it. Merger is good enough for me.

"Anyhow, like I said, that killed about one-third of the initial number. Invader soldiers accounted for about a third. It was flooding, of all things, that did in the rest."

"Come here," he said, beckoning us to rise and follow him to the windows. He gestured at one of the screens displaying a Mercator projection of a satellite's eye view of the world. "Look at that. Brand new–honest to God–continents."

We looked. And even though I'd had a rough idea what to expect I was still shocked.

Continents was an exaggeration. The singular would have been more exact. Roughly centered in the North Atlantic, midway between the Eastern U.S. seaboard and Portugal, there lay an island, maybe twice the size of Iceland. Hard to say; the Mercator projection always threw my sense of scale off. I'll always believe Greenland is enormous. Anyway, it was big, but not continent class. The new continent proper was a kidney-shaped mass interrupting the open expanse of the Pacific and weighing in about the same as Australia. It took me another moment to realize that the archipelago twisting away like a cornucopia from the southwest of the new continent was actually the Hawaiian Islands, or what remained of them above water. The Strait of Japan now resembled more a river delta, the open water between Japan and the Asian mainland paved with a cracked mosaic of islands, large and small. Finally (and I'll admit this took me a second or two to spot–Americans and geography, damn you stereotypes with a basis in reality), the Baltic sea was now little more than a bay in the North Sea. A sort of subcontinent, jutting south from what had once been the deep cut nearly severing Finland from Sweden and Norway, now plugged that gap clear to Denmark.

Other alterations were more subtle. Coastlines had changed, low areas submerged by the sudden water displacement. The Low Countries were no more. The English Channel had widened considerably. Florida was missing entirely. Not so subtle, that.

Gordon released a slow whistle. "I was expecting a couple new additions to the map, but I had no idea it would be this extensive.

We're going to have to revisit continental drift progression and retool the Pangaean puzzle pieces."

"This doesn't come as a complete surprise then," said the General. An observation not a question.

Gordon pointed a finger and adjusted his target point on the satellite image to accompany his recitation of, "Atlantis, Mu, Lemuria, Hyperborea."

General Brown blinked, his new found optimism obviously shaken. "Atlantis?"

"Their names, not mine, General. I'm just quoting the texts I've read."

"What texts, comic books?" Nonetheless he didn't sound utterly skeptical. How could he discount any hypothesis, however outré, given the reality on the ground?

Hoping to steer the General back to his briefing, I interjected, "So, merger, flooding, enemy action, three-quarters of the population dead. What happened next?"

He must have decided to give Gordon the benefit of the doubt. For the moment. "Some areas weren't hit as hard as others. Boise came through with fewer than ten thousand killed. Mountain Home Air Force Base is close enough that we were able to respond quickly. Once I knew what we were dealing with....Fine, I still don't know what we are dealing with. But once I had a certainty that we were facing hostiles, we were able to respond pretty quickly. We managed to bomb the local Invader base and sent in a makeshift force of ground personnel to mop up. Honestly, I'm proud of them. We handed guns to clerks, meteorologists, and mechanics, then trucked to Boise to face a disciplined, alien force. But I'm getting off track."

"You said some areas weren't hit as hard as others," I said. "So we're not alone? Other sections of the US are intact?"

"Enclaves of the United States, sections of other countries. And most of our battle groups at sea survived. I'm no sailor, I can't begin to imagine what those boys went through, riding out global tsunamis."

"What's left of our country, sir?" asked Gordon, subdued and thoughtful.

"D.C. is gone. Hell, most of the Atlantic seaboard is a write-off. The Midwest isn't much better. Less damage from the merger, and, of course, little from flooding except up the Mississippi River valley. But the Invaders have bases salted throughout the plains states, apparently protecting their agricultural interests. The fighting was, by all reports, pretty brutal. But it isn't all dark. Big swathes of Texas remain free. Quite a bit of the Gulf Coast is free, or becoming free—a cordon expanding from Fort Polk. Every day I hope to hear word of the liberation of Montgomery."

There was too much to absorb. I tried to focus. "No civilian government, then?"

"We are, de facto, under martial law. I try to maintain civilian functions and officials as much as possible, though. I swore to uphold and defend the Constitution, goddammit. I want there to be a country to relinquish authority to."

"So you're in charge, then?" Gordon asked.

"It's a bit confused," the General said. Reluctantly, I thought. "The Joint Chiefs didn't survive. The Pentagon is gone. I hate to say it, but the functioning military enclaves behave more like a council of warlords. If this thing drags on, if this war takes a turn for the worse.... Hell, let's not look at worst case scenarios. You gentlemen bring me a ray of hope. So let me continue the briefing.

"We retain satellite capability, as you see, so we are able to maintain some communication worldwide and can gather intel. The story isn't pretty. Europe is a total loss. The merger was devastating, the floods nearly as bad. And what survivors there were, were not, it seems, able to muster much of a defense.

"Russia is in chaos. My worst case scenario is already a reality there: Invaders facing off against local military commanders who've set themselves up as independent warlords. What reports we've gotten suggest a continual battle royale, with everyone's nose getting bloodied. We can't look for help from that theater, except insofar as the big dust-up keeps the Invaders there pinned down, unable to assist those here."

"That wouldn't happen in any case, sir," said Gordon. "The Hyperboreans would not consider allying themselves with the Atlanteans. From their point of view we're doing them a favor."

"What's that? Intel suggests that the Invaders are divided into factions, but not that they are in outright conflict."

"Fifty thousand years of antagonism, General. Open war has been their status quo for millennia. Peace breaks out for a century or two at intervals, but they always locate new casus belli. And they can usually amuse themselves with a spot of civil war while they wait. Temporary alliances of convenience do crop up, at least until one party finds a tactical advantage in treachery. That is one advantage we do have. They are very unlikely to combine resources and pick off one enclave at a time."

General Brown absorbed that in silence for a minute. "I'm beginning to think debriefing you will prove profitable, Professor Cameron"

"It is still your turn, sir," I said politely. My curiosity was still not assuaged. "What about the rest of the world?"

He nodded, conceding an obligation to continue. "Australia is in reasonably good shape. They've fought the Invader to a standstill. Our latest evaluation of the satellite imagery suggests they may even be on the cusp of an offensive.

"China is...Did you ever seen those nature documentaries when the armies of two different ant species meet? It's like that. Tooth and nail. Desperate fighting. We think the Chinese even detonated a low-yield nuke in Chengdu. Conditions are similar in India. High-population countries. Wipe out a few hundred million people, they can still field makeshift armies. Still, I wouldn't wager either way on those contests.

"The Middle East and North Africa are hard to figure. Israel is holding its own. No surprise there. The rest is uncertain. Lots of open terrain in that part of the world. So the merger was less devastating. Flooding hit the coastal cities pretty hard but left effective fighting forces in the interior. We've pieced together stories of suicidal cavalry charges undertaken against Invader bases and some pretty effective ambushes. On the other hand, we've gotten confused accounts of what are either mass surrenders or some sort of religious movement, a Cult of the Invader. Worshiping the bastards.

"Sub-Saharan Africa is almost entirely occupied and pacified. You can see on the map there a lot less green than there used to be. Major deforestation, agricultural land supplanting jungle. What little resistance exists is largely ineffective. South America is in little better condition. There are pockets holding out, but the countries down there took as much of a population hit as we did, and they aren't displaying quite the resilience." The General shrugged. "A well-funded military, a large industrial base, and an armed populace do yield certain benefits I suppose."

"Pretty grim," I said. "So how are those benefits serving us? I used to hear jets overhead in the early days."

The General sighed. "We are doing well in some respects, poorly in others. I have substantial resources at my disposal. Mountain Home was unhurt. We've even received reinforcements from other squadrons who were unable to return to their original bases. The local Army National Guard and the Army and Marine Reserves provide a small, but effective, ground force. And surviving service members have trickled in from elsewhere. I even have Special Forces at my disposal: a few Rangers who were on leave, a couple of Green Berets from Fort Lewis who were deer hunting in Eastern Washington on Doomsday. A few more from this or that MOS. Individual stories vary. Even have a few swabbies and a coastie or two.

"I'd like to think I've made good use of them all. We pounded the nearest bases in the first week. Cleared a safe zone of several hundred miles. In that respect we've done well. But after that first week, something changed."

"Let me guess," I said. "You began to lose planes. Unexplained explosions."

"Right. We probed and scouted..."

"And discovered the ziggurats were protected by heat barriers," said Gordon.

"I'm no longer surprised at how well informed you two gentlemen are," said General Brown. "Yes, the bases are surrounded by heat shells of substantial dimension and, apparently, of exponentially increasing temperature toward the center of the shell. We tried standing off at a distance, launching missiles from over the horizon. No effect. The missiles detonate from the heat too far from the structures to do any damage. We did discover that the shells do not reach all the way to the earth, for obvious practical reasons. They don't want to flash fry themselves. So we tried a ground assault with TOW missiles."

"And the vehicle mounting the missile, or the poor bastard packing it, erupted into a fireball," I said, the memory of the deaths of Jim, Luisa, and Tonio, still fresh and painful, burnt into my core.

"Precisely. We had early success with the technique. I still have hopes for it, employing a more stealthy approach. Word from Texas is that a diversionary force can be effective, but those boys have more manpower than I do."

"Early success," repeated Gordon. "They can learn, these invaders. Don't underestimate them just because they lack firearms and internal combustion engines. Their society, as abhorrent as it is, has survived virtually unchanged for tens of thousands of years. But stuck in a rut doesn't mean stupid. Their leaders will employ whatever is required to maintain their dominance."

"I wish that were all I had to worry about," the General said. "As things stand, we're looking at a stalemate, or a contest of slow attrition. Or we would be, but for one factor. Those new lands that popped up on the map suffered little damage from the merger. Those are basically pristine Invader homelands."

I groaned, understanding where this was heading. "You're telling us that the Atlanteans have a virtually bottomless supply of reinforcements, and we..."

"We have what you see, yes Mr. Gates. We have a minuscule population and virtually no remaining industrial capacity. We can maintain a modest level of energy production so long as the remaining hydroelectric dams survive, but materials manufacture and agricultural production are minimal. Subsistence, no more. We have no reserves to draw on. The Invaders can simply ship them in."

Gordon asked, "Didn't you tell us that our fleets are mostly intact?"

"True, but they can't span the globe. The Seventh Fleet did interdict a resupply convoy headed for Australia. A notable success. Since then, the enemy armadas are protected by the same heat barriers that cover the Invader bases. We can take a toll with submarines, luckily, otherwise we'd be overrun within a couple of years. As it is...well, we can defend a perimeter while fuel and ammunition hold out. After that I'm afraid numbers will ultimately tell."

We were all quiet for a minute, pondering a grim future of wave after wave of fresh Atlanteans coming ashore, battering against a gradually shrinking cordon of desperate soldiers and, eventually, civilians.

"Nukes?" I said.

The General shook his head. "We've considered that. The job would require so many warheads that the resultant fallout would constitute slow suicide. I'm not interested in Pyrrhic victory. Even the Chinese quit after one."

We returned to our despondent reverie.

General Brown was the first to lever himself out from the funk. "Well, then Professor, this is where you brighten my day with some good news. I've briefed you, now it's your turn."

We'd been standing near the windows for some time. Gordon led a return to the chairs and settled in to rehash his account of finding himself seemingly trapped within a ziggurat. He related the tale of skulking, survival, and scholarship. The General took a few notes when Gordon provided a broad outline of Atlantean history, including the initial ritual that created the two Earths, like global-scale cell division.

"It is an interesting story, Professor," the General said when Gordon began to wind down. "I'm sure Intel and PsyOps will find it instructive. But I admit I was hoping for a bit more. I'm not sure how a history lesson or your ability to read the Invader's language is going to help me kick their asses."

"Always close with your best stuff, General," said Gordon. "Remember that I mentioned a ritual, some sort of procedure–science, magic, makes no difference–that rent space-time, dividing us into two separate worlds."

"Yes, you did. And preposterous stuff, too. Except there on the satellite map over my shoulder lies the proof. Well?"

"So we, or specifically I'm guessing, the Chinese, accidentally effected a reunion of the two worlds." Gordon held up a hand. "My guess is that the initial experiment in the ChiCom's new supercollider went awry. Maybe, maybe not. The point is, the Atlanteans, or the Invaders, or, as Nick's wife called them, the Claimants, created the initial rift." Gordon paused, a gifted lecturer employing dramatic silence as ably as an actor on stage or a litigator in the courtroom. "And that means they could do it again."

Silence as the General absorbed the implications. "Wait. Apply the brakes, Professor. What you're saying is we can send them back?" I saw then the expression that must have molded my features when realization set in, when hope sparked from dead ashes.

"In theory," said Gordon, though I thought not too confidently. Was his confidence faltering as the possibility of putting his theory to the test neared?

"So we capture one of their wizards, or high-priests, or whatever you want to call them. And you speak the lingo, don't you? Then convince the son-of-a-bitch to cast the same spell." He nodded, muttered "yes, yes, yes," while the plans and schemes swirling behind his skull almost threatened manifestation. He'd had his moment of prospective joy. Now he'd reverted to General, the man responsible for seeing to the realization of the prospect. Joy gave way as he shouldered another burden.

"I read the lingo, sir," said Gordon, as always anxious for clarity. "To be precise, I don't speak it yet. But reading and writing will serve."

"What? Yes, of course. First thing, before I even call a staff meeting, is to put you in a room with as many linguists as I can assemble, military or civilian. Then the staff meeting. There is work to be done."

Chapter 17

I SAW GORDON ONLY BRIEFLY DURING THE NEXT FEW WEEKS. WE MANAGED to meet for lunch a few times, and for dinner at the restaurant employing Trina. She would emerge, beaming, from the kitchen to serve us herself. The work had renewed her in some fundamental way. We moved into a small apartment where she repeatedly demonstrated that she had shed her early concern over bringing a new life into the world during the apocalypse. I was happy for her and concealed my own anxiety for the future. I mean, we'd found a little enclave of peace, but the existential threat hadn't abated. Would having a baby be an emblem of hope or a gesture of thoughtless selfishness?

I had no idea.

Gordon was kept busy. He shared with me what he could. He was obviously relishing it. His work seemed rather dryly academic to me, but given that he was an academic, I was willing to be pleased for him on his own terms.

There was an additional factor in his calculus of happiness: Lieutenant Ibsen had been appointed as Gordon's minder, shuttling him to meetings, scouring the territory for accomplished linguists, arranging his schedule... And escorting him to dinner, in mufti, on her own time. I don't think it was simply a matter of conscientious performance of her duties.

I was left to my own devices. Stewing in my own unproductive juices. Pleasure in others' happiness could only carry me so far. Every morning I considered hiking down to the police station to interview for a position. Or marching down to the General's office to offer my enlistment. Surely any activity was better than loafing around the prison cell of the apartment. Any contribution to the struggle was honorable. But something held me back. I felt I still had a role to play in Gordon's scheme, a role beyond bringing him safely to Boise. If I was in uniform I'd lose what autonomy I retained. I might be tasked with duties that would preclude me from contributing.

I walked the streets each day, slowly reacquainting myself with the rhythms of a vibrant city. I observed the military personnel go about their duties, sensing a gradual rise in excitement, a growing briskness to the step, an edge of excitement in speech. Word was leaking that something big was in the works.

The walks were insufficient. The school where we'd spent our first days allowed me access to the cramped weight room. I burnt off excess nervous energy, trying to coax my body back into pre-Doomsday condition. And I steered clear of pubs, permitting myself no more than a beer during dinner, two or three on the weekends.

So while my mind remained on edge, filled with doubt and anxiety, physically I appeared well. I avoided suspicion or scrutiny from Trina and Gordon, both of whom were preoccupied with their new lives anyway. When life is trending positive people enjoy the delusion that pay raises, wedding engagements, and unexpected legacies are the general lot of life, spreading like lice in a kindergarten playground. And that was fine. Misery may love company, but I was picky about the company. I preferred to see my wife and friend happy.

ഗ്ഗ

A gentle snow was painting the city a uniform white one morning in early January when a knock at the door drew me out of bed. I wasn't particularly tired. Loafing isn't strenuous. Trina barely acknowledged my departure. She was working long hours and treasured her sleep. I padded as quietly as I could from the bedroom.

Gordon, a nervous grin stretching across his face, awaited me on the other side of the door.

"Get dressed, Nick. We've got an appointment."

"Good morning to you, too," I said. I opened the door wide and turned my back on him, heading for the kitchen. "Come on in. Want some breakfast?"

"We've already eaten, thanks," came an unexpected voice. I shuffled a slow u-turn. Vicki Ibsen, in uniform, was entering the apartment behind Gordon. "Nice robe."

"Thanks. Former tenant's castoff." I avoided delving into the specific implications of 'We've already eaten.'

"If you're brewing a pot, I wouldn't mind some coffee," said Gordon, plopping himself down onto the plaid couch, its muddy crosshatching minimizing the years' accumulation of mystery stains.

I shoveled cereal into my mouth while the coffee percolated. I waited until the last fragrant drips fell into the pot, occupying myself with rinsing, drying, and re-shelving the cereal bowl.

"Coffee's ready," I announced, carrying my own mug to the bathroom where I managed a few sips before stepping into the shower. Uninvited guests and old friends can prepare their own damn cups of java.

I didn't indulge in a long, hot drenching. This obviously wasn't a social call. For all my snark and feigned nonchalance, I was horribly curious what brought the two of them here so early. I was scrubbed, shaved, and dressed in fifteen minutes.

I slurped down the remainder of my tepid coffee as I rejoined them, noting a sudden disentanglement of hands where the two sat adjoining on the couch.

"OK, spill it," I said. "What brings you around? Don't tell me you were out of corn flakes."

Gordon sat up, straightening his back and leaning forward eagerly. "There's a planning session starting later this morning. The General wants to determine how best to snatch a priest from the ziggurat at PSU."

I nodded, rolling my hands in a "go on" gesture.

Gordon cleared his throat. "I've been putting in fourteen-hour days the last couple of weeks, trying to pass along everything I've learned about the Atlantean language. There's a good dozen people now who can read and write the basics."

"Congratulations. Maybe Boise State can award you an honorary Doctorate of Linguistics. There is, I presume, more?"

"With that knowledge disseminated, my value as a potential translator is outweighed by the value of my knowledge of the hidden entrance to the ziggurat and familiarity with some of the interior." He spoke slowly and precisely, his concern that I get the point bordering on patronizing. No, not bordering, deliberately over the top.

"So, you're in on the caper, then. They letting you carry a gun?"

Gordon turned pleading eyes on Vicki. "You see how he wounds me? I come bearing an opportunity for him and he mocks me."

"An opportunity? What are you dancing around here?"

Gordon grinned triumphantly. "I've convinced the General's operations officer that someone intimately familiar with the streets and byways of Portland should join the planning session. And maybe join the mission itself."

It was my turn to sit up straight. "Wait a minute. They bought that? The streets and byways aren't exactly what they used to be. I haven't been to that part of town since Doomsday, I don't know the new ins and outs."

"True. But not every landmark has changed. What familiarity you have with the unaltered terrain might just mean the difference between success and failure."

I wondered how much force that line of reasoning had conveyed, and how much was simply Gordon's personal leverage. I could imagine him saying bluntly, "You need me. I want Nick along. End of story." But he'd never admit that to me, or that he'd stuck his neck out for my benefit, or that he'd feel safer having me along.

I nodded. "You're assuming I'd go. As usual, you assume correctly. Just let me write a note for Trina, then we can go see the General."

ℵ☉

The conference room felt undersized. The table, a stretched ellipse with the short ends sliced off, seemed to have been deprived of its destiny furnishing a larger chamber. Every chair was occupied, and assorted aides stood lining the walls. In front of each chair lay mounds of notebooks and loose papers. A laptop computer connected to a projector occupied a position a few spots down from the head of the table. A retractable screen hanging from the back wall displayed the innocuous introductory slide of a PowerPoint presentation: The Department of Defense was responsible for the following material, which had been classified as Secret.

Was there some concern of Atlantean spies? More likely an operations clerk simply continued to follow directives and protocol whether appropriate and relevant or not. We are creatures of habit even with the world crumbling at our feet.

Gordon, Vicki, and I were seated near the foot of the table, paper cups of coffee transitioning from tepid to cold before us.

General Brown called the session to order and quickly turned the meeting over to his operations officer, an Air Force Lieutenant Colonel named Marsh.

"Operation Valiant Wolf consists of...is something funny?" Marsh brought his comments to an abrupt stop at some inefficiently stifled sniggering from our end of the table.

"Nothing, sir," said Gordon, under the appalled gaze of Vicki Ibsen. "Sorry. Please continue briefing Valiant Wolf."

I bit down on my lower lip.

Colonel Marsh nodded to the Lieutenant operating the laptop. A new slide popped up on the screen. "As I was saying, the operation consists of three primary components: team delivery, target extraction, and team recovery. Air transport will be by helicopter. We will establish two staging and refueling depots, here and here."

He and his assistant conducted the briefing flawlessly, a perfectly choreographed and rehearsed performance. I struggled to stay awake. Body heat in the confined space more than compensated for the niggardly central heating.

The gist of the preliminary briefing was that a team would fly to Portland by helicopter, stopping a couple of times to refuel at bases set up by advance teams. Then, after snatching the priest, the team would return the same way. Colonel Marsh required roughly half of an hour to explain it, at which point he handed over the briefing to another officer.

Captain Gaines wasn't a big man, but compact, fit, exuding confidence and competence. The insignia on his uniform spelled out US Army and Special Forces. He must have been one of the hunters on leave from Fort Lewis. I found my attention focusing again.

"Short version: I lead an eight-man team. Insertion point ten klicks from the target to avoid detection. Infiltrate, retrieve the target, then, depending on conditions, return to the insertion point, or radio for extraction outside the heat barrier.

"That's the short version, easy. Now, details. Map, please." A close-up satellite view of downtown Portland and its immediate surrounds appeared on the screen. What a mess. I'd driven through some of it the night of Doomsday, so the extent of the damage was not a real surprise. But seeing it again, as a whole, rekindled my dismay and anger. The neat grid pattern rising up from the river to the hills was smashed, a handful of heavy gravel dropped on a waffle. Here and there the initial pattern peaked through, most of the rest just a confused clumping. Only three river crossings stood, and one of them was Atlantean. I had been lucky getting over the Willamette that first night.

"As you can see, clear landing zones near the target are at a premium, and the prospects aren't much better within a ten-mile radius. I understand we have a local to provide us with some expert advice." Captain Gaines was stone-faced and his tone equally neutral. Whether his words concealed sarcasm, anger, or were to be taken at face value, I had no clue.

I stood up. Time to prove my worth, if I had any. "Nick Gates. Portland Police Department. There are cleared zones on the east side: some farmland and some neighborhoods razed by fire. But then you'd be faced with river crossings, and those will be guarded."

"Yes," said the Captain, and this time he failed to suppress the sarcasm contained in that single syllable.

I let it slide off. I'd written enough traffic citations while enduring the snide opprobrium of the violators. I was inured. "As you can see, the west hills still remain forested." It was true, though to a much lesser extent than prior to Doomsday. The Atlanteans had logged and built up much of what had, for us, been parkland. Still, woodland remained. I walked towards the screen and gestured to an area near the top. "You can see here, off Highway-30, it is relatively clear. Some small scale Invader fishing huts merged with our industrial river port. Their fishing is concentrated east, along Interstate-84, so this spot was probably sparsely populated even prior to the merger." The barest twitch of an eyebrow raising told me I'd begun to impress the captain. A hair, an iota, a barely registrable quanta.

I continued. "If this satellite photo is recent, I'd suggest a landing here, near this intersection and this parking lot. Looks clear of power lines and back here you're far from traffic signals, so it appears to allow enough room to land a helicopter. It would be a hump from there, but you'd get your insertion far from visual range of the target. From that point you could approach undetected. Maybe. A local, an expert guide would certainly increase your odds."

My statement caused a short flurry of photo analysis and consultations with flight operations experts. Captain Gaines decided the interruption gave sufficient pause for a tête-à-tête. The room allowed no illusion of privacy, but we stepped into the least occupied corner.

"I'm already saddled with one civilian, Gates," he said without preamble. "Why should I take you along too? You're a cop, fine. I'll assume you are competent in your field. But this is a war. We're planning a raid, not a drug bust. People are most likely going to be killed. By us."

So, maybe I'm not completely inured. He'd got my back up after all. He wanted a pissing match? Fine, I'd shoot for distance and accuracy.

"You're a soldier, Gaines. I'll assume you are competent in your field. General Brown tells me he's had some success against the Invaders. With bombs, missiles, and artillery. Not at close quarters. How many Invaders, how many people, have you killed up close? Close enough to watch their eyes go dead? Why should you take me along? Because I've actually done this sort of work. Now, if you're happy with the length and circumference of my dick, can we get back to planning this little outing?"

The internal roil of emotion can often be observed externally. It isn't in the eyes themselves. Despite what the poets would have us believe, they convey no emotions. But the face around the eyes–the brow, the cheeks, the workings of the muscles–can betray much of the mind's struggle. In the case of Captain Gaines it was a short battle, and humor won out over contempt, anger, and embarrassment.

"OK, hung like a goddamn Clydesdale, Nick. Outstanding. Glad to have you with us."

So it was decided. Much of the rest of the day was taken up by logistics such as payloads and fueling needs. Gordon briefed Captain Gaines on what he could remember of the interior and the defenses of the target ziggurat. I employed most of the time wondering how Trina would react to the news of my volunteering to return to Portland.

ꝏ

She reacted remarkably well, as a matter of fact. She returned home from work at the usual hour–late. I saw no profit in waiting and simply followed the hug and kiss of arrival with "I'm on the retrieval mission with Gordon."

A widening of the eyes and a slight parting of the lips were her only visible reactions. That was enough to spell dismay. But she was, and remains, a trooper.

She took her time and replied with composure. "Of course you're going, Nick. Not being able to help people, the realization of...of futility almost killed you, honey. Now that there's a chance to be involved, to make a difference, I know you have to go. I'd hoped...well, it doesn't matter."

She disappeared into the kitchen and returned with a glass of red wine and a bottle of beer. She dimmed the lights and we sat sipping in silence, which I broke to tell her I loved her.

"Of course you do, Officer Gates," she said, "and I love you too. You'd better come back to me so I can keep reminding you."

ꝏ

I met the seven others who were assigned to the mission along with Gordon and Captain Gaines. I was surprised to find I recognized four of them: Corporal Manse, Private Hebert–the soldier from New Orleans–and their other two squad mates, Privates Purvis and Washington. I hadn't noticed the Ranger tabs on their uniforms at our first encounter.

Sergeant Caplan was Captain Gaines' hunting companion. They had been stalking white tail when Doomsday struck. The sergeant was tight-lipped, either taciturn or shy. My money was on taciturn.

Sergeant Prentiss was an Airman, part of one of the Air Force's elite para-rescue teams. He over-topped the tallest of us by several inches and outweighed the heaviest by twenty pounds, all muscle. He was genial and voluble and I took a liking to him immediately, as I imagine most people did.

The team was rounded out by a Marine, Lance Corporal Garrett, Force Recon. He was built like a greyhound, lean, all bony planes and long muscle. He kept aloof, observing the world with a faint smile. He and Sergeant Caplan could form a duet, harmonizing silence.

I expected a deal of inter-service rivalry, but was disappointed. The Ranger squad was rambunctious, full of that heady cocktail of youth and bravado. But I felt that, tonight at least, the Ranger's spirits were somewhat bridled. The new world accounted for that to some extent no doubt; the catastrophic changes had dulled the enthusiasms of all survivors. More immediately, I think, was the presence of the other hard-bitten team members, each looking the part of an experienced special forces veteran. I don't think they were put off much by me. And Gordon, even at his most ferocious, does not inspire awe.

If I was going to infiltrate a compound guarded by brutal, fanatical soldiers, I suppose this was a pretty good bunch to do it with. Madness. I'd done my part, hadn't I? But no, Trina was right about me. I had to see this through. And Portland was my town. If these boys were going to engage in mayhem, breaking and entering, kidnapping, or whatnot, I was going to be there to keep an eye on them.

We met at the diner, the owners pushing a couple of tables together and hovering about with nervous, almost obsequious attention until Trina politely shooed them away, coming out of the kitchen to take our orders personally.

A couple of pitchers appeared and glasses were filled. I doubted all of the Rangers were of legal drinking age, but stickling over it seemed petty. If Captain Gaines wasn't going to play the martinet, I wasn't going to grouse. These boys were going to watch my back.

We had the diner mostly to ourselves. The bones of the traditional coffee and hamburger establishment remained: a long lunch counter, booths lining one wall. The owners, however, had given the decor an upscale makeover. The tables, including the tabletops of the booths, were sleek, dark hardwood. The lunch counter had been re-purposed as a bar. The color scheme was muted, dark browns and deep maroon, the lighting soft.

"So, Nick," said Sergeant Prentiss, breaking the silence that followed the pouring of the first round, "I hear you've been up against these lobsters. What kind of fighters are they? Tell us what to expect."

"First of all, to be fair, Gordon's seen the elephant as well," I said. "That's the expression, right, 'seen the elephant?'" I received just about as many uncomprehending stares as I did nods of agreement, so I went on. "They're disciplined. Brave, fanatically so. They keep coming, no matter how many of them you've gunned down before their eyes."

"X-Box practice, huh?" asked Private Washington. "Line 'em up and shoot 'em down."

"Video games don't run two feet of steel through your guts, Washington," I replied, "like what happened to my partner on Doomsday."

"They just try to stick you?" asked Private Hebert. "They haven't picked up guns yet?"

Gordon said, "A hide-bound people, Private. They do not adopt novelties. I imagine that, given enough time, their ruling caste will begin experimentation, but for now we are facing pole arms and arrows. The officers carry swords, and, Nick tells me, will engage."

"Indeed, Professor?" asked Sergeant Prentiss with a broad grin that softened his mockery. Gordon's didacticism doesn't always travel well between social circles. All four Rangers had buried their faces in beer glasses to mask their expressions.

"Don't forget," said Captain Gaines, "that indoors a close-quarter weapon can be as effective as a rifle. Do not underestimate your foe."

I raised my glass in salute. His words would carry weight where Gordon's–or mine–might not.

"With luck," the Captain continued, "we'll be in and out without needing to fire a shot."

"About that," I said, then took another swallow. The beer was pretty good. At least one of Boise's local breweries was still producing. "The goal of the mission is to capture one of their priests. But if you find yourself in a scrap with one, shooting isn't going to help much. Might buy you some time, but to finish one off, you need to use a blade."

I received a lot of skeptical looks for my warning.

"Think of it as full body-armor," put in Gordon. "Including the head. Probably designed as a general missile-weapon defense. The priests rely on bodyguards to protect themselves from hand weapons, but arrows and similar high velocity projectiles demanded a more personalized remedy. Snipers, a hail of arrows–these are factors a personal bodyguard may be unable to contend with. Luckily for the priests, the same protection functions against small arms fire as effectively as it does against arrows.

"But if I may reiterate what Nick said, try not to kill them. We're tasked to retrieve at least one alive."

Sergeant Caplan spoke up, all heads swiveling his way in surprise. "We've seen so much impossible shit, bullet-proof priests shouldn't spook you. The Captain enlisted civilian experts. Listen to them."

And that, apparently, was enough to satisfy all of them.

ꙮ

The next day I went shopping.

Corporal Manse had decided to take me under his wing at some point during the previous night's unofficial, beer-fueled planning session. He determined that I should be properly kitted out. He swung by the apartment early in the morning to escort me to a sporting goods store and an Army/Navy surplus store.

Trina's watchful eye had helped me curb the impulse to keep up with the competitive level of consumption the rest of the team had indulged in. So prompting my lazy ass into action at the ridiculously early hour proved less uncomfortable than it might otherwise have been. Manse looked absurdly fresh. It is wrong to hate the young; the passage of time is no fault of theirs. But still.

After breakfast we set off in search of a pair of boots. Manse was insistent on this point, and equally insistent that I don them immediately, offering the perfectly valid reason that I had little time to break them in. Of course that rendered the remainder of the outfitting session a pinched, cramped, and chaffed experience.

I picked out a combat vest with pockets for sundry items that I hoped not to have to use. Operating under the bullshit theory that things you have are the things you wind up not needing, I proceeded to fill up the pockets with first-aid gear, a flashlight, batteries, half-moon speed loaders for the .357, protein bars, a compass, chemical heaters, glow lights, and a spool of military-grade cord. I felt absurd, like a grown man playing soldier. I suppose I was at that. Doing it under the eye of an actual soldier made it even more awkward. But Manse didn't appear to notice. I caught no hint of condescension.

Manse wandered off while I browsed the clothing selection. I bought a used set of what Manse termed BDUs (battle dress uniform), in an outmoded camouflage pattern. I found a well-worn canvas jacket with a warm flannel lining that fit equally well either over or under the combat vest.

I found the corporal examining the edge of an oversized survival bowie knife. "You serious about bullets bouncing off the priests, Nick?" he asked.

"Serious as syphilis," I said. "One of the bastards almost knifed me because of it."

"What did you do?" Manse asked.

"Dropped my gun and stabbed him with a sword."

"A fucking sword?"

"A fucking sword."

"Do you still have it?"

I was pretty sure the saber was in a box of odds and ends in the apartment, waiting to be unpacked after Trina and I found more permanent accommodations.

"Yeah, I still have it. I don't think it'd be too practical inside a helicopter, though. Wearing a sword isn't something you think about doing much," I said, examining a glass display case full of blades. "How do you walk without tripping over it? Do you smack people with it every time you turn around? Do you have to keep one hand on it while running?"

"OK, Nick, I get the point. You won't be bringing your sword along. Too bad. I think that'd be cool. So maybe you should pick out something else."

I settled on a variation of a bolo knife, a heavy, single-edged chopper, its fourteen-inch blackened blade swelling to a broad point. About four inches of the back edge had been ground into serrations, which would be very useful if I needed to do some carpentry on the mission. The black plastic grip bore raised checkering for a non-slip grip, and a wide, D-shaped guard stretching the length of the handle protected the fingers. The sheath strapped neatly to the combat vest.

I added a box of .357 ammunition to my pile. I'm sure the rounds I'd commandeered on the road were perfectly fine. I just felt more comfortable going into harm's way loaded with ammo I'd bought for myself.

This whole excursion was making me superstitious.

"Taking a revolver along?" asked Manse.

"Yeah. Gordon, uh, Professor Cameron is most comfortable with my service pistol, a .45 Glock. It doesn't make much difference to me what I'm using, so I'd rather leave the .45 with him. And I know Captain Gaines is barely tolerating civilians tagging along on his operation. I don't want to hear what he'd say if I asked him if the Army could lend me a gun."

Manse laughed. "Probably 'pound sand.' But why a six-shooter? I'm sure you can find an automatic somewhere."

"I'm going to be surrounded by you Special Ops types. If it becomes important that I have more than six shots at a time, we're fucked anyway." I felt the need to knock on a wooden ladder, or break a mirror with a black cat or something, so I quickly added, "The speed loaders just about make up the difference, if it comes to it."

Thing was, I'd carried this pistol on the jaunt across Oregon and I'd come through unscathed. I knew it was foolish to fetishize the .357, to treat it as a talisman. It conveyed no mystical protection, no aura of good luck. But still...

Corporal Manse nodded, seemingly satisfied. "Fine. I think we've got you squared away. And like you say, you've got a vicious gang of killers watching your six."

࿇

The mission was set for the next afternoon. Trina took the night off from the restaurant and busied herself in the kitchen. She chased me out each time I attempted to enter her sanctum for a talk. It didn't help matters that I heard the occasional sob in between the sounds of clattering pots and knives slicing into chopping blocks. Everyone handles stress differently. Some exercise, some drink. Some exercise and drink simultaneously, but never more than once. And some cook. I left her to it after one last foray to snag a beer.

Trina made enough for eight. Considering the dinner party would consist of the two of us plus Gordon and Vicki, I could rest easy knowing Trina would have leftovers to last until my return.

At Trina's insistence I donned slacks and a button-down shirt. She was still selecting earrings when the doorbell rang. I slipped on a pair of loafers and trotted to the sitting room to get the door.

Vicki cleaned up well. Scratch that, she cleaned up fantastic. Gordon looked like Gordon, except happier.

"Come on in. Let me take your coats." It sounded so banal, so normal. A bit of civilized adult socializing to distract our minds from impending danger. A touch of bravado or insouciance perhaps, a last cigarette before the firing squad. But what else were we to do? Stage a drum circle and weep? No, we'd sit down at a fine meal and enjoy genteel company. A reminder of what we were fighting for, what Gordon and I were about to hazard our lives for.

Trina emerged from the bedroom, rivaling Vicki. Hell, no contest on my scorecard; Trina won hands down.

I hid a smile, observing the scrutiny to which Trina subjected Vicki. At earlier meetings she'd shown nothing but polite, growingly cordial interest. Now that it definitely appeared that Vicki had her sights set on Gordon, Trina had dialed up the focus, searching for flaws, determined that any woman after Gordon be worthy of him. Ironic, considering the shifting level of esteem in which Trina held Gordon. But if it kept her mind occupied, off of tomorrow, I was happy to keep my smirk to myself.

Aperitifs led to dinner, then after dinner cocktails. As dinner parties go, it was not a success. I cannot fault the food, which was excellent, or even the company. We simply tried too hard. Our levity rang false and everyone felt it. Gordon begged off early, citing the need for a good night's sleep prior to our departure. I couldn't have argued with that if I'd wanted to.

I did not, however, raise the same excuse when Trina kept me up late. There was tenderness and a foreboding of finality in our lovemaking.

Chapter 18

THE HELICOPTER LIFTED OFF FROM MOUNTAIN HOME AIR FORCE BASE into the bright orange glare of the setting sun that sank slowly on the western horizon like a deflating basketball. The operational team–us–was the last to depart. Support teams had flown out in sequence throughout the day, setting up fueling points and miniature field hospitals in case of emergency. A platoon of assorted, heavily armed troops left about an hour prior to our departure, providing a reserve force, there to pull our asses out of the fire if required–or possible.

Trina had declined to accompany me south to the Air Force base, preferring to say goodbye in privacy and in the relatively familiar surroundings of the apartment. A wise choice I think. No distractions, no onlookers.

General Brown arrived to personally see us off. He stood aside as Captain Gaines ran through the operation one more time. Sergeant Caplan conducted a final weapons and equipment check, raising an eyebrow at my revolver and absurdly oversized knife, and querying Gordon about the Glock, "You sure?"

"They're entitled to their sidearms," said Gaines. "From all reports they've put more rounds down range than any of us recently."

And that was the last word I heard for hours. Earplugs muffled the howl of the helicopter engine, but conversation was a practical impossibility. We sat on canvas bench seats that depended from the interior fuselage by crisscrossing canvas strips. Passenger comfort had not been a priority in the design criteria.

Sunlight faded and died away as we beat westward, depriving me of any view of the disordered world below. I tried to get some sleep. I'd always read that soldiers could sleep anywhere. Apparently I was no soldier. The noise, vibration, and uncomfortable seating were more than I could overcome. It appeared none of the rest of the team were soldiers either. All sat bolt upright–no nodding heads or drooping eyelids to be seen beneath camouflage-pattern caps.

We refueled twice, the second stop outside of Hood River being little more than a top-off.

I'd been accustomed to enjoying the lights of Portland on flights home, picking out the freeways and major roads from the streaming flow of headlights, trying to approximate which neighborhood glow contained my house. The near uniform darkness–broken only sporadically by the red glow of firelight–reminded me forcefully of the reality that the months in the haven of Boise had dulled: the world had changed.

Well after midnight, but with hours still before dawn, the helicopter lowered, wobbling and rocking several feet above the road surface. The pilot hovered precariously, relying only on instruments and night-vision equipment.

It was pitch black inside. Gloved hands tugged at my arm, politely suggesting I get off my ass, then shoved me toward the door. I could just make out departing figures, the heads descending a couple of feet, so I was able to judge the drop and my exit without twisting an ankle. My thick rubber-soled boots and bent knees absorbed the impact. I stumbled forward to clear room for the remaining passengers, keeping my head low beneath the whirling blades, and my eyes narrowed to avoid kicked-up dust and debris.

When the last man disembarked, the helicopter rose, hesitated, then drifted away, a black silhouette against a cloudy night sky. The whole thing had taken about thirty seconds. Of course, it wasn't a silent procedure. Any Atlanteans along several miles of the strip of land between the hills of Northwest Portland and what had been riverside shipping and industrial facilities would have heard something. We could expect that word of–something–would make its way to all Portland area ziggurats. Not terribly worrisome, though. Little could be deduced from it, and certainly not the reckless stunt we were about to attempt.

Sergeant Caplan counted heads while Captain Gaines checked our position on a map illuminated by the red-filtered light clipped to his combat webbing. I didn't need the light. As my eyes adjusted, I took in the surrounding landmarks and forced myself to compensate for missing structures whose absence would disrupt my mental topography. I waited politely for Gaines to complete his review. He'd displayed leadership and independence, and now he could consult the expert to confirm his reading.

Which is basically what happened. Truth is, he was pretty much bang-on. The helicopter pilot had delivered us to within a hundred yards of our planned landing zone. All this efficiency made me briefly question my presence. But then Gaines suggested saving time, just following the highways.

"Shine your light right over there," I said, pointing toward the river. He complied, and the gleam of his flashlight reflected crimson off of the high water submerging the far lane of the highway. "Unless you brought boats, we're going to have cut over the hill. The water is just going to get deeper eastward."

He shrugged. At least I think he did; the light bobbed up and down. Hiking the west hills was the plan anyway.

I traced the proposed route for him once more on the map, through Forest Park, along roads paralleling a series of reserved green spaces, then dropping in to our destination from the west. Then, upon Gaines' whispered "Let's go," I led the way south, up into the hills. As the elevation increased, warehouses and industrial parks gave way to residential neighborhoods and parkland.

That's how it had been at any rate. In the early going we found little change. The streets still ran as I remembered. It was too dark to see the true condition of the buildings and houses. I was, in a sense, glad of the minimal visibility. I could imagine it all intact, undamaged, and not face the probable reality that all the unmerged homes had long since been searched by Atlantean troops. All I'd see in the light of day would be kicked-in doors, smashed windows, and old blood stains.

It was chilly. The exertion of the uphill hike helped warm me, but not enough for comfort. The darkness prevented us from moving fast enough for that level of body temperature. A blessing, really. There was no way Gordon and I could keep up with our peak-conditioned escort if they were moving at full clip. We'd be exhausted, limp bags of sweat, blisters, and pulled muscles within two miles.

The first check came as we ascended into Forest Park. I'd led us off a residential road onto unpaved trail and we climbed. As we neared a junction with another trail that would lead us in a wide, roundabout loop to the crest of the hill, a reddish glow exposed Atlantean construction, illuminating a section of stone wall and a flagstone-paved clearing.

We stopped for a consultation. "Block house," Gaines opined. "Good field of fire."

"Yeah," I whispered. "We could tell from the satellite photos that the forest had been thinned out. Too much to hope that they'd not fortify the high ground." This was not a ziggurat. I'd sketched our route well wide of the ziggurats shown on satellite. A patrol outpost, maybe. Whatever it was it required us to detour through thick, damp rainforest. In the dark. Ferns and undergrowth clutched at my legs and feet. Pine branches slapped me in the face. I was unhappy.

We took a ten-minute rest about an hour later, munching on plastic-packaged military rations and guzzling from canteens. We were behind schedule. The ridge proved to be a patchwork of fortifications, so we'd been forced into numerous detours. My feet were sore, my back was beginning to ache, and I was thoroughly miserable. I heard not a grumble from anyone, so I kept my bitching to myself.

One bright spot: the remainder of the trek would be mostly downhill.

☙❧

The eastern sky was paling as we left behind the last stretch of forested cover. We faced scuttling from building to building for the next couple of miles. I didn't care. No more jabs in the eye from tree branches, no more wet spider webs in the face, no more brush tripwires.

We sat on the hillside above Goose Hollow, the land rising past that shallow dell before dropping steadily to the river. Goose Hollow was only sporadically merged. The eponymous tavern itself, I was pleased to see, had escaped. But beyond this little neighborhood, the cityscape was radically altered. As the sun hunched skyward, the extent of the amalgamation of structures grew more evident. The dawn light exposed a maze of narrow, artificial arroyos, exposed watercourses, and here and there an unchanged stretch of street falsely promising unhindered passage. Cleared areas showed starkly. Sections had been razed to the foundations by Atlantean workers. Salvaged materials from demolished buildings, ready for transport, were stacked neatly in the nearest visible work sites. While all of the team understood what had occurred, only Gordon and I had previously experienced the crazed mishmash of interlocked structures on a citywide scale.

"Shit," Manse whispered, his tone awed and subdued. Profane mutters of agreement followed before Gaines instructed us all to put a sock in it. We holed up for the day in an apartment building dating from the 1930s. The place had been ransacked, but in an odd fashion. Furniture was notable by its absence. Kitchen drawers lay empty on grimy linoleum floors. But televisions, computers, and stereo equipment still sat untouched. The smell of decaying bodies permeated the upper floors.

We bunkered down on the ground floor. Those not on watch stretched out on the floor since the beds of the former tenants were all missing, presumably now furnishing Atlanteans with hitherto unknown comfort.

I pored over the map once again with Captain Gaines. I craved a few hours of sack time, but we still faced crossing 405, and I was supposed to be the expert. It wasn't clear how many freeway crossings still stood. And it wasn't clear if those that stood were unguarded. I pointed out the overpasses nearest our position and leading most directly towards the former campus. Scouting, dealing with guards—that was Gaines responsibility. Duty done, I commandeered an empty bedroom and, after fitfully tossing and turning at least twice on the warped hard-wood floor, dropped into the sleep of the exhausted.

ཱྀ

The overpass was indeed guarded. A square blockhouse squatted in the middle of the span, red torchlight burning through wide doorways in each wall. The four soldiers on duty inside were clearly illuminated, along with most of the expanse of the overpass and a stretch of the former freeway beneath, though no light was truly necessary to reveal what lay below: the reek of stagnant water rising to street level in a nigh visible miasma. The freeway's retaining walls were now channel embankments, trapping water into what was essentially a long, befouled lake. Long-handled tools and rectangular buckets were stacked on the sidewalk, leaning up against the guard rail. Enough light from the guardhouse reached the perpendicular street to show a cutting into the near embankment, stair-stepping down.

The Atlanteans were prodigious canal builders. My guess was they intended to take advantage of the existing channel to run a short trunk line paralleling the Willamette.

I briefly pondered discussing the theory with Gordon, an indication of how disoriented I was by the late hour. Crazy. It wasn't too long ago that this time would have coincided with the early part of my shift. We grow accustomed to new routines so quickly. The old habits fade, though they too can be speedily resumed.

Atlantean long-term infrastructure planning wasn't my concern. The four armored soldiers blocking our crossing were.

Technically, of course, they were Captain Gaines' concern. I wondered what he had in mind. Send the four Rangers–two on either side–hand over hand along the outside of the guardrails, knives in their teeth, then slip over for a bit of silent throat slitting? A sudden rush, overwhelming them with numbers, butt stocks, and fists?

Turned out he had something more pragmatic in mind. He and Sergeant Caplan threaded silencers onto their big Heckler & Koch USP .45s. They low-crawled into position, lay prone, braced themselves on their elbows, and fired, a sequence of muted coughs. Two of the Atlanteans had just time to look surprised at their toppling comrades before joining them.

We crossed the overpass at a run, only to plunge into the maze once again. We wended our way eastward. Our route required us to go about what used to be four blocks before turning south. This took some doing, necessitating frequent backtracking after promising passages culminated in dead ends.

Eventually we reached the Park Blocks, a stretch of undeveloped blocks running north and south, home to benches, statues, childrens' playgrounds, and lines of trees. Portland, at least, hadn't developed it. The Atlanteans hadn't got the urban planning memo. They'd built up the area heavily, yet since it was primarily discrete, unmerged construction it provided a relatively straight run south toward our target. Relatively, because there was no exact overlap between our grid pattern of roads and structures and the Atlanteans' street plans. The buildings here reminded me of the jeweler's shop I'd darted through so many weeks ago. This was likely a neighborhood of skilled craftsmen, supervisors, and overseers. The lower floors might contain a workshop or office. The upper floors probably living quarters and a section where the women would be locked away from the world.

The Atlanteans in this quarter hadn't completely escaped merger. I could see the dim shape of a spreading oak canopy blossoming from the roof of a house. Another tree, snapped at the base, lay at a diagonal in the wreckage of a house, scattered stone blocks evincing the force of the collision. But compared to our trip so far, this last stretch was a stroll up an open boulevard.

Portland State University capped the south end of the Park Blocks, an urban campus sprawled across and intermingled with the southwestern rump of downtown Portland where it met 405's sweeping curl from westward to northward (or southward to eastward, depending, of course, on direction of travel).

The merger recommenced in earnest here. Few people could have lived through the transition, through the ruinous fusion of solid structures. It looked nigh impenetrable to me. So here is where I turned over guide duty to Gordon. He'd wormed his way out, he could lead us back in.

"Right then, gentlemen," Gordon whispered, "follow me." He crouched to slide open the window of a basement apartment in a tenement building that was now about seventy-five percent fused with the granite slabs of a cyclopean temple. The sandaled foot of an angularly carved, monstrous Atlantean deity shadowed the windowed entrance, requiring us all to duck low, passing beneath the ominous bulk of that threatening sole.

The oppressive dread of a crushing doom stuck with me as we continued. Our passage through twisting hallways—either purposefully constructed interior hallways or hallways formed by the merger of alien and mundane architecture—reminded me claustrophobically of spelunking. I was continuously aware of the weight of stone, steel, concrete, and rebar resting above me in perilous equilibrium.

Wavering flashlight beams lit our way since we had no fear of discovery in these improbable catacombs. It was an eerie journey. Sections of tile flooring, a slice of a classroom glimpsed through a gap in Atlantean walls, a half a bulletin board still festooned with pinned notices of club activities and bands. Constant reminders of what this merger had buried. At times brick or yellowed grass beneath our feet indicated we were passing through what had once been outdoors.

The cramped route—often so narrow as to require slipping along sideways, or belly-crawling over an obstruction—did not allow for speed. The team took advantage of the pace to take in Atlantean wall frescoes, ugly, squat icons set in recessed niches, and other partially evident glimpses of an alien lifestyle. Their interest flagged within an hour as nerves and impatience gained the upper hand.

"Sure he knows where he's going?" came a whisper from one of the Rangers. I think it was Hebert.

A trick of acoustics carried the whisper to Gordon who shot an answer over his shoulder. "You had better hope so. If I'm lost, good luck getting back out."

That rejoinder must have got everyone thinking. No one had left a trail of breadcrumbs. We were reliant on Gordon's memory. He'd been living in and exploring these dark, choked corridors for weeks. Stumbling blindly through the maze held no appeal. Flashlight batteries would hold out only so long (though there must be areas where light leaked through) and we hadn't brought food for more than a couple of days.

"Worrying is not an authorized component of this operation, soldier," said Gaines, deadpan.

"The Professor knows where he's going," Caplan said. "He's just fucking with you, and now so's the Captain." Sergeant Caplan must have a case of nerves to display such uncharacteristic logharea. This lab rat routine was starting to get to everyone.

And then we were in the library. Just like that. One minute we were walking through an Atlantean sub-basement, the next, after ducking beneath rebar poking from the bottom of a stretch of concrete wall, we were walking though the lower stacks of the University library.

A crawlspace opened behind a pile of disassembled shelving. On hands and knees in single file we crept through, a column of heavily armed mice. The crawlspace terminated in a room filled with bulky equipment sprouting pipes that branched in all directions. The room was silent, cold. A whispering tug of air directed us to another mouse hole.

"This is it," said Gordon, a decibel above a whisper. "This leads into the ziggurat. I don't mean to tell you your business, but from here on silence is imperative."

"Once more, for the slow learners," said Captain Gaines. "We follow the Professor to the library and try to snatch at least one target there, if we're lucky. If not, we look for living quarters. If you get separated, hurt, or have to retreat, this is the rally point. Hold the entrance. We do not leave without, at a minimum, one live target. One that's likely to stay alive. This is a wasted trip if the target kicks. Understood?"

Heads bobbed in crisscrossing beams of light, accompanying grunts of acknowledgment, a hushed, guttural "hu-ah."

Gaines grabbed my elbow and led me aside. "Why don't you stay and guard our escape? You've already done your part."

"I've been watching out for Gordon for a dozen years, Gaines. I'm not going to bail now. Let's just get this over with." It was a tempting suggestion though.

We rejoined the rest, completing final preparations. Backpacks were stacked and weapons checked.

"Lights off," whispered Gordon. Then, as the boiler room plunged into darkness, he added, "Follow me."

He pushed aside a woven hanging, letting in a faint glow of torchlight, and squeezed through a low aperture, slithering forward on his belly. We followed one at a time, emerging from between the legs of a rectangular side table fronting a thick tapestry.

That decorative pattern repeated the length of the hallway every few paces. And it was an impressive hallway, despite being–according to Gordon–a little used lower-level route to long-term storage rooms and pantries stocked with bulk staples. Walls of iron-gray stone rose at a slight inward angle to reach a twelve-foot ceiling. The inward cant induced a sense of claustrophobia, hinting at the immense tonnage of quarried stone poised, tomb-like, over our heads. Torches in brass sockets were set at thirty-foot intervals, casting their eerie, unwavering orange light. The ubiquitous Atlantean gods were represented by ugly votive idols atop each table.

To our left, the hallway continued with monotonous, unbroken regularity. To our right, it terminated at a broad, ascending stair that rose to a wide landing. From where we stood, I could just see the stairs continuing from the left-hand side of the landing. A brutish statue carved from reddish stone stood on the landing, overlooking the hallway below. One of the war gods, I guessed, animalistic in feature, a work of crude angularity, armed and armored.

Gordon led the way. Captain Gaines walked at his side, his sidearm–silencer in place once again–at the ready. Sergeant Caplan, similarly armed, brought up the rear. We made for the steps, tension evident in each exaggeratedly silent footfall.

The scale of the ziggurat's interior was in keeping with that of the exterior. Massive. Its dual role as fortress and temple was apparent from the thickness of the walls and the omnipresence of iconography.

But Gordon soon showed us another aspect of the ziggurat, the hidden, out-of-the-way passages on so different a scale they might have been in another structure entirely. These were the side halls for servants, ways to quickly and quietly fulfill the needs and demands of the lords and masters without subjecting lofty eyeballs unnecessarily to the sight of lowly menials. They were cramped, unadorned, and less likely to lead us into the path of a late wandering priest or a platoon of guardsmen tramping in unison toward a shift change.

Gordon seemed to have his bearings. He led us with apparent confidence, turning without hesitation left or right, and invariably upwards.

The lights in these narrow service halls were more widely spaced, leaving us in an unrelieved, uniform dimness. Sounds seemed magnified, our own footsteps the heavy, clumping tread of giants. That keenness of ear perhaps saved us from our first contact–a shuffling up ahead telegraphing someone's approach.

Gaines darted to the nearest door, eased it open for a quick peek, then waved us all through, back into the vast hallways of the fortress proper. The door closed behind us just before (we hoped) whoever it was had rounded the corner. We waited what seemed an eternity, giving him time to pass out of sight or hearing, hoping no one would stumble upon us here, exposed in this hall from which several doors and two crossing halls were visible.

Our luck held. Unseen, we ascended narrow stair after narrow stair until my thighs tightened into leaden slabs of pain. At last Gordon opened a door letting out into an upper hallway, less inhuman in scale but more ornate in furnishing and decor. Bright, nonsmoking torchlight broke into scintillating reflection from multicolored mosaics inset in the walls and was mirrored by highly polished floors of glossy black stone. Rectangular lengths of limestone framed doorways. Gordon led us to one such doorway and through, into a room lined from floor to high ceiling with small wooden cubicles. The library at last. We entered, tugging the door shut behind us.

The suppressed hope of finding a late night/early morning scholar absorbed in research was dashed. We were the library's only occupants. The library was a sight though, the pigeon hole shelving that masked the stone walls behind held thousands of documents, each square receptacle chiseled with characters at once alien and naggingly familiar. I wondered if there was a card catalog. Reading tables filled most of the central space, though there were also a half-dozen shoulder high sections of shelving set back-to-back that housed even more written material: loose sheets, engraved copper plates, brass-bound books, and always more scrolls. Light was provided by a wheel-shaped chandelier, wide enough in diameter that I briefly tried puzzling out how they'd fit it through the door.

I stretched my legs, trying to ease the knots. Gordon immersed himself immediately in a scroll plucked from the nearest receptacle. I sensed a general easing of tension. We'd arrived. Unnoticed and unharmed.

Captain Gaines must have noticed it too. "Professor, it isn't time for study hall. There are no targets here. We need to get to the living quarters, and we're burning darkness."

Gordon, with evident reluctance, re-rolled the parchment and tucked it away in his rucksack. "We've climbed near the upper levels of the ziggurat. You may have noticed we've entered a more upscale zip code. The theocrats like to live near the library, so most of the doors lead to their luxury suites."

"Are you sure, Gordon?" I asked. "How do you know?"

"I had some near misses of the soil-your-shorts variety. I ducked behind that bookcase over there for three hours one night when a priest wandered in, probably trying to look up the answer to some nagging conundrum that prevented him from sleeping. I stuck my head out the door when he finally left and watched him enter one of the rooms down the hall. I had similar close calls. Trust me Nick, I do know."

"Can you still recall the door?"

"Doors, actually. Like I said, similar close calls."

"OK, you heard the man," Gaines said. "Let's grab a couple of targets out of bed then regroup at the rally point. Lead the way, Professor."

We left the illusory safety of the library and returned to the hallway, turning right. Facing down the hall we could see two doors on our left and one on our right. Ahead, the corridor terminated at a stairway that ascended to a doorway set midway up the wall. Another hallway intersected ours to the left at a ninety degree angle at that point, probably one of four constituting a square walkway surrounding the apartments on this level. If we kept walking, we'd wind up back where we started.

Considering that the library was set on the outside edge of the perimeter hallway, perhaps all the doors on the right opened onto utilitarian chambers: labs, meeting rooms, etc. Or perhaps some were rooms with views for the most privileged priests, the equivalent of corner offices. I wasn't curious enough to open all of the doors in order to check. We'd just trust Gordon's memory and nab a couple of victims from these inner rooms.

We crept to the nearest door in response to Gordon's pointing finger. Sergeants Caplan and Prentiss were on door-opening detail. Lance Corporal Garrett was positioned right behind him, tasked as first to enter, followed by Gaines, then by Gordon and I. The Ranger squad would watch our back, or come in and pull our asses out of the fire if we'd stumbled into something unexpectedly hot.

Caplan checked his roll of det-cord and nodded. He was ready if the door proved fractious. But a two-man team was unnecessary as the door proved unlocked and swung open easily and noiselessly. Garrett rushed in, followed by a shoving cluster of five of us.

We were too eager, on edge. It wasn't a pretty room-entry, but pretty didn't matter.

We were in an antechamber. A row of brass hooks held a collection of robes and priestly headgear. Wall frescoes ran from floor to ceiling and a trio of chairs provided a small conversation area centered around a short table. A tiny pantheon of plug-ugly deities was grouped on the surface of the table. An open doorway led to the next room of the apartment.

The bedchamber lay through the archway. Two other doorways opened onto other rooms that we didn't bother exploring. A thick mattress rested on a low platform of heavy timber frames, only dimly visible by the light filtering in from the hallway.

Our target was a shadowy lump in the middle of the bed, fast asleep.

Sergeant Caplan flicked on a flashlight, spotlighting the sleeping priest for the benefit of Garrett and Prentiss. Prentiss leapt bodily onto the target, pinning him beneath his weight and slapping a hand over his mouth. Garrett followed immediately, retrieving thin, hairless arms from beneath blankets and slipping plastic quick-cuffs around the priest's wrists, sliding the binding loop tight.

Prentiss had to move his hand momentarily to allow Garrett to apply a gag, but the priest was able to muster only a confused grunt before the muzzle slid into place. It sounded deafeningly loud to my ears, but probably couldn't have been heard as far as the hallway.

Success. We'd bagged our prize. We could repeat the feat next door for redundancy and get the hell out. Smooth, unhurt, victorious.

And then the gunfire commenced.

Someone (Prentiss I think it was) had the presence of mind to stay with the prisoner. The rest of us scrambled toward the hallway, pushing, shoving, and cursing in our haste, Gaines hollering for a sit-rep.

"We've got lobsters," came Corporal Manse's shouted reply as our shoulder-to-shoulder, sprinting pack neared the finish line.

I reached the doorway a step behind Gaines, shoving ahead of Garrett. Gaines passed under the lintel and I got my head out the door. The four Rangers were ranked across the hallway in firing position, the extended butt stocks of their M4-rifles tucked tight against their shoulders. A half-dozen Atlantean soldiers were sprawled along the hallway, a line of blood-leaking dead men leading from the steep stairway.

Stalking unperturbed down the last stairs came another Atlantean, robed and capped in the style I'd come to dread and hate. The door at the head of the stair behind him was open to the night sky. The priest's hands were following a smooth sequence of practiced gestures, like a fraternal organization's recognition sign. And he was chanting in gibberish.

"Shit!" I grabbed Gaines by the shoulder and yanked him bodily back into the antechamber. "Get your asses in here!" I called to the Rangers, trying to invest my voice with the sort of command authority Captain Gaines could deliver.

I was too late. A blast of heated air washed past the doorway. Screams accompanied an acrid smell of burning hair and fabric.

Captain Gaines tore free from my grip, a look of fury on his face as he wrenched loose. He plunged back into the hallway. The rest of us followed.

The squad of Rangers was burning. Hair and camouflage caps were torches, lighting distorted, melting facial features. Their uniforms sent licking tongues of flame in all directions, beginning to melt the webbing of battle harnesses.

"Mother fucker," said Gaines, and began firing at the priest, the whisper of the silenced rounds inaudible over the screams of the dying soldiers. The priest staggered at the impact, but continued his approach, his hands raised and his lips beginning to move once more.

"No!" I said and dashed forward, trusting Gaines to not plug me in the back. I slid the heavy knife free from it sheath as I ran. I had time to build up momentum. There was weight, speed, and angry force behind my arm as I buried the blade in the priest's skull. I carried his still standing corpse before my rush, his body cushioning my impact as we fell against the stairs. I bounced away, rolling off to one side, the embedded blade tugging free, trailing blood and brains. Behind me I could see Gordon, Caplan, Gaines and Garrett futilely attempting to douse the flames with bare hands and robes snatched from the antechamber. But of more immediate concern were armored legs appearing in the doorway above me at the head of the stairs. And the opening of the door that led to what Gordon had indicated was the apartment of another Atlantean priest.

I tried accomplishing several feats at once: switching my machete to my left hand, drawing my pistol, and standing up. I succeeded in none of the above. I dropped the big knife to clatter on the stone floor, trapped my fingers in my combat harness, and rose up a few inches before falling on my butt.

Gunfire crackled again, bullets zinging above me, some flattening against stone walls or ricocheting away. Most, however, found home in the armored legs or lower torsos of the soldiers who'd been clattering menacingly downstairs.

Even dead and dying the soldiers proved nearly lethal to me. The leading lobster, pulsing red jets from holes in thigh and lower abdomen, toppled my way, leading with the glittering sharp point of his spear.

I seemed to observe his fall in slow motion, suffering the maddening illusion that I had time to move out of the way but was frozen to the spot. I did manage to jerk my head to one side, the wide spear blade sparking against the floor a hair from my neck, the point of one of the protrusions nicking my ear. I did not, however, avoid the full force of his belly flop, absorbing the brunt of over two hundred pounds of man and armor.

The force drove the breath violently from my body. My head smacked against the floor as I was pushed, skidding backwards, along its smooth surface. I saw sparks through a yellowish haze.

I also saw—dimly—Garrett hitting the newly emerged priest with a textbook flying tackle. Somehow (misery loving company?) it made the contusions and bruises along the length of my body more bearable. Or perhaps it was my struggle to take a breath that occupied all my immediate attention. I felt like a marlin flopping on the deck of a boat.

Other bodies clanged down the steps. Some rolled to a stop, dead still. Others curled up, belly shot and dying in agony. A helmeted head bounced off of my foot, and a falling pole arm rebounded from the armor of the dead man atop me.

I didn't care. All I wanted to do was breathe.

Hands reached down to haul the corpse away. Another hand grabbed me by the belt buckle, just below my navel, and pulled hard, hoisting my lower back a half a foot off the floor. Air—sweet, painful air—flooded my lungs.

"On your feet, sir," said Caplan.

Other hands helped get me there. "Damn it Nick, are you OK?" asked Gordon.

"Now I know what a waffle feels like," I said, pausing for a breath between each word.

I looked around, taking in the aftermath of the last few seconds. Prentiss was leading the first prisoner from his room. Garrett was trussing the second, working the quick-cuffs like a rodeo cowboy in a steer-wrestling competition. Caplan began working dog tags from the smoldering necks of the four Rangers. The moans and screams of wounded men filled the hall, a pleasant conversational volume after the racecar bellow of gunfire in this enclosed echo chamber of a hallway. The smell of charred meat and scorched hair and gunpowder roiled in a malodorous stew.

I didn't want to die here.

"Move, people," said Captain Gaines. "Down to the rally point. Garrett, you're on point. Prentiss, you've got the targets. Professor, you're assistant warden. You too Gates, if you're up to it. Caplan, we're over watch. Move out."

We hadn't been silent. This place was a hive and it was going to be swarming all over us within seconds. I snatched up my fallen bolo and we moved out, darting back into the servants' utility corridors.

We pushed forward as fast as we could, burdened by two uncooperative prisoners. I drove myself as hard as I could. If I let my bruised muscles stiffen up, I didn't think I'd be able to keep up.

Pounding down the first stretch of stairway as rapidly as my legs would absorb shock drove tremors of pain through my bruised frame. It only got worse from there. But I wasn't allowed the luxury of wallowing in self pity. We'd barely cleared the first hallway, starting down the second stair, when we heard the clatter of soldiers tramping down the stairs from the level above.

"Discourage them," said Gaines.

I glanced over my shoulder, keeping one hand on the wall so I didn't tumble down the stairs and break my neck–a stupid way to die. Why do the work myself when there were countless Atlantean soldiers haunting the hallways, eager to take on the task themselves?

Caplan turned and trotted back up the few stairs he'd just descended. He was tugging a black, baseball-sized grenade loose from his combat harness.

Sergeant Caplan rejoined us in the hallway below shortly after the bang ended and the screaming began.

We kept moving, eyes pausing nervously, expectantly, on each doorway we passed. Angry shouts reaching us from above told us that Caplan's grenade hadn't caught all of our immediate pursuers .

"Pick 'em up and put 'em down people," said Gaines, a trace of worry inflecting his words, a barely detectable tremolo.

A side door swung open as the midpoint of our column jogged by. A man wearing an apron over his white kilt stood in the doorway, a tall woven-basket brimming with coarse flour straining the muscles of both arms. He watched us with eyes almost as wide as his gaping mouth. Gordon pivoted instantly at the creak of the swiveling hinge, placing the man in his sights in a smooth transition to the Weaver stance. He held it for a moment as I jogged painfully by on his unarmed side.

"Shit," he said, lowering the weapon and moving back in front of me. "Shit. I almost killed him. Shit."

Repetitious profanity, constrained vocabulary. Gordon was rattled. "But you didn't," I said. "Excellent threat recognition. A Plus. You assessed the target and held your fire. Aced the exercise." And then I saved my breath for more jogging.

ꕥ

They were waiting for us the next level down.

A door blasted open under the press of a charging squad of Atlantean guardsmen. They hit the tail of our column, swarming over Sergeant Caplan. He got off two rounds before contact. I turned my head in time to see a spear blade nearly sever his left arm. Caplan tucked his M4 tight against his side. He must have thumbed the selector to automatic, for, as a wave of metal broke over him, I heard a truncated jack-hammering riff, then a brief silence before more screaming.

Captain Gaines had skirted the scrum, Caplan having been between him and the ambush. When I looked over my shoulder again I saw him walking rapidly backwards, ripping off controlled bursts into the surviving Atlanteans who were trying to disentangle themselves from the dead and wounded piled atop the sergeant's body.

I stopped, allowing Gaines to catch up. I pulled my pistol and took aim.

"Save your rounds," said Gaines in a cold, emotionless voice, and pumped a final .223 into the last standing lobster. "Keep moving."

I turned on my heel and kicked up the pace, regaining my position flanking Gordon.

"Perhaps volunteering wasn't your optimal choice," he said. It was a sign of the true Gordon re-emerging, unhappily perhaps, but sticking his nose out nonetheless.

"Ah, it was my day to do the dishes," I said. "The joke's on Trina."

Our banter was flat, forced. Gallows humor was still a novel and unwelcome experience and Caplan was still freshly swinging from his.

A hastily erected barricade awaited us at the next floor. Garrett chucked a grenade over the top and retreated back up the stairs, prodding Prentiss' captives ahead of him. A single haphazard volley of arrows clinked harmlessly against the risers below us before the grenade cleared a path, leaving a wreckage of piled furniture and men, torn and punctured by the erupting sphere of spinning metal shards.

We moved through. I watched Garrett kick aside the mangled body of a soldier still vital enough to clutch weakly at his leg with one hand while struggling to lift his spear with the bleeding, three-fingered remains of the other. I'm sure the hall must have been full of the din of the screaming wounded, but the concussion wave of the exploding grenade had traveled up the stairs. My head was still a ringing echo chamber, a clanging bone tocsin.

After that it appeared that we had outraced or bypassed the interior defenses. We descended through level after level unmolested. Our two prisoners began to wake to the seriousness of the situation and became fractious, bolting for doorways, or slowing their pace, or—at one point—attempting a mule-like refusal to continue. Prentiss tolerated none of it, dealing with each mutinous balk with a shove or a rifle barrel digging into the spine.

The priests weren't much to look at, hardly intimidating in these circumstances, trussed and gagged and prodded along at gun point. They were shaven-headed, a night's stubble displaying individual hair loss patterns. Each was barefoot, wearing only a calf-length skirt of embroidered linen, a soft fabric of blue, shifting from corn-flower to amethyst depending on the light. Each bore a blockish tattooed design around his midriff, lettering that looked either runic or cuneiform depending upon the angle, but somehow striking me at the moment as more comic than menacingly diabolical. The memory of the agonized faces of the Rangers, melting away beneath a sheathing of flame, prevented me from developing any compassion for the plight of our prisoners.

We reached the final stair and trotted down into the hall containing our concealed entry point. Prentiss handed off control of the captives to Gordon with a cheerful, "Can you babysit? I'll be back by midnight." He fell to the rear of our procession and dropped prone to cover our escape. I got it pretty quickly: we'd be at our most vulnerable crawling through the exit one-by-one.

Garrett turned back to assist. He forced the nearest prisoner to his knees then lifted aside the concealing tapestry with the barrel of his rifle. The priest got the idea, and after a cuff upside the head, acquiesced, squeezing into the darkness beyond. Garrett followed on his heels, keeping one hand on the priest's ankle.

Gordon watched the process carefully and emulated the Marine. I think he was disappointed that his prisoner didn't require a motivating smack in the noggin.

I was next. I was about to lower my bruised and protesting body to all fours when things began to happen fast. A door opened a short way down the hall, a wide ceremonial door elaborately decorated in bas-relief. An ill-tempered bellow preceded the lumbering bulk of a glyptodont, his plated hide scraping the uprights as he squeezed into the hall, prodded on by an unknown number of Atlantean soldiers.

"Oh shit," said Prentiss in a quiet, resigned voice, "it's blaze of glory time."

"Move it," Gaines told me, plucking a grenade from his harness.

I dropped and scrambled. I heard Gaines say "fall back, Prentiss" before the detonation of the grenade and the remorseless hammering of full-auto rifle fire temporarily deprived me once again of the ability to hear anything but a constant ringing inside my skull.

I emerged into the flashlight-illuminated boiler room. I knee crawled aside to give Gaines room to enter and tried to observe what was happening out in the hall. Gaines slid through on his belly and spun, rifle presented back the way he'd come. I didn't have an angle on what he was seeing. Muzzle flash and spent brass bouncing against my thighs showed he was firing, and a faint metallic popping joined the bell choir in my head. But the slump of his shoulders and the mouthed profanity told me what I needed to know. He heaved himself to his feet and gestured us on.

Prentiss was dead. The only question was to what extent he'd been able to hinder our pursuit before his violent expulsion from this mortal coil.

I saw Gaines roll a final grenade through the opening before he followed us. He didn't move with any excessive urgency, so likely he considered his parting gift sufficient.

I relieved Gordon of his prisoner escort duty, allowing him to move to the front and guide us back through the maze. The priests were docile, responding to prodding direction, seemingly more intent on protecting their tender bare tootsies by careful foot placement than upon escape. I was able to spare a couple of backwards glances, checking for possible pursuit, but also keeping an eye on Gaines.

His attitude could be a concern. Despondency and compensating action—a suicidal revenge assault rationalized as a rearguard action, perhaps—wasn't out of the question. And how could I blame him? He'd just lost almost his entire task force, one of whom had been, from all evidence, a good friend. He was in command, he'd take responsibility, shouldering the weight of each man's death as a personal failure of leadership or planning.

I understood that level of almost immobilizing frustration. I still bore the weight of guilt for the deaths of Tonio, Luisa, and Jim. And more than once I had seen the reproach in the eyes of a citizen who I had been too late to, or incapable of, assisting. I'd read in those eyes the damning question, "Aren't you a policeman? Aren't you here to help me?" I had experienced the entirely unjustified self-loathing

Gaines must be enduring. There was truly nothing he could have done, and yet...

Eventually, I hoped, the realization would dawn that he'd succeeded in his mission. (Although here I chided myself about counting our chickens. We still needed to cart our basket of eggs to the helicopter.) If Gordon's theory bore fruit, Gaines would be the man who'd commanded the pivotal mission of the war, the mission salvaging our entire world's civilization, perhaps the single most consequential military action in all human history. That conclusion might bring him out of his funk. But for the moment he was just a man who'd watched his men die in horrible ways, powerless to prevent it.

We needed him, though, to get us to the extraction point and call in our chopper. I was a little fuzzy on the details and I doubted that either Gordon or Garrett was one hundred percent clear on the procedure.

Pursuit, at least, did not appear to be an immediate problem. Prentiss' last stand and Gaines' grenades had, it seemed, given any survivors pause. Or perhaps no live officers were left on hand to issue the directive. Personal initiative did not appear to be a typical virtue of your garden variety Atlantean. Without a priest or an officer to organize a chase, the surviving foot soldiers would just sit there and bleed.

By this time the prospect of pursuit caused me little anxiety. We'd wormed deep into the labyrinth of merged edifices, Gordon leading with growing speed, more confident of the way out than the way in. Absent an energetic blood hound, a trailing posse would be hopelessly lost within minutes. Picking up our track would be a monumental feat of luck, good luck or bad luck depending on the perspective. Since the Reunion had beaten any vestige of moral equivalence out of me, I would have unequivocally called it bad luck.

ꟸ ꟸ

We emerged, blinking, into the bright pink-orange light of dawn, harrowed, disheveled and bloodied but with our prisoners intact. It could conceivably have felt like a moment of triumph, but we crept out furtively, darting glances at every shadowy point that might serve as concealment for an Atlantean ambush, a last minute turning of the tables.

We saw no one. But a clamor of bells warned us that the Atlanteans were not sitting idly on their hands. The alarm knelled. We were hunted. Shouts echoed through the crazed acoustics of the warped urban architecture. Our prisoners raised their heads in a surge of hope. A rescue was afoot.

Gaines took a long drink from his canteen and spat. He looked us all in the eye, seeing I don't know what, maybe hunting for a sign of blame or anger. Whatever he was after it was enough for the moment because he squared his shoulders and said, "Right, we'll never make it to the primary extraction site. We need a clearing for the bird. Nick?"

I thought a minute, turning a slow circle on my heel, as if I could see a wide open stretch of ground invisible to the others. "How about the river?" I asked. "Or does the chopper have to land?"

Captain Gaines freed a radio from his harness. The days of the dedicated radioman with his suitcase-sized radio phone strapped to his back were receding in the military's rear view mirror. Unless we lost this war, in which case our survivors would be communicating by thumping out messages on hollow logs to announce the arrival of an Atlantean patrol.

"Find a path," he said while fiddling with a dial.

That was a simple enough task. I'd discovered during the night of the transition that several of the streets leading towards the river remained passable. Skirting a fusing of a convenience store and a rectangular-pillared portico I found a mostly intact road, its surface broken here and there by sections of street composed of closely fitted stone blocks bearing deep wagon wheel ruts. I led us on, Gaines trailing while talking quickly, but apparently calmly, into his handset.

I tried to set a fast pace but my body was having none of it. I forced myself to keep moving at the best clip I could attain, knowing that if I stopped for any duration, my deeply contused muscles would seize up on me. The continuing Atlantean hue and cry provided a pretty good incentive to heel-and-toe it as well. I had an expanding headache, the kind that would soon make me look back longingly at hangovers I have known.

Gordon and Garrett were pacing me on either side, just a step behind. Only the burden of keeping the prisoners in check prevented them from leaving me a limping, dwindling figure in their dust. "The river is still in the same place, Nick," said Gordon.

"Let's see how spry you are after an armored Atlantean lands on top of you," I replied. "It's like having the hardware-store shelves collapse on you. In the hammer aisle." But I did try to shuffle faster.

The steeper downhill gradient that developed as we drew closer to the river aided my endeavor. Gravity, our indifferent friend.

The sounds of pursuit expanded as additional outposts joined the search, creating a wide net. It would tighten once a hovering helicopter pinpointed our location.

We made it, unspotted, to the Tom McCall Waterfront, portions of which remained. But most of the riverbank was much lower than I was used to, not a concrete esplanade but a brick-lined tow path broken frequently by steps leading down into the thick brown flow of the Willamette. The steps probably terminated in submerged jetties intended for the unloading of the barge traffic that was the Atlantean commercial life-blood.

We clambered down from the abrupt terminus of the street, past the layers of asphalt and aggregate and plumbing and wiring conduits. We halted at a stair, a plateau of the waterfront towering ten feet over us to our left.

Captain Gaines held a brief conversation with his radio, then told Garrett, "Smoke."

The Marine popped a cylinder into the grenade launcher mounted beneath his rifle and shot the smoke round spiraling into the air. OK, perhaps the Atlanteans wouldn't need to wait for the chopper noise to narrow down our position.

The pursuit sounds abruptly altered as the cordon became a tightening semi-circle. We were pinned. Safety now depended upon winning a race: helicopter against infantry. And infantry had a head start.

My ears had mostly recovered by now. A soft grumble in the distance grew as the chopper, flying low and following the channel of the river, approached fast.

"Garrett, help them with the harnesses," Gaines said. He hauled himself back up to street level.

"This ain't the Alamo, Gaines," I called after him. "We've got an escape route."

He didn't respond. In his mind, I guessed, buying us time to escape at the cost of his own life would be his atonement for the deaths suffered on his watch.

I didn't try again. Hell, for all I knew we'd need every second.

The chopper neared. Garrett gave Gordon and me a bare-bones primer on hooking up to the evacuation harness which would soon be lowered from the helicopter. He finished just before the noise, water spray, and air blast of the hovering chopper made instruction a practical impossibility. And just before the pop-pop of controlled sniping came from up above. Gaines had engaged our pursuers.

"Damn it," I said, unheard. I pointed at the four men with me and then gestured up at the helicopter. Not waiting to discover if they understood–or would comply with–my desire for them to go first, I turned and heaved myself painfully up the artificial cliff to join Captain Gaines.

He'd created three corpses already. The Atlanteans were arriving from all directions, but in twos and threes, soldiers from smaller garrisons and guard posts. A quick count tallied no more than twenty yet, too few for a rush to be anything but suicidal. Not that that would stop them.

Gaines sensed me behind him. He looked over his shoulder, frowning and lifted a hand to wave me back. I shook my head and drew my pistol, lowering myself prone beside him. Gordon and the prisoners were the important ones. If time must be bought, two would be better than one. And if escape was a possibility, I wanted to ensure that Gaines took advantage of it.

It must have been obvious that I wasn't going to move voluntarily. He gave me a resigned, on-your-own-head-be-it look and turned his attention back to target practice. No one was near pistol range, so I spared some time to observe the evacuation.

A cable had descended from the hovering Blackhawk. Garrett was busily strapping a shaking and uncooperative priest into a lifting harness at the end of the cable. He tugged tight a final belt and thrust high a thumbs-up. A winch began to turn, coiling the cable about a drum. The priest was hoisted from the stairs, twisting and thrashing, swaying out over the river and back over the heads of the three men waiting their turns below.

The lobsters had drawn closer when I looked back. They had also grown in numbers despite twice the previous number of bodies lying sprawled on the street. Still not in reasonable pistol range however. Maybe with a long barreled and scoped hunting pistol, but not with the .357. It was a close quarters killing tool. Gaines didn't look to need my help at this point so I tried not to worry.

Worrying, I turned riverward again. The cable was lowering for the second passenger. Garrett was prodding Gordon forward. Good man. The bare minimum for success was Gordon and one priest. The rest of us were gravy.

An increase in the rate of fire brought my attention back to my more immediate concern. About two-dozen soldiers were surging forward, pole arms lowered at the charge. Gaines switched the firing selector to three-round burst, emptying the magazine quickly.

While he thumbed the magazine release and worked at slapping home a replacement, I took a two-handed grip, propped up on my elbows, and fought to keep a bobbing, shifting target in my sight. I squeezed the trigger, missed, and took a breath. I exhaled half of it while applying pressure with my forefinger, allowing the discharge to surprise me. Just like training at the range. The Atlantean stumbled, twisting, and sprawled to the ground, his spear skittering along the street ahead of him.

I fired again and missed again. But this time my aim was thrown off by startlement. A jack-hammering barrage of high-caliber bullets tore up the street and ripped into the advancing soldiers, toppling them like so many fleshy, blood-spraying dominoes. The side gunner in the Blackhawk had joined the defense.

I levered myself up off the ground. "Come on," I yelled at Gaines. Unless a priest appeared on the scene to turn the helicopter into an erupting ball of flaming steel, spiraling into the river, we should be home free.

Gaines, apparently of the same mind, sprang to his feet. We dropped down to the stairs again. Garrett was awaiting the descending cable. The Blackhawk crew was assisting the second priest aboard.

Gaines insisted I go next, still stubbornly holding onto the possibility of an atoning martyrdom. Or just being a solid leader, last man out.

The ascent in the sling was a dizzying carnival ride, the marginal enjoyment of the slowly rotating view of the city diminished by the buffeting down-force of the rotors and obstructed by the upward misting from the surface of the river. It seemed to take an eternity, but it required less than a minute. The crew was fast, and I was just the latest production to roll off of their assembly line.

A helmeted crewman hustled me to a seat beside a trembling priest. Some sympathetic soul had draped a woolen blanket over his shivering frame. I removed it momentarily to thread it between his cuffed wrists, before spreading it out over the rest of him. I wanted his hands where I could see them.

Gaines swung aboard, gesturing and yelling "Go go go" before he was even unharnessed. I wanted to tell the side gunner to keep an eye out for anyone who looked like one of our captives, and to keep up an unbroken stream of lead on him if he showed. But conversation without a microphone and headset was an impossibility. Nonetheless, I kept a weather eye on the body strewn street as it slowly receded in my view. If I was going to go out like a moth in a candle, I wanted to see it coming.

The street disappeared as the pilot swung the gunship around and began a low-level, twisting exit of the city, following a course that must have been mapped out to slip around ziggurat heat shields.

ഇ൬

I watched the earth slip past beneath us as I absorbed the fact that we'd escaped. That we'd succeeded. The naked reality of the Reunion lay bare below us. The crazy-quilt patchwork of fused architecture, the burnt over swathes of ground with skeletal frames of razed houses, and roofless stone blocks of lifeless Atlantean buildings broke the monotony of blackened soil. The roads appeared and disappeared at random, like seasonal watercourses in the desert at the end of the rainy season that churned to life from a sudden deluge only to sink into oblivion in the thirsty sand.

I watched Captain Gaines staring down grim faced at the same vista and hoped again that all the sacrifices would prove worthwhile. I thought about all the weight descending on the narrow shoulders of Gordon, the value of all those lives depending upon his deductions and acumen. The fate of all we survivors riding on his guesswork, and I had to wonder again if all of those weeks spent alone and terrified of discovery, trapped inside an alien fortress, might not have frayed a few synapses, triggered certain minor delusions. What if this entire venture, all those deaths, had been a lunatic errand?

No. The answer remained the same. I knew Gordon. Yes, anything could happen to anyone, mental illness was no respecter of persons, but I knew Gordon. I would have sensed if his combo platter was short an Americanized ethnic entree. He was sound, his *mentis* was *compos.* I had to believe it. Manse, Jim, Tonio, Luisa. All of them. Their deaths–personal and real, not abstract like the snuffed-out lives of those who'd once inhabited the ghost structures below–had to serve a purpose. And that purpose was to get Gordon and our captives to a safe location to work an ancient ritual once again.

Confused thoughts these, the fuddled workings of a drowsy mind. I fell asleep.

ꟸ

My fear of stiffening up if I ceased moving was well founded. I stubbornly refused to be carried out of the helicopter and nearly took a header onto the tarmac as a result. Garrett kept me upright when my legs failed to heed instructions.

It was dark. I'd slept through refueling stops and meals. My stomach's protestations nearly equaled those of my bruised frame. Someone must have alerted Trina that we were en route and that I was alive. I was happier to see her than I was the hamper of sandwiches she'd brought. Really.

A medic pronounced me fit for release into Trina's custody, provided I spent at least half an hour in a hot bath before going back to sleep. Gordon and Captain Gaines were sufficient for debriefing. The report of one beat-up cop wasn't going to add anything of immediate value. Lieutenant Ibsen spirited the two of them off in a town car. MPs, under strict orders to maintain the gags and wrist cuffs in place, drove the prisoners away in separate Humvees. I went home with my wife.

Trina prevented me from drowning in the bathtub. Then I slept again. When I woke Trina set to work, diligently warming and loosening my muscles. I didn't allow a bruised rib or two to interfere with her efforts.

Chapter 19

I DIDN'T SEE GORDON FOR TWO DAYS. WHEN I DID—FOR A BRIEF LUNCH AT the restaurant served by a hovering Trina—he was accompanied by both Lieutenant Ibsen and an armed bodyguard. General Brown was taking no chances on damage to an invaluable asset.

"It's a hell of a set-up, Nick," Gordon said around a forkful of filbert-stuffed quail. "It's a researcher's dream, except instead of graduate assistants I have everyone in uniform with any facility for interrogation or linguistics looking over my shoulder, with a secondary team of professors from Boise State taking notes."

"Writing down the ritual?" I asked.

"The ritual? We're nowhere near that point yet. Remember, Nick, I deciphered the basics of the Atlantean language in script. I'm only just now learning how to speak it. Knowing what a symbol means doesn't correlate directly with the knowledge of how to pronounce it."

"What? How long is this going to take? Do you need to earn another doctorate—Advanced Atlantean Linguistics—before we can pull this off? I don't know if we have that kind of time." I was steamed. Good men had died providing him the live anthropological samples he'd requested. Was it all just an academic exercise for him?

"Restraint, Nick. It's me, your friend. No, I don't need to earn another degree. I just need to comprehend enough of the lingo to ensure that our guests aren't playing us false. And anything additional I, or the rest of the team, manage to garner during the learning process can be helpful in the end game. Practical, usable intelligence, incidental to whatever historical and anthropological data I might glean for my book." He added the last because he knew me, he knew he'd defanged the hothead and I wasn't going to bite.

"At least tell me you are past the ABCs."

"I am. According to Saraeghon and Ankiado—our two prisoners—my glottals are stopped and my fricatives are fucked, but I'm becoming more comprehensible. I'm progressing, and what I am unable to get across vocally I can communicate in writing. And vice versa."

"So when is the moment of truth?"

Vicki leaned forward. I don't know if it was her frowning stricture against revealing military secrets or if Gordon really didn't know, but he said, "Too early to tell. Soon, I hope, but I don't want to spring our project on them just yet. They might balk, clam up if they learn too early what we want them to do."

I stabbed my fork idly into my platter of salad. Gordon knew what he was doing. I trusted him. Didn't have a choice in any case. "Fine, I'll let it rest. But I want to be there." I switched gears. "So what *have* you learned about them?"

"A bit. Mostly confirmation of what I thought I'd gathered from the library. They do call themselves Atlanteans and they are in a state of nearly constant warfare with the other civilizations. It's fascinating; they have almost no conception of progress. I mean, look at their buildings. They appear to have been constructed fifty thousand years ago. Obviously impossible. Even discounting earthquakes, natural erosion would have reduced them all to rubble. No, they simply maintain the existing structures as they are without improvements or novel upgrades, or when needed, reconstruct *the exact same building.* To the Atlanteans the world is–or rather was, prior to the Reunion–at its zenith of cultural perfection. Only the subjugation or extermination of the Lemurians, Hyperboreans, etc. remained to buff a high gloss on history."

"That phrase going in your book?"

"The highlight of the prologue," Gordon said.

"What about the heat magic? Did you learn any way to circumvent it?"

Lieutenant Ibsen said, "Nick, please. You were never a detective were you?"

"I liked being a patrolman."

"I'm sure you did," she said, patronizing me with a capital P. "Be glad you never bucked for promotion. You'd be an awful interrogator. You can't start out questioning the subject with 'why did you kill her?' First thing the perp would do is lawyer up. Similarly with

POW's, you've got to lay the groundwork, build a rapport. You don't jump straight to demanding military secrets."

"Watch a lot of cop shows, Vicki?" She'd put me in my place, but I'd be damned if was going to take it lying down. "Fine. I was just curious. So when will Trina and I see you two again for dinner?"

ꕥ

"What happens now?" Trina asked that night.

"You mean if Gordon ever gets around to his big experiment?"

"Yes. What should I expect?"

I discarded a number of flippant answers. She always deserved better than that. She always deserved better than me, though I'd given up making that point. It exasperated her. "If it works, I suppose we look forward to rebuilding our world. We clear away the rubble and put the pieces back together again. Gordon and the rest of the eggheads can have great fun observing a social experiment performed on a grand scale and you and I can have fun being modern day pioneers." More or less a straight answer. I never claimed to be a saint.

"And if it doesn't work?"

"Then eventually we lose. The Atlanteans keep raising more armies while we run steadily lower on gas and ammo. With any luck, you and I live out the rest of our natural lives within a steadily shrinking defensive cordon and die before it collapses. We leave it to the next generation to go down fighting atop the new city walls of Boise. Bright side: no matter what, we probably don't have to endure the daily threat of violent death."

"So the world might be doomed, but we'll be OK? Just a matter of living either during our civilization's ascendancy or during its final decline?"

"A neatly packed nutshell, my love," I said.

She rested her head on my shoulder. "Since either way I spend the rest of my days with you, I'm content."

Have I noted that I'm not worthy of her?

ꕥ

A month and more passed before Gordon announced he was ready. I'd had an inkling the time was nearing. A great deal of military activity had commenced, uniformed personnel were moving briskly about, a great deal of helicopter traffic whirled by over head. General Brown was obviously preparing for something and I doubted it was another offensive. An ineluctable tingle of excitement crackled over Boise. People spoke in hushed, rapid tones, laughed more loudly than the recent norm, and gushed the latest rumors, some of which struck me as nearly as fantastic as the truth.

Trina and I were sharing another meal with Gordon and Vicki, this time at Vicki's apartment. I noticed a certain amount of masculine appurtenances but declined to speculate. If Gordon wanted to keep his shacking up with the Lieutenant on the down low that was his prerogative.

Vicki surprised me by turning out to be a more than tolerable cook. I don't know why that should have come as a surprise, but it did. I let the food and small talk carry me through to dessert, after which I could no longer restrain my curiosity.

"Enough, Gordon, spill it. It's soon, right?" I added for Vicki's benefit, "I'm no detective, just spell it out plain for a flatfoot who's slow on the uptake."

Gordon chuckled. "OK, Nick. Yes, you're right. General Brown has been dispatching observation teams with cameras and satellite up-links. Really we could have tried the ritual a couple of days ago, but we're giving the teams time to get into position. We'll be able to observe the results firsthand."

I noticed Vicki didn't caution Gordon or attempt to forestall his revelation. The plan was too far advanced to be stopped, I guess. Or maybe she was finally of the opinion that I wasn't somehow an Atlantean deep-cover double agent. Hell, I was a suspicious sort myself. It helped with the police work. Vicki was all right in my book, short words and large print as it might be.

"I want front row seats for Trina and myself," I said. "I was there laying it on the line with you."

"You don't need to sell me, Nick." Gordon sounded a touch wounded.

"Sorry. You're right. I've just got a lot invested in this. I mean, I know we all do, but..." I ran out of words, but Gordon understood what I was trying to articulate.

"I've already bent General Brown's ear. He didn't even blink, just nodded."

"Fantastic. So what is the plan? You wave a knife at the two priests and tell them to make with the magic?"

"'Make with the magic?' What's with the tough guy dialog, Nick? And you know damn well it isn't magic, just manipulation of the current physical law paradigm." Gordon took a sip of the post-post-prandial beverage, a dessert wine a bit too sweet for my liking. He failed to entirely conceal a grimace of distaste. "But to answer your question, no we won't be physically threatening them. We've passed that point. It took some... persuasion. But the two of them have come around to the view that a re-separation of realities is in everyone's best interests. So they've been rehearsing me and a dozen volunteer linguists in the ritual."

"Wait, what's that? I thought the two priests would be performing the song and dance routine."

"No dancing, Nick. It's all verbal. It's a sequence, a sonic sequence establishing a pattern of vibrations. And the two of them aren't sufficient to produce it. If you remember the history I related to you and Trina after I showed up on your doorstep, the initial ritual required the combined efforts of a number of the 'mightiest wizards.' Our two guests just don't have the lung power to pull it off unaided."

"So you and a handful of volunteers from the audience are going to fill the shoes of mighty wizards, steeped in ancient lore or some such shit? Come on, how is that going to work? Someone is going to muff a line here or there. There's no way all of you will run through the whole piece note perfect."

"It might take a couple of tries," Gordon said. "We've been rehearsing." He was repeating himself, a standard Gordon indication of defensiveness.

"Look, if it's just vibration, why don't you sit the two of them in front of a microphone? Those PsyOps guys have loudspeakers. Crank one of those up and you've got more than enough volume."

Gordon's mouth opened to provide the reason why my suggestion was the incoherent raving of an imbecile child. But no words emerged. His mouth snapped shut and he turned to exchange looks with Vicki.

"I'll call headquarters," Vicki said, rising to her feet.

ꕥ

The spacious assembly hall of the capitol building had been declared acoustically sound by Gordon's tamed priests. The two were ensconced upon the speaker's dais in padded chairs and supplied with pitchers and water glasses. Technicians were fussing with microphones and tweaking reverb and squelch and whatnot, trying to meet the priests' exacting specifications as relayed by a harried Gordon. Other uniformed techs were setting up a series of monitors, relaying some of the same views as General Brown's war room—satellite imagery and key perimeter views—but also displaying a series of Atlantean fortifications. Ziggurats primarily, but also a fortified bridge crossing and a mountain pass. The angles were low. In some cases the camera lens was partially obscured by blades of grass. The resolution and picture quality would have driven television executives to spontaneous thrombosis. But it didn't have to be clear, it only had to be. Or soon, we hoped, not be.

I thought about the placement of those cameras. The excursion to capture the priests had made me cognizant of the level of planning and the man hours and sweat involved in executing a mission. I hoped all these had come off casualty free. Even assuming they had, I felt for the poor bastard low-crawling through the weeds to plant his camera, filthy, sweating, and fearing discovery at every moment.

Discounting the assorted electricians, the chamber was sparsely peopled. The priests, for one, found the presence of too many bodies to be sound deadening—or so Gordon interpreted their petulant remarks. More importantly, perhaps—considering who was calling the shots—General Brown wanted few witnesses to the event, worried that rumors of a failure would cripple morale.

In all, only about twenty of us would witness the attempt. The General was there with an aide and a selection of ranking officers and Idaho state panjandrums. A couple of enlisted men sat before the bank of monitors. Gordon and Vicki were there. Captain Gaines sat in a corner, fixing a brooding stare on his hard-won prisoners.

Wanting to snag a good seat, I'd arrived pointlessly early and spent much time moping because Trina was unable to attend (she didn't want to take time off from the diner) and wishing I'd brought a flask along. To celebrate with after the triumph, of course.

Two MPs armed with truncheons and tazers flanked the priests. No one was willing to rule out the possibility that they might seize the opportunity to roast the lot of us. Gordon didn't know (though he was determined to winkle it out) if the priests remained bulletproof, if that protection required some periodic renewal or if it was some physical alteration they'd permanently imbued themselves with. No point in taking a risk. A blow to the head would stop short any shenanigans, and while a bullet might do the same, it just might also destroy an invaluable asset.

I staved off boredom until the stage was set and the players ready to perform.

"Any heroic exhortations or words for posterity, General?" Gordon asked by way of announcing all was in readiness.

"Quit wasting time," the General said. Not exactly 'damn the torpedoes' -class rhetoric.

Gordon muttered something to the priests, then took a seat near one of the MPs, tugging free a small notebook and a pen. Ever the anthropologist. With a ring-side seat for an epoch-defining event, he was taking notes for his next paper.

The room grew silent as a tomb—an unappealing and disturbingly apt thought given the chilly marble walls of the chamber. Only the hum of electronics drowned out breathing and heartbeats as the dominant ambient noise.

At some signal I failed to catch the two Atlanteans began intoning. They vocalized paired baritones, the blend of voices seeming to drop to a bare octave above bass. The tones made a sort of music of the guttural Atlantean speech, reminiscent of Mongolian throat singing, though more distinct, the division between words clearly evident to even we non-Atlantean speakers. The language was primeval, without being primitive. It was spartan, functional, devoid of nuance and grace notes. Such frippery was not so much trimmed away as deliberately eschewed. The microphones carried the chant to the speakers arranged about the room and I felt almost enveloped in the sound, as if the emptiness of the council chamber was filled up with a viscous fluid, a marine abyss reverberating to whale song. I could almost see the vibration, a ghostly presence imagined at the limits of my peripheral vision.

The hairs on the back of my neck stretched to their full height. It reminded me that I needed a haircut.

I found myself leaning forward in my seat, anxious, expectant. A glance around the room showed the same attitude was nigh universal. It would have been comical if not for the seriousness of our endeavor. Only the priests and their two guards remained erect.

The ritual droned on, rising and falling in pitch and intensity, the vibrations in the imagined fluid–an ether, for want of a better word–followed suit. A penny on a drumhead, I felt, would have trembled and skipped in perfect sympathy with the chant. The incantation plodded, dragged, rushed. It was simultaneously interminable and timeless. I know how long it lasted, but only because several people timed it. Without such mechanical assistance I would have been unable to even guess the duration. I was adrift in the sound waves.

The chant ceased as it had begun–without warning. Abruptly.

I straightened along with the other witnesses, as if the move was choreographed. The sounds following the ritual felt harsh, rude, like someone loudly breaking wind in church. The susurration was like the release of a collectively held breath: the shifting of chairs, the rustling of papers, and the crackling of cramped vertebrae.

Then the spell dropped and the overwhelming need to know dominated. Every eye turned to the monitors.

One of the techs swiveled about and shook his head. The cameras broadcast the same images of ziggurats and other Atlantean structures. Unchanged, solid, as fundamentally threatening as they'd been since the Reunion. Still there.

I heard a gasp. A farrago of profanity. I'm sure I added an ingredient or two.

We'd failed.

Caplan. Prentiss. The Ranger squad. Sacrificed in vain. Luisa, poor hapless Tonio, and the stalwart Jim, unavenged. I'd failed them.

I looked up from the floor where my gaze had fallen. My despondency was echoed in every face. Captain Gaines appeared on the verge of a total emotional collapse. Only the two priests appeared unmoved, though that could just be my cultural unfamiliarity with Atlantean mores. And Gordon, who looked more puzzled than floored.

What now? Resign myself to defeat I suppose. Spend with Trina what years were left before the inevitable triumph of the Atlanteans. And inevitable it was. Their continents and islands, left hale and vigorous by the Reunion, would continue to provide generations of men and weapons while our devastated population dwindled and our fuel and weapons were spent.

I foresaw a spate of suicides. An explosion of military activity, perhaps enough to provide a false reprieve. If I were lucky a stalemate would linger long enough for my death from old age.

I focused my attention on the two priests. The open pit of depression that had just yawned beneath our feet might lead to someone working out his frustrations on our prisoners. We'd need their knowledge to delay the defeat. I prepared myself to back up the MPs.

Or maybe join the lynch mob myself. Maybe Saraehgon and Ankiado had deliberately muffed it. Maybe they'd completely pulled the wool over Gordon's eyes–they might have performed another ritual entirely, one that would hasten our doom.

I could see from the furrowing brows around me that others were leaping to similar conjectures. Despondent, disappointed profanity began to give way to angry mutterings, emotions beginning to overwhelm the self-possession of even this uniformed bunch. They might as well have been sporting cartoon thought-balloons. What had the priests done? The ziggurats remained. Our two captives remained. What had they changed and how soon would it bite our asses?

If they had somehow done for us, I just might want to get some preemptive payback.

I'd promised Trina that no matter what the outcome, we'd be able to play out our string together. How could I face her if it turned out we'd been hoodwinked? Dammit, Gordon.

I rose to my feet.

"Sir!" a voice called from by the bank of monitors.

I turned. One of the technicians was waving a finger excitedly at the screens. "Look, sir. Look!"

General Brown was looking. So was I and everyone else. I didn't get it. I saw the same views as before: the cameras fixed on Atlantean still-life, the composite map of earth constructed of imagery from orbiting satellites. What was I supposed to be looking at?

And then I saw it. The imagery was real time. I was looking at a map of the earth. The earth as I'd always know it, the familiar seven continents. I hadn't noticed it because it was exactly what I was conditioned to expect instead of what I would have seen minutes ago. The new land masses–Atlantis, Lemuria, and the rest–were gone! Absent from the map. No longer existent, in this universe at any rate.

A rumble of recognition grew to a spontaneous cheer. The ritual had worked. We'd won! Two Earths existed once again, inhabiting parallel universes. Yes, a vast number of Atlanteans, Lemurians, Hyperboreans, etc., still infested our soil along with all of their weapons and vast fortifications. But with the re-separation, the physical laws of their universe should no longer apply. Magic would no longer function here. Which meant that the heat shielding protecting the ziggurats was gone. No endless sources of reinforcement and resupply existed any longer. We faced a mopping-up operation on a grand scale, but that's all it was. Mopping up.

And after the mopping up, the rebuilding. We had to put the pieces of a shattered civilization back together. Gordon would get one hell of a book out of this. Me? I'd have to consult Trina. Perhaps she'd like to rebuild our lives here. Maybe. But our house was intact and I could imagine it beckoning us. And I imagined that NeoPortland just might need a sheriff. What competition could there be? And certainly a renascent city could use a restaurant. They say location is paramount, and Trina could have her pick.

The End

About the Author

Ken Lizzi is an attorney and the author of an assortment of published short stories. When not traveling–and he'd rather be traveling–he lives in Portland, Oregon with his lovely wife Isa. He enjoys reading, homebrewing, exercise, and visiting new places. He loathes writing about himself in the third person. *Reunion* is his first novel.

http://about.me/ken_lizzi